I0741515

Michael J. Martineck

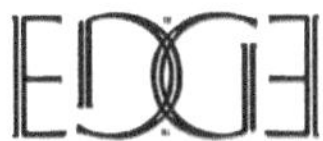

EDGE SCIENCE FICTION AND FANTASY PUBLISHING
An Imprint of HADES PUBLICATIONS, INC.
CALGARY

The Link Boy
A Freeworld Novel

Copyright © 2017 by Michael J. Martineck

EDGE SCIENCE FICTION AND FANTASY PUBLISHING
An Imprint of HADES PUBLICATIONS, INC.
P.O. Box 1714, Calgary, Alberta, T2P 2L7, Canada

The EDGE Team:
Producer: Brian Hades
Acquisitions Editor: Michelle Heumann
Edited by: Maylon Gardner
Cover Design: Jack Kasprzak
Book Design: Mark Steele

ISBN: 9781770531505

EDGE Science Fiction and Fantasy Publishing and Hades Publications, Inc. acknowledges the ongoing support of the Alberta Foundation for the Arts and the Canada Council for the Arts for our publishing programme.

Library and Archives Canada Cataloguing in Publication
CIP Data on file with the National Library of Canada
ISBN: 9781770531505
(e-Book ISBN: 9781770531499)

FIRST EDITION
(20170611)
Printed in USA
www.edgewebsite.com

Publisher's Note:

Thank you for purchasing this book. It began as an idea, was shaped by the creativity of its talented author, and was subsequently molded into the book you have before you by a team of editors and designers.

Like all EDGE books, this book is the result of the creative talents of a dedicated team of individuals who all believe that books (whether in print or pixels) have the magical ability to take you on an adventure to new and wondrous places powered by the author's imagination.

As EDGE's publisher, I hope that you enjoy this book. It is a part of our ongoing quest to discover talented authors and to make their creative writing available to you.

We also hope that you will share your discovery and enjoyment of this novel on social media through Facebook, Twitter, Goodreads, Pinterest, etc., and by posting your opinions and/or reviews on Amazon and other review sites and blogs. By doing so, others will be able to share your discovery and passion for this book.

Brian Hades, publisher

Acknowledgment

Special thanks to Christopher Martineck. I'm very glad you could dust off that degree and help your brother out.

Chapter 1

Edwin McCallum held a roller over a canvas laid out on his kitchen table. It dripped white gesso. The oil painting showed a woman standing atop a stone wall, back to the viewer. All grays and blues, he had decided five minutes after finishing it that canvases were too expensive to burn or slash. He'd cover the piss-poor attempt at art in a thick layer of primer and move on with his life.

A chime went off in his ear and his cuff vibrated. The device, wrapped around his wrist, was double-strapped black carbon fiber and it pulsed purple-white from a screen curved to fit tight to his forearm. The machine knew this was an entitled period of time off. Not a lot of people called this late, but he had ordered the machine not to disturb him, just in case. Which meant this call came from someone with power. A lower order.

"We've got an alert two blocks from your location," a dispatcher sent into his ear.

"We out of uniform operatives?" McCallum's lips felt gummy. How long had it been since he spoke?

"This guy's a 360," the dispatcher continued. "Full bill."

"Oh good." McCallum set the roller down on a tray. "Thought I'd been demoted."

"Sorry, Detective. You are the closest op by four minutes."

"Any info?"

"No data. Just a general alarm."

He jammed his feet into some boots and took the time to tie them. "So this could be a raccoon in the trash?"

"The customer is not answering calls."

McCallum glanced at his wrist. Dispatch had sent his cuff a map, showing the exact location of the alarm's origin.

He knew the neighborhood. He'd make it in two minutes by cutting through an alley across the street and hopping a fence. Did he remember CPR? First aid class was a long, long time ago.

"You call in an ambulance?" McCallum asked as he hopped down the stairs of his apartment, four at a time.

"Yes sir. Prepaid."

"Shit. This guy worried about something?"

"Says here," the dispatcher said, "he thought someone might want him dead."

McCallum plowed through the doors and ran.

— «» —

Father Demiana DeFalco sat in the Bishop's chambers, twisted in her chair so she could get her arm up on the back and rest her head on her shoulder. She re-crossed her legs. She turned to try a different angle, then huffed and turned back, propping her head on her fist. She'd been waiting for forty minutes, silently praying for strength. The Bishop needed to show his power and authority. She needed to show humility and compliance even though this display of arrogance by the Bishop diminished her, the Office of the Bishop, the dioceses of the Buffalo Catchment and, in fact, all of the Catholic Church. Who, in God's name, did this pompous—

Please, Lord, give me peace, she said to herself. She exhaled and let the wave of calm pass across her. It washed away her angry clutter and smoothed the prickly, pointy spikes she could feel sprouting through her skin — the ones that popped out when she got riled. The ones that made her say things that got one called up to the Bishop's chambers on a Thursday night.

Demiana changed the order of her legs, fluffed out her long black skirt, and flipped her long black hair. She probably should've had it up in a bun. She checked her cuff. 11:55. Nearly midnight? Why did the Bishop believe her time to be worth so much less than his? Were they not both devoted to God's work? Wasn't this, then, the Lord's time he squandered? Not that she was going to be doing the Lord's work this late — now who was being pompous — still, she was going to—

The door opened behind her. She popped up straight, smoothed her skirt, and folded her hands in her lap. The Bishop rounded the desk. He could have chosen to sit in the red velvet chair next to her. But, no. He needed his place to be behind the vast expanse of walnut and brass, with a 500 pound cross over his head, and tomes of leather and paper framing his shoulders. The books were ancient and wise, and probably, she bet, unseen by human eyes since this guy was a toddler.

"Dinner ran late," he said in his century-old voice. He took his wide chair quickly, hands covering the curls of the arms. He pressed his white, hairless head back into the red leather, closed his eyes, and opened them in what Demiana knew to be the slowest blink ever. The darkness of the room and the blackness of his shirt and jacket made his round pillow of a head seem to float, disembodied.

"I am reassigning you."

Her mouth opened. She tried to close it but, "Sir, while I wish I would have crafted my homily with more care, I do truly believe—"

The Bishop raised his hand as if stopping traffic. "It is a special assignment. A tragedy-of-the-commons mediation."

"Mediation? You want me to run a mediation?"

"Yes."

"I've never… I've trained, but I've never been sent out."

"So you feel you might fail?"

Her mouth opened again. This time the words weren't ready. "Yes. I guess I could fail."

The Bishop grinned with only the right side of his mouth. "There is no failure," he said. "There is learning about limitations. Oh yes. There is that. You will learn about your limitations. What you should be doing. What you should *not* be doing."

The Bishop flicked his fingers. "Dismissed."

— «» —

Neelesh Fhor walked out of school into the steamy midsummer midnight air. He slogged across the parking lot, arms and head feeling like they'd gained mass by 50 percent during the course of the day. They don't teach you in school that teaching is a physical job. The kids get to sit most of the time. Teaching, at least the way Neelesh did it, burned more calories than roofing.

Moisture clung to everything, so his blue teardrop car sat covered in teardrops. A Saab Sonnet with a single door on the front. He twisted the handle and used it to slide the door over the roof. The front window became a second back window. It harvested dew along the way. Some would drip onto him as he drove since he could, technically, drive with the front door covering the back. Which was kind of cool, despite the sprinkling. Cool until you started spitting bugs.

He walked into the car, stood between the two bucket seats, and drew his finger through the condensation on the hood. He noticed a girl in stripes bending back a piece of chain-link fence. May. May Podlowski, third grade. She wasn't in any of his classes, but he knew the name because he tried so hard to learn them all. He might have her in his class in a few years. If he stayed at the school. If she stayed alive.

"Ms. Podlowski, what are you doing?"

"This way's faster."

"Where are your friends?"

"No one's around tonight." She let the fence bounce back. Tiny, with blond pigtails. Neelesh was impressed she bent it back in the first place.

"There's no one to walk home with tonight?"

"Caddy is sick. Lisa ditched me. I couldn't find Moira or Latasha. And—"

"And the boys?"

"I don't walk with the boys."

"You'd rather walk home alone at midnight than walk with the boys?"

May nodded her head.

Midnight, second shift. Ambyr Consolidated, keeping families together. Or, at least, keeping kids off the streets. Which Neelesh always found to be a laudable practice, until it ran up hard against other practices. Like now. School 64 — the whole education profession, really — proffered hundreds of rules. Some you kept in spirit, some you ignored, and some you took so seriously you didn't even have to think about them. They became reactions like arms wheeling for balance at the edge of a manhole or hands leaping back from a flame. Or driving away before a little girl gets in your car.

Unfortunately for Neelesh, 'never be alone with a student' contrasted with 'leaving a youngster alone in a parking lot.'

Neelesh scanned the area. No one. The other teachers left faster than him or lingered for reasons he couldn't imagine. All the other kids scooted like mice. He thought about drafting some other, older kid to escort May. But there was no one. Then he thought about letting her go on her way. She did this all the time, right? Cut across the practice field, through the alley, and into her neighborhood.

"You live close?" he asked.

"Four streets over. I count them."

He closed his eyes and motioned for May to come over. She ran towards his car, orange and white school bag flapping behind her.

"Just this once. Tell no one. You're supposed to walk with friends."

Chapter 2

Demiana got to the pub close to one o'clock in the morning, having taken just enough time to change her skirt from ankle length to well above the knee and her shirt into a sleeveless blouse. Her collar hung loose around her neck. She didn't want the boys thinking she was anything other than a priest who took her vows to heart, regardless of how much skin showed — because screw it, it's hot outside. The humidity would return her hair to the way God intended in seconds, so she didn't even bother playing with it.

The crowd parted when she entered. Once they noticed the collar, people had a tendency to give her a little extra space. She never had any trouble getting up to a bar. Her friends said it was the reason they still liked to go out with her. Bartenders gravitated towards her. Of course, they always had.

Demiana wore a smooth, plain black ceramic cuff. No ornamentation, no frills. She tapped it and told it to tell her friend Karen she'd arrived. She couldn't see her through the jungle of arms and shoulders and midriffs. She'd never hear her over the band playing from somewhere. Mandolin, fiddle, bass — no vocals for the moment, thankfully. She could tell this crowd was getting ready for a sing-a-long. If they started "Sixteen Tons" she'd never get situated.

She smiled at the two boys standing between her and the polished oak. In their early twenties — too young for her by a few years, not that she was in the market — they both smiled back and ushered her through. She ordered a gin and tonic, insisted on paying for it, tapped her cuff on the bar to authorize the transfer, and turned. She loved moments like this — alone in a pub with friends nearby. Out amongst the real people, in their chosen setting, doing what they wanted — listening to forbidden music, glancing at new faces, sliding against each other, nodding, bending, bouncing to a beat, while backed up with familiar comforts. New... but not that new.

Her cuff tickled her wrist. An orange arrow pointed at her stomach. Demiana grabbed her drink and followed the compass needle as it lead her around the bar, farther from the band and closer to her friends.

"Oh my God," Karen squealed as she hugged her, with next to no pressure. "You made it."

Other acquaintances had congregated in the bar's far corner, where the music tapered enough to allow for conversation. The 'pushing 30' area, Demiana called it. She waved and mouthed greetings. Karen received the only actual contact. She wanted to talk to her more than the others. Karen, in her plain white frock, blond pile of hair high off her neck, barely any makeup — because, again, screw it, it's hot — did not appear to be here in pursuit of attention or sex or to wash memories of the day out of her head. She came to be. Demiana surmised they were the only two like it in the place.

Karen pulled Demiana close to speak right into her ear. "How'd it go?"

"He didn't say a word about it." Demiana sipped her cocktail.

"Crazy little fuck. What did he want?"

"To flex, I guess. Remind me he can move me around like a doll in a house."

"You can take the priest out of the boy," Karen said, "but not the boy out of the priest."

"Did you mean that to be gross?"

"I don't mean half the shit I say."

"He's putting me on a mission."

Karen raised her left eyebrow.

Demiana raised hers to match. "I know. A mediation."

"That's not your thing."

The song stopped. A few people shouted through the rest of whatever they'd been saying. In a second, the whole noisy pub lay silent. Demiana knew why. The 300 or so gathered were all going to sing.

"Day O," the band's lead singer howled, a cappella.

"Day ay ay O," the crowd returned.

"Daylight come and me wan' go home."

"They just disappeared it," Karen yelled as the crowd chanted through the song's opening. "The song."

"I heard," Demiana said. "Ambyr holds the rights. They made it vanish from everywhere, even the Church archives. It's causing a bit of a stir."

"Hey, maybe that's what you're going to negotiate?"

Demiana shook her head. "That's for the big hats."

The band joined in as the singer started the first refrain. "Work all night on a drink a' rum."

Karen took Demiana's head and pulled her ear to her lips.

"You're being set up," she said.

Demiana sang, along with the crowd, "Daylight come and me wan' go home."

— «» —

"Can we drive with the door open?" May stepped up into the front of the car, sidestepped between the bucket seats, and dropped down.

"I'd prefer it," Neelesh said. The air, thick with bugs and moisture, was better than any privacy with an 8-year-old girl.

May clicked her seatbelt and Neelesh rolled out of the parking lot, tires making most of the sound. He checked the charge. He'd be fine if she wasn't more than five miles out of his way.

"How's your summer block going?" he asked.

"Fine." May watched the road out before her, squinting her eyes from the breeze. "I never been in one of these."

"They're not that popular. Not everyone likes the wind in their hair."

"I like it." May sat up straight, trying to get her pigtails to blow backwards. In the tight neighborhood, he'd never get the car above 15 miles per hour. He repressed the urge to floor the accelerator and to get their hair blowing. He wanted this girl out of his car before anyone saw. He wanted her safely at home. Done.

"Does it go fast?" May asked.

"When I take it to the track."

Ah, the track, Neelesh thought. Driving free — no governor on the motor, no ops pulling you over for smiling the wrong way, no children.

He turned a corner. They passed a group of four kids walking. He didn't look to identify them. Didn't want to give them a full view of his face, like a guilty person.

"You really should walk in groups," Neelesh said. "Even if they are stinky boys."

"I know."

"You promise me?" Neelesh turned onto May's street. "You promise I won't have to do this again?"

"Promise, promise, promise."

"Which house is yours?"

May sat up to look over the car's side window and pointed. Neelesh pulled over and stopped.

"Thank you, Mr. Fhor"

May hopped up and out the car. Neelesh reached back and pulled the door over him, and listened for the lock.

He thought about speeding away. His brain kept telling him he needed more distance between him and the girl. He didn't want to make a show of things, though. He lumbered away like the hot lazy night expected.

—— 《》 ——

McCallum ran through the alley between the two buildings directly across the street from his apartment. Five-story brick and mortar places, he believed they dated back to Buffalo's first boom. A good 250 years in the past, when people could be bothered to arch windows, sculpt corners, and scallop a cornice. He'd done pencil drawings of both buildings years ago, when he moved in.

The buildings had smelly, littered passages behind them, barely big enough for a normal-sized man. While this was mostly an Ambyr neighborhood, he thought the second building might be owned by BCCA/Hong Kong Holdings. Could've been India Group. Didn't matter. All that mattered were the nine-foot fences companies loved to erect between their properties for reasons that could only be justified by fence manufacturers and installation crews. They had nothing to do with Systems Security. He knew that for a fact.

McCallum ran up the flat planks at the end of the alley. His momentum gave him just enough height to get his hands on the top. 48 years on the planet did not disqualify him from chinning this stockade.

"Crap," he exhaled has he pulled himself up. He threw his arms over. The boards stung his armpits. This sucked so bad. Was he even beating the uniforms to the customer? The victim, he corrected himself. The vic was probably lying in his bed with his hand on his heart.

McCallum got his legs up and looked down the alley. The bracing on the back of the stockade was six inches thick and fairly straight. He ran, jumping over the junctions, confident in his balance, but hoping the beams could take the impact. Some of this wood could be from Buffalo's last boom, too.

He didn't look down. His eyes were somewhere around 15 feet up, now. He looked at the customer's apartment building. It had a few lights on. Not enough to signal trouble. It had a courtyard in back, abutting the fence he was using as a highway. He leaped over one more junction, squatted, grabbed the cross beam with his hands, and let his body drop and unfurl. Three feet to the grassy lawn. Easy.

"Looks like you're there," he heard in his hear. Dispatch, tracking his movements.

"Yeah," McCallum said between puffs. "Could you get the door?"

"No problem, sir."

McCallum stopped. "I think there's a problem."

He had a tough time seeing the figure in front of him. A man, a few inches shorter than him, wearing a tight, flat black body suit. It absorbed what little light made it from the stars and distant streetlights to this little lawn. The man ran from the apartment building with care, choosing silence over speed. He stopped. The full head and face mask prevented McCallum some seeing what he assumed to be the same stupefied expression he felt on his own face.

"The door is signaling open," dispatch said.

"Got something else," McCallum said. "Something pertinent."

The man in black took a fighting posture. Thai Krav Number 1. McCallum knew it, and groaned.

"Crap," he said. "You really want to do this?"

The man hopped two steps, spun, and kicked.

Crap! McCallum kept the exclamation internal. He realized immediately that creep had been trained. Fucking crap.

He blocked, tried a grab but had to cross his arms and block again. The guy had speed. McCallum figured he had a good 15 pounds up on the guy. That might matter. Might not, the way his feet were flying. McCallum shifted to the right to get air behind him. Getting backed up to the fence wouldn't help.

Fight Thai with... something else, he said to himself.

McCallum kicked, aiming for the head. The man in black pushed the leg to the side and punched with his left, into McCallum's stomach. He took the pain. He'd expected and welcomed it. The punch brought the man's arm in nice and close. McCallum grasped the wrist, pulled the arm, rolled into the black body, and brought the man to the ground. He kept hold of the man's left wrist, fully extending his arm. He stomped onto the man's chest, positioning the toe of his boot on the man's prone neck.

"Dispatch," McCallum said. "ETA on back-up?"

"One minute, 40," the dispatched replied.

The man in black reached his right hand up to meet the left one, which McCallum held near the man's black bracelet. McCallum shook his head and pressed his toe down on the soft trachea. The hands parted. McCallum heard a slight ratchety sound, like a fishing reel. The guy held something in his right hand. There was a glisten between his left and right.

McCallum's foot folded. He collapsed over top of the man in black like he'd lost the use of his left foot.

Which he had. The burning, lightning pain came after the fall. He turned, clawing for his left ankle. The man jumped up. A line almost too thin to see retracted into his cuff. McCallum squeezed a wound he couldn't see, stifling the blood he could feel.

The shadow disappeared over the fence.

"Dispatch?"

"Yes, Detective."

"That ambulance coming too?"

"About 60 seconds."

"Send one of the EMTs around back."

"Are you OK?"

"Not as far as 'nights off' go."

Chapter 3

McCallum closed his eyes when he heard the footsteps out in the hall. Heels hard on the tile, lots of force from not a lot of weight. He recognized the gait as easily as he would have the voice or face, and decided to fake a coma.

"Eddie," Detective Supervisor Andrea Kim said. "Come back to us, Eddie."

Artificial sugar, McCallum thought. Insulting. Did she think she was fooling him? A decorated op? A detective? He… wasn't fooling her, either.

"You're supposed to wake me with a kiss," he said, keeping his eyes shut.

"This ain't no fairy tale. Come on. Time to make an oral."

McCallum opened his eyes. Andrea stood next to the bed. She wore navy pants and a white sleeveless blouse that contrasted with her dark skin, and showed off her etched muscles. She did this on purpose. At 5'4" with round, overtly feminine features, she knew she didn't naturally project command.

"How are you doing?" she asked.

"Adequate," McCallum answered. "Think I still got a good flow of narcotics going."

"More than you think. The docs said you had your Achilles tendon sliced clear through. The cut was so clean they guessed it was a surgical instrument."

"A wire."

Andrea's lips pressed and poked out. She raised her left wrist. Her com-link was a set of large gold beads. She tapped it to turn on the recording and nodded at McCallum.

"Yes, sir," he said. "Ambyr Systems Security operative Edwin McCallum."

"You were attacked?"

"Melee with a person of interest at approximately 12:05 AM while responding to a customer alert. I'd subdued the POI when he produced a wire. It uncoiled from his cuff. Because I had a leg on his chest, he was able to cut through the back of my leg."

"And"

"And subsequently flee."

"Totally flee. We got nothin'. How'd he fight?"

"Like a pro," McCallum said.

"You get anything?'

"Male, 5" 10", 175 pounds, in about as good a shape as you."

"Not what I meant," Andrea said. "I'm asking you. Eddie."

McCallum understood. He didn't get his current grade through connections, sex, or graft. He had a different perspective. Sometimes that perspective helped see things that could close up a policy breach. Sometimes it didn't.

McCallum looked up at the bright, white ceiling. "A blank canvas."

Andrea gave him a moment to reflect. He couldn't tell if she was disappointed or tired or hoping he might recall a detail he'd overlooked.

"The customer?" he asked.

"Deceased," Andrea answered. "Throat slit to the spine. Gloves 'n goggles are poking him now. They also said something about a nice, clean cut. Surgical quality."

"We got a decent budget?"

"The blank should not have injured an operative. Sends down a whole pile of money. We'll find him."

"When I—"

Andrea lowered her head. "We. Not you. I will formally recognize your professionalism and devotion to the company, but you ain't goin' anywhere for a while."

"How long?"

"I'm not in the game of guessing." Andrea tapped her cuff. "Why'd you pretend to be asleep?"

McCallum made a thin smile. "I'm still a little silly from the drugs."

"Or you were going to work this investigation from the bed. Because no one said you couldn't. Which is the other reason I'm here." Andrea tapped her cuff again. Restarting the recording, McCallum figured.

"Edwin McCallum," she said. "You are hereby suspended."

— ‹›› —

Neelesh stood before the bleary-eyed eighth graders hoping they didn't notice his bleary eyes. He had to fit in a mandatory workout when he got home, and then try to fall asleep with an elevated heart rate. Up at seven, here at eight. Day students until three. Back at five o'clock for the night shift kids. Teach until midnight and repeat. *No.* He couldn't stand here looking forward to midnight. That was no way to go through life. He wouldn't allow it. If he let his mind slide that way, eliding the nights and days and weeks and years, he'd end up like... every teacher he'd ever known. No one thinks he or she is going to shrivel up and dry out, but every teacher does. It's just a matter of time.

Not him. Not yet. Neelesh did three jumping jacks. He would put desiccation off as long as he could.

"Hey," he said to the class, "anybody remember what we were talking about?"

They chuckled a bit. Not much. Too early.

"Pre-Buy-Up social structure. OK. Everyone, with me now. 1... 2... 3— yawn."

They chuckled a little bit more now.

"I know this is not that interesting."

"Then why are you teaching it?" Nicholas Pawchek asked from the back, apparently looking for his own laughs — Which he got.

"Good question," Neelesh nodded and spread his arms. He took a deep breath and held it as he looked out over the 35 girls and boys in their khaki pants and red sports shirts, some attentive, some asleep with their eyes open, at the zenith of their learning years. Neelesh loved teaching eighth grade, the final year of general education. Soon, they'd all be sifted and separated, sent off to highly specialized programs. This would be last time some of them ever learned something they didn't have to.

"Why would Ambyr Consolidated invest thousands of dollars in teaching you all about history? Does anybody really need it? Is knowledge of the ancient Romans going to help you to be better clerks or nurses or crane operators? Is it to help you at home, raising your own kids? Balancing your own income accounts? Help you save for a house, wash dishes, or sort your laundry? How exactly is any of this worth anything at all?"

Neelesh stomped his foot on the ground.

"Too soft," he said. "Wish I'd worn the boots today. Help me out." He stomped again. He flipped his hands, encouraging the kids to stomp with him. Thump. Thump. Thump. They each fell into the rhythm. The room filled with a soft, slapping thunder.

Neelesh jumped and landed with both feet and swept his arms over each other. The kids ceased.

"That is why," he said. "History is the ground beneath us. We came from it. We will return to it. The school is built on ground, just like society is built on history. A catalogue of mishaps and triumphs; a long, long list of dos and don'ts. We can't see what's ahead of us. None of us can. Humans are future blind. But by glancing back, by learning what *has* happened, we can, at the very least, make a guess at what *might* happen.

"We learn, so we can live."

The whole class stared at him. He rarely had such full attention.

"Really?" Amy Lin asked.

"No," Neelesh said. "Not really. This whole class was written by company employees to make you believe you're living in the best of all possible circumstances. That this is as good as it gets."

The kids' mouths opened. They looked at each other, then back at Neelesh.

"And they've got to do something with you while your parents are at work, right? Can't have you doing math drills all the time. So. Where were we? Pre-Buy-Up Mayans, I think."

— «» —

"You are Father Demiana DeFalco," the woman said.

Demiana nodded.

The woman scowled. Her skin had the color and texture of peach silk discovered in the attic of a great, great aunt.

Norma Fielding, consul for India Group, Demiana's cuff whispered in her ear.

"You must state your name for the record," Norma said.

Demiana looked around the small conference room. A bamboo table for eight, lighting fixtures too boring to notice, chairs puffy enough to allow for one hour of comfort and no more.

"You are Father Demiana DeFalco," the woman said.

Demiana nodded. "You don't think there are ten cameras recording my nod?"

"You must state your name for the record."

Demiana looked at the man two chairs to her left. Mid-fifties, sloped like a hill, remnants of chestnut hair circling a pale, spotted knoll. The cuff whispered, *George Chan, consul for BCCA/Hong Kong Holdings.*

"And you, sir?" she asked. "Do you need me to speak as well?"

"My company's technology is sufficiently advanced to determine your identity," he said. "*We* can move forward whenever you are ready."

"Oh, I'm ready."

"Please, Father," Norma said. "State your name for the record."

"I will set the rules for these meetings." Demiana's voice rose in pitch, as she tightened the vocal cords to keep them from quivering. Her neck heated and prickled. "If either party present is in disagreement with these stipulations, they may end the function at any time. If you understand me, please nod."

She looked into the Norma's eyes and waited. The woman's head lowered one degree and returned. Demiana glanced at George. His head bounced as he chuckled.

"OK, then," Demiana said. "What would you like to know?"

Norma straightened in her chair. "Your parents were both Ambyr employees, correct?"

"Yes."

"You were raised Ambyr and went to Ambyr Consolidated Schools until how old?"

"Through college."

"And yet you don't believe we should expect any bias towards your company in this tragedy-of-the-commons mediation?"

"Hey," Demiana smiled. "Who's got more gripes with a company than its own employees?"

Norma's face failed to change.

Demiana continued. "I have given my heart and soul to the Lord Jesus Christ and the Catholic Church that does his work on this Earth. I have no prejudice above my devotion to peace, charity, and truth."

"You have renounced your allegiance to Ambyr Consolidated?"

"There was never a need. My vows trump all other considerations."

"Your communications facilitator is of Ambyr design? Ambyr supported?"

"My cuff is paid for by the Church and is Church property. While Ambyr currently sees to my data needs, the contract is not binding. Many members of my order use India Group data draws. Others use Hong Kong. My preference is entirely due to the learning curve established by my upbringing, but I could, at any time, address my data needs through your company. Or the other.

"Unlike employees of any one company, members of the Catholic Church frequently spread commercial transactions out over the three companies. We are encouraged to, so as to keep even the impression of entanglement at bay. You may find it interesting that my current health insurance policy is actually held by India Group. I have taken a vow of poverty, but what savings I do have are held in a Hong Kong Bank."

Norma looked at her own wide, eggshell bracelet. "You are unmarried."

"Yes." Demiana snickered.

"You're not seeing anyone?"

"No."

"Man or woman?"

"I've taken a vow of chastity."

"And you are keeping your vow of chastity?"

"You're not persuading my otherwise."

George chuckled again.

"You joined the priesthood later than normal."

"I heard the calling all my life. It took me till 24 to answer it, which is not uncommon. The average age for someone taking their final vows is 37."

"Can you tell me why you chose to answer the call at 24?"

Demiana lost her smile. She titled her head and tapped the table. Norma kept her eyes fixed on her, like lasers trying to burn their way through her skin and bone.

"If you've never heard the calling, it is difficult to describe."

"Try me."

Demiana paused again. She looked at George, who'd also lost his smile. He did not seem like he was poised to cut in.

"There is something bigger than the companies, an entity that deserves our love and devotion. Providing that love and devotion is a fulltime job, so if you're really, really into it, you can't very well keep another job, can you?"

"You chose to escape the rigors of corporate life."

Her neck warmed again. The nasty words bubbled up in her gut. She couldn't. She couldn't say any of the things she wanted to shout at this wilted bureaucrat whose whole existence seemed to be based on lessening the value of others.

"The Lord showed me that I could do more with my life."

"It seems convenient."

"Is there a question in there somewhere?" Demiana asked. "The standard agreement stipulates that I sit here and answer questions in order to show my qualifications to conduct this mediation. It says nothing about statements."

Norma swallowed. "It seems like a convenient choice, don't you think?"

"It is not for me to judge. The Lord does the judging. I believe what the Bible says in Romans 2: *For in passing judgment on another you condemn yourself.* Any other questions?"

"I'm good," George said.

Chapter 4

"Sounds like paradise," Aga Graber said. Her head filled the screen on McCallum's wall. Colorless, waxy skin bounced too much light. Her nose, from this angle, looked like an architectural feature. Her hair hovered around her head in a spray of black and gray fuzz so uncoordinated that the monitor seemed to be on the fritz.

"One man's paradise is another man's Hell." McCallum sat on his couch, left leg elevated per medical instructions, the rest of him trying to get as far from the leg as possible.

"I'm thrilled. You get to do art all the time. What are you working on?"

"Getting well."

"I had some interest last year in your acrylics on glass."

"Between the painkillers and the actual pain, I don't know if I'm going to get anything done."

"Sweetums," Aga said. "There should be no 'between.' Take more painkillers. I'm sure I don't need to list all the great artists who took advantage of various mood-enhancements. You've been laid out by opportunity. Exploit it. Then I will exploit you."

"You may have to take me in if I can't get working again."

"Another time-honored artistic tradition. This may be a turning point in your career."

"That's what I'm worried about."

"Pfst." Aga swept a hand across the screen, dismissively. "Rent, food, water — they all take care of themselves. It's art that needs attention. So what did the doctors say?"

"Two weeks horizontal. It could take months to get back to normal. If it ever does. I'm not ... at my optimal healing age."

"You are darker than usual and your usual is basic black."

"And you've actually been cheering me up."

"Use it, darling." Aga clenched her hands together and shook them at the screen. "Use this dark time in your life to make something that counts. Make that blackness a forge. Press your coal into a diamond."

Yes, McCallum thought. *Use the anger and frustration, use the time to make something new...* except for that gnat in the back of his head, the man in the black body stocking. The killer. The unresolved.

His leg, mostly his calf, ached. His meds would be wearing off soon. He had to think hard about another dose. Aga continued to stare from the wall. Unmoving, not unlike a photograph. Like one of those watercolors that reaches for realism. On either side of her image, leaning against the wall, were stacks of canvases with paintings on each. He considered each unfinished. He had never, to his mind, finished a piece of art in his life. There was always some stroke to even out, detail to refine, color to mute or embolden.

Aga had never received a McCallum original for her gallery to sell because McCallum never let one go.

— «» —

Neelesh clasped his hands and surveyed the class, fresh from lunch. He liked this time. He didn't know how much information he pumped into them, but while they digested they gave the appearance of learning.

Neelesh announced, "Unified in purpose, diverse in tactics."

The mumbles of the children ebbed. Three-quarters of the eyes rose to focus in his direction. Generally speaking.

"Anyone know who said that?" he asked. "Anyone?"

"An old guy," someone said.

"A dead guy," another added. Children snickered.

"Yes," Neelesh said. "Trick questions, actually. No one knows. It is attributed to Christopher Louis, the first Chairman of Ambyr Consolidated. If we were in a Hong Kong or India school, we would probably be giving someone else credit. What is important is not who said it, but why. What does that statement mean and why does it get repeated?"

Neelesh waited, arms raised.

"Too much tofu today? What? Unified in purpose, diverse in tactics."

"It's the..." Donna from the third row raised her hand. "The mission statement? It's part of our mission statement?"

"Close," Neelesh said. "It's actually simpler than that. It is the reason the companies won. The reason monarchies and democracies and all the other forms of government are gone. It is the best-of-the-worlds theory and the core of what we'll be studying in this block."

Many sat back. Eyes began to roam. Economic history did not grip 13-year-olds, Neelesh knew. He'd been one not so long ago. What did reach out and grab their little minds?

"This is a story of death, pirates, and power. It is all that is wrong with humanity and our struggle to make things right. Our history shows us first how to survive, then to grow, and ultimately to prosper. History shows us how to use our natural instincts, our gifts, and each other to make the world a safer and more hospitable place. Our best tool for that is the corporation, and it starts in the year 1600 with the East India Company — the mother of all companies and our first glance at an honorable society.

"Bring up Chapter 1..."

— ⟨⟩ —

The man looked nice enough. Younger and better dressed than those who usually found their way to weekday mass. His blond hair was feathery, with layers perfect for fingers... or so it seemed to Demiana.

"Father DeFalco," he said as she passed, on her way up the aisle.

"Huh?" Oh God, did I look too long? He knew me?

"Steven Hosland." He rose partly, perhaps to slide deeper down the dark oak pew. "Ambyr consul for the mediation."

"Oh. Yes. We haven't met."

"Do you have a second?"

"I seem to," Demiana said. "I mean, my time is being directed in your direction now, so..."

"Sorry I didn't make the first meeting."

"It wasn't mandatory."

"I know, it's just that—" He sat and motioned to the end of the pew. "That I'm rejecting you, so why plop down at a meeting, right? Then my boss said you can't reject her without sharing some air, so here I am. It's nothing personal."

Demiana sat down on the edge of the bench, legs pressed together. She fluffed out her skirt. She lowered her head a tad and looked at Steven.

"You just made it personal."

"It's just business, is all."

"I'm not in business."

"No, I guess—"

"So you're meeting me in the flesh, in a house of worship, to tell me what, exactly? If it's to inform me that my services will not be required, well that's not just impolite, it's unnecessary. Your decision regarding my acceptability goes to my superior. Not me. If this is a perfunctory gesture, you should have at least bought me a drink. I don't date. Anymore. But I do enjoy a well-made martini."

Steven looked around without moving his head. Eventually his eyes settled back on Demiana's.

"Scratch it," he said. *To himself*, Demiana thought. *He is trying to change tactics*. "They told me to kick you."

"Who?"

"They. Grades lower than mine. Lower than my bosses. They told me, orally, to kick you in an oral. Nothing to trace."

"Why?"

Steven shrugged his shoulders. Demiana sat back in the pew. She gazed at the altar under the 20-foot cross. Candles glowed at either end, small flames, steady from the lack of activity in the church.

Steven said, "Felt bad about it, is all."

"Yeah," Demiana said. "You tell them the rejection was rejected."

"What? Can you do that?"

"Sure." Demiana continued. "Why not? The Church sets the rules. You tell them that."

"I don't even know if I can. They didn't exactly leave me a number or anything."

"We will proceed. On schedule." Demiana rose and walked up the aisle. "It was nice meeting you."

She walked faster.

Chapter 5

Neelesh flicked his hand. The classroom's computer noticed and changed all of the personal screens in the room.

"On the last day of the year 1600, Queen Elizabeth granted a charter to the British East India Company, or as it is more properly known, The Governor and Company of Merchants of London, trading with the East Indies. This is not the first corporation in the world. Who had the first?"

One third of the class looks at him, the rest were already doll-eyed, minds drifting.

"Ting Ting," Neelesh said. "Who had the first corporation?"

The girl snapped her head up. "The... um... Romans."

"Excellent."

"In fact, other nations had already set up ventures into the same region. The East India Company was the world's first joint-stock corporation of any note. It is one of the reasons for its more than 250 years of success and why it's worth studying today.

"A joint-stock company brings, for the first time, the chance for economic fairness and equity to the masses. Anyone can buy stock — a little piece of a company. If that company makes a profit, that money is divvied up amongst the people holding the shares of stock. Profit is shared jointly. Until this time in history, most money was related to land ownership and that land was handed down family lines. For a good life, you had to be born into a wealthy family or marry well. Now, suddenly, with a stroke of the Queen's quill, anyone could be rich. Questions so far?"

A hand. Sam Qui. Neelesh pointed and nodded at the boy.

"Is this going to be on the test?"

Teachers are supposed to say there are no stupid questions. There were, however, Neelesh decided, some detestable ones.

"I don't know," Neelesh said. "Let's decide as a class. Anyone think that should be on the test?"

Several heads nodded. Again, about a third. These kids were tough today. Not even sarcasm got their attention.

"Sorry," Neelesh said. "Yes. And an extra five points on that exam to anybody who can tell me why."

One hand. Amy. She always paid attention. He'd hoped for one or two others, but pointed to her and nodded anyway.

Amy said, "Because this is how the companies started."

Neelesh smiled. "Good. Good. It is more than that, though. This is when the companies did something good. When they started giving everyone a chance for a better life. Joint stock wasn't the whole reason. The East India Company was also the first LLC or limited liability company. Anyone want to take a stab at that? No? How about liability? What does it mean when you're liable for something?"

"It's your business," a girl from the third row said.

"Excellent," Neelesh replied. "It's your business. It's your responsibility. If the company borrows money and fails and can't pay it back, you are responsible. You are liable. But this is *limited* liability. The people who own this company are only responsible up to a point. Anyone want to guess why that's important?"

Blank faces. He hated the blank faces.

"If we all go up to the roof…" he said. Some faces came back. Quizzical and alive. "Let's go up to the roof because I have a new kind of umbrella that will let you jump off and float lightly to the ground like a dandelion seed."

"Really?"

"Sadly, no. Let's pretend though. We go up there and I hand it to you, Carey. Do you take it and jump?"

Carey Moseur from the forth row looked side-to-side and giggled.

"It'll be fun," Neelesh said. "Drifting down like Mary Poppins. Do you do it? Do you jump?"

"I don't know," the girl pushed through her tight, embarrassed grin.

"No, you don't know. You've never heard of this magic umbrella before. You've never seen one used. There is a lot of risk in taking this leap of faith. Now supposed I put up a net. You can't get hurt even if my umbrella fails. What, then? Would you try then?"

Carey looked around again. Neelesh waited.

"I guess. With a net, sure."

"Why not, right? Could be fun." Neelesh addressed the whole class. "With a net you are less likely to hurt yourself. A net limits the risk. And that is what Queen Elizabeth does to the liabilities associated with this newfangled company. She limits them. A limited liability corporation is born. And what does that do? Why the heck should we care?

"Because now we can leap. We've a net so we can try our new umbrellas. You and I and all the other cobblers and farmers and peasants who have managed to stash away a couple extra pennies can take a chance on a new company and not risk losing our shops or farms or freedom if the company fails. We can take chances. A chance to advance. If you're clever, frugal, and do your homework, you can build wealth. For the first time in centuries, a person can move up in society under his own power. On the far side of the aristocracy lies meritocracy. Through the East India Company, people get a glimpse of it, and they like what they see."

Oscar D'Arran's hand went up. Neelesh pointed to him.

"Is this umbrella stuff going to be on the test?"

Neelesh said, "Is Mary Poppins a symbol of private enterprise stepping into guard the population from an ineffective parental state? That's the question."

Neelesh looked out over the field of stunned eyes. He finally had everyone's attention. He laughed and swatted his hand at them. "No, Oscar. That is not something I want to type into a test question."

Not if I want to keep my job, he added in his head.

— «» —

McCallum sat on a stool, one easel in front of him to hold the canvas, another set a little lower to support his outstretched left leg. The white canvas stared at him, gazing into him. A big, rectangular eye. It knew. It knew all his faults and failures. It could see his doubts, his foolhardiness, his stupid-ass belief that the canvas could be transformed into something he wanted. Stupid, pathetic man. Go back to chasing toilet paper thieves.

He couldn't paint this way. He had to stand. But if he stood, his leg throbbed. His own blood beating out a song of pain. If he sat, he couldn't move his arms right. His angle of attack was always down and to the left. Down and to the left. Like that black body-stocking fuck who sliced through his Achilles. Down and to his left. My left, McCallum corrected himself. His right. The assailant was right handed. There. He just ruled out 10% of the population.

The victim, the guy who took out the protection policy, he had known someone wanted to kill him. He dished out for a full security service, but he didn't site the reason. He never told Ambyr Systems Security who or why or what might happen. When a woman pays a premium, she always knows. She says right up front that so-and-so is going to hurt me, or worse. And they're always right. Ex-boyfriend, husband, or co-worked who gets bent too far — the only mystery is when the hurt will happen and how bad it will be. If the victim had known someone wanted him dead, he must have known who. He must have. The victim had known the guy who cut up McCallum's leg, the guy who needed a kicking. A real good kicking.

Unproductive thought. McCallum picked up his pencil. He would sketch, then paint. He would not tumble the details of this case over in his head, polishing them like sea glass, because that produced nothing. Nothing he could use. He always said he could use more time. This time, now. Alone, unpressured, able to produce whatever he wanted. He could do a big piece. Get a bigger canvas, maybe three. He could finally do a triptych. Fort Niagara. Three seasons… No spring. No one did spring anymore. If he wanted to paint fantasies like growth and rebirth, he'd be better off with unicorns and dragons. People bought those. People liked those. People believed in those things.

His leg lay out before him. A bridge. A suspension bridge, running through its supports, leading nowhere. He ran his pencil down the pure white canvas, roughing in two vertical lines meeting near the top of the space, then two horizontal traveling under them.

— «» —

Demiana wore a black blouse and black jacket. She kept her collar dangling around her neck. She'd chosen black boots, black tights, and a short black skirt because… why? *Why?* she asked herself strolling into the conference room. To impress? To shock? To say, 'I'm different'? She had no idea. She thought maybe God helped her dress. Guided her hand through the closet. Wasn't that the kind of minor miracle everyone prayed for every night? God, help me get through tomorrow. This outfit would help. It blended tradition and sass. Glory be to the Father.

George and Steven stood as she rounded the round table. Norma did not. She didn't even look up from her portfolio, which Demiana could see displayed the morning news.

She had requested this room from the hotel because of its size. It fit four people, maybe two more if they were friendly. The round table meant no sides, no teams, no hierarchy. She worked well this way. Or, at least, she hoped she did. She'd never done one of these before, and she felt really bad about not mentioning it — possibly because of hubris? Was that the right sin? Ha. There's no right sin.

Demiana cleared her throat and said, "In the two years since my ordination, I've been assigned almost exclusively to the dairy arbitrage. Because the companies do not mingle currency — and hate negative cash flow — they don't buy from each other. They will, however, buy from the Church. In order to keep the price of certain commodities stable, companies will buy and sell to the Church. I've been facilitating the buying of milk from a company that had too much, helping them avoid a drop in price, and selling to a company that had too little, helping them avoid a price spike. The companies prize stability, and trust the Church not to manipulate prices or force a commodity bubble. Yes, the Church makes money, but what I liked was that people

— kids and babies — got what they need to live, and on a regular, affordable basis. If Jesus walked the Earth today, I think he might have something to say about commodities flow. A parable of the arbitrageur: How a fair market can force a rich man to feed the poor. He talked a lot about feeding the poor. Anyway, that didn't come up in our interview."

The three looked at her. George twinkled. Norma made her lips into a sphincter. Steven jammed his jaw side to side. Demiana registered all three expressions, filing them away in her memory for later analysis.

"Father," Steven said. "Your double shot of honesty there is top shelf. It really hit the spot. But in light of this new intel, your rookiedom in the extreme, I'm thinking we've got to close this whole thing up."

Demiana folded her hands on the table and smiled. "The time for that has passed. Objections needed to be aired at the interview."

"Yeah. Still, we can vote. If two of us are in agreement that this is no longer a floating boat. You know, we can junk the proceedings. What do say, Hong Kong?

George turned to Steven and laughed. "I've got no problem with her."

Steven moved his attention to Norma, who had already swung her head to face him. Her lips continued to squeeze and protrude. Demiana wondered if they might be stuck that way, like her mother claimed her eyes would if she continued to cross them all the time. Or stuck her tongue out. That's what this group needed — a tongue sticking. Except for George. He seemed all right.

Norma continued to stare at the Ambyr consul. Demiana continued to keep up her smile, though it got more difficult by the second. Had she gone too far? Had she, once again, let too much information blabber from her heart? Better question: Did she even care? She didn't feel ready for this assignment. Steven was right. Passing buy and sell orders between a couple of people who all wanted the same thing did not lead to a formal mediation, with people, in the flesh, for weeks or months, with millions of dollars and the reputation of the Roman Catholic Church at stake. She did not belong at the table.

Norma knew that, too. That's why she had tried to intimidate her at the interview. She didn't decline her, though, when she had her first chance. Odd. It was like she wanted her, Demiana, to withdraw on her own. Which she couldn't, because the Bishop personally threw her into this mess. He knew better than the others how ill prepared she was for the task. Odd, again, like Steven telling her his bosses wanted her out.

What the fu— Nope. What the fudge. What the heck. No, no. How curious? That sounded pretty priestly. And she was a priest. She needed to be a priest. She could be nothing else, she knew, in her ever-blabbering heart. That meant following the Bishop no matter how Byzantine his orders.

Following did not mean sitting idly by while others played with her fate. She glanced at Norma, who held her gaze. Demiana could see the woman weigh the matter on the scale in her head.

"Steven?" Demiana asked. "How long have you been captaining this whole mediation boat thing? In the extreme?"

"I'm not—" He stopped himself. His eyes darted around, like he might find a better answer on the wall or table or floor or George's head. "That's part of the interview process and that time has passed."

"Just wondering. You know, had a double shot of top shelf wonder."

Norma looked at Demiana from the corners of her eyes. Her lips failed to loosen. Her eyes returned to Steven, taking in his blue suit and silky yellow shirt. His rush of blond hair, flying back from a nonexistent breeze. His lack of creases, wrinkles, spots, gray hairs, or sag.

Norma blew a bit of air out her nostrils, looked down at her cuff and said, "India Group will brook no more delays on this matter. Let us proceed."

Chapter 6

McCallum had never been capable of taking naps, but the late afternoon light had a long, deadening quality that he hated, so he tried. He almost reached sleep when his cuff vibrated. In his ear he heard, *More cleaning power than ever before. CoreClean.*

"Yes," he said out loud. He didn't want to talk to anyone whose ring was a CoreClean ad. He wanted the ad to continue even less.

"Mr. Edwin McCallum," a young female voice answered.

"Yes."

"This is Lizzie with PanHealth. According to our records, you have not engaged in any physical activity for three days."

"Yes."

"With your contract, you agreed to a four-and-two exercise program."

"I'm familiar with the details."

"Until now you have been very good in keeping your schedule. Do you think you will be able to work out today?"

"No."

"Is there a problem?"

"I'd label it that. I got hurt on the job. Can't walk. Doctor's orders."

"Can you be more specific?"

"Isn't it in my file? You're my healthcare provider. Don't you know I'm laid up?"

"There is no mention of it in your file."

"I was in the hospital. I had surgery. I don't know a lot about medical records, but I'm damn sure the company keeps 'em."

"Your annual check-up is the last entry."

McCallum sat up. He ran his fingers through his hair. "You can tell from my cuff that I haven't moved around much, right?"

"That is what our records indicate."

"Can you go back three days and see where I was?"

"We're not authorized for location services," the woman replied. "We track proprio data only."

"And three days ago?"

"It appears you went for a midnight run."

"A short one."

"Five minutes. Followed by a one minute workout routine."

"You've got to check with my doctor."

"If you could have their office resubmit to us. Perhaps they haven't logged in."

"OK. I'll get a hold of them."

"In the meantime, you really do need to work out."

"I can't."

"If you do not continue to take your health seriously, sir, we may have to suspend your contract. You will be liable for pending or future healthcare costs."

"Pending?" McCallum asked. "Do I have any charges pending?"

"Current charges pending total $18,250."

"From when?"

"They entered the system about three days ago."

"From where?"

"St. Mary's trauma."

"And what does that tell you?"

"You should reconsider your exercise program. That is a substantial fee. We would hate to turn that fee over to you."

"Does the cost come with any other details? Can you tell what was done to me?"

"I'm sorry, it's been redacted."

"Re-what?"

"The info is being withheld by Systems Security."

McCallum yanked on his hair then smoothed it back. He looked around for his pain meds. "How's my heart rate now, Lizzie."

"Elevated."

— ⟨⟩ —

Neelesh reached for the bowl of chole. His mother waited. She put nothing on her plate until he'd tasted whatever she'd made. She had a straight back, high features, with black hair pulled back so tight she looked bald viewed head on. She didn't chatter away tonight, Neelesh noticed. She wasn't waiting to see if he liked dinner. She waited for something else.

"What?" he asked.

"Dr. Cohen is dead."

"That's awful." Neelesh felt a heavy door slam inside him. The rush of air passed through him with a chill. The home that was him now had a room closed off forever. "I didn't know he was sick."

"He wasn't."

Neelesh looked up from his plate. Sukhbir Fhor wore an expression Neelesh could not remember seeing before. He looked not at her, but at the expression, the dour mouth and wide eyes.

"What happened?"

"I heard he was murdered."

Neelesh rolled his eyes. "Where'd you hear that?"

"Gloria, at work."

"Don't you think it would've been in the news? An actual murder? Around here? It would be the top trending headline all the time."

"Gloria knows someone who lives near there. He saw it. Then the SS told him to forget about it."

"The SS? Systems Security?"

"They want to keep it a secret."

"A friend of a friend, huh?" Neelesh took in a fork full of curry.

"It's true."

"Why, Mom? What makes you believe in a secret murder?"

"The secret."

"The secret makes you believe in the secret."

Sukhbir held her expression. Neelesh felt like he'd just met her. This grade nine vice-president of customer care for an energy company, with over 100 direct reports. The woman who had raised him on her own, with no other family around, while working and continuing her education. Stern. Unflappable. Her hobbies consisted of making sure he did well in school and cooking. A pillar you tie your boat to when the storm's coming in. That was the Sukhbir he'd known for his whole life… until this moment, when she started relaying flimsy gossip with the shadow of trembling death on her face.

"The curry is delicious," he said.

"Be careful," Sukhbir said.

"What's that supposed to mean?"

"Dr. Cohen…"

"Yes."

"He looked out for you."

Neelesh drooped. "He was my doctor. That was his job." It seemed like a lie as he said it. The man had been much more. "I guess I'm going to need to find another one now."

A tear massed in the corner of Sukhbir's right eye and began a slow journey down her cheek. Neelesh watched it. His face fell with it.

"I'm sorry," he said. "I didn't know he meant that much to you."

Sukhbir tipped her head back. She huffed out a laugh. "That's funny. I hated the bastard. It's you that means a great deal to me."

Neelesh brought a spoon full of chole to his mouth, then realized he hadn't chewed up the parcel already there.

— «◇» —

Demiana stood outside the hotel waiting for a cab. What had she been thinking with this outfit? Yes, she kind of had to wear black all the time, though she'd never been explicitly told that. She'd never seen any other members of her order don a different color, either, though. Not while on duty. She'd never felt more on duty than today. And now, standing here, in a heat that made it tough to breathe, the word 'folly' kept playing in her mind. Her bracelet said 92 degrees. The humidity made it feel like 102. Black stockings? Really? The Lord hadn't been guiding her hand, he'd been trying to teach her a lesson. About what, she had no idea. Too damn hot to think.

"How 'bout that drink now?"

Demiana turned her head and saw Steven.

"I can't decide what to comment on, the inappropriateness of the question or that fact that you would even ask it? I'm thinking you've got to be naive at the quantum level, so I shouldn't got all hyper-sarcastic on you. Still, you've got to understand that I'm not even supposed to talk to you now that the mediation sessions have started, right?"

Steven tipped his head right and left, juggling his eyes around. He kept his lips pressed tight. He stopped, fixated on something over Demiana's shoulder.

"Can you help me? I've dropped my... lip balm in that fountain."

"And, what? You want me to give it last rights?"

Steven started towards the fountain inside the hotel lobby. He turned as the doors swooshed open and walked backwards, beckoning Demiana to follow.

It would, at the very least, be cooler.

The fountain consisted of three bronze towers, each spilling a sheet of water into a square basin. Steven sat in front of it and patted the seat next to him. The air refreshed Demiana. The water attracted her. She sat down out of curiosity.

Steven took off his jacket and rolled up his sleeve. He had a gold com bracelet, laser etched on the thick sides. The edges had a severe cut. Most people preferred more rounded corners. Demiana found it gaudy, but in a good way.

"Here," he said. "Help me look around."

Steven plunged his left arm into the water, submerging his cuff.

"Doesn't lip balm float?"

"No." He looked her in the eyes.

Demiana took off her jacket. Her black blouse had no sleeves to roll. She turned, putting her back to Steven and dipped her arm into the basin until her cuff was under water. Steven scooched in behind her and put his hand on her upper arm and his mouth next to her right ear.

Steven whispered, "They want me to delay the proceedings by any means necessary."

"Who? And why?"

"I don't know."

"You said they gave you orders orally? Who does that?"

"A person. A flunky."

"Then how do you know it comes from a low grade? What's the show of authority?"

"I don't... and I just do, alright?"

"It's OK. You know I do this all the time."

"Run silent using a hotel fountain?"

"The Church has founts. Basically the same thing. We use them for confessionals now. Are you Catholic, Steven?"

"Wouldn't know how to start."

"Did you know I've taken an oath not to repeat anything you say to me in the sanctity of confession?"

"No," he answered. "Does this count. Is this sanctity?"

"Well," she said. "I'm also obligated to tell you the truth. So, no. This doesn't really count. Seeing as how we've gone through all the trouble of looking for your lip balm and all — why don't you just trust me and tell me what's going on."

Chapter 7

Demiana adjusted her skirt, flipped her hair back, and walked into the club like she'd been a member all her life. No one stopped her. She hated to admit it, but she looked like she belonged. Looks weren't deceiving. She did belong here, though not for the reasons the other patrons possessed. She did God's work, she told herself. Or, well, the Church's. Close enough.

Within a minute, she figured out why no one had stopped her at the door. The place was maze of white marble with wide hallways — it had once been an art gallery of some prominence, she'd been told. It suffered from very little light. Murmurs drifted through the corridors, mixed with the occasional moan. She ignored those and pressed on to a covered courtyard at the center. A glorious circular silver bar marked the middle, lit by steel torches. The stone top and location called to mind an altar, though in a much different kind of church.

There were but a half-dozen people ambling about, not quite paring off. The men wore dark suits, the ladies this year's versions of tight and sparkly, even though two of them really couldn't pull it off. At least they were dressed. The two bartenders were bare to as far as she could see. Maybe they had on shoes.

What was this, again, an Ambyr club? No Boodles, she remembered. What decent gin did Ambyr make?

"Hendricks and tonic," she said, sliding an elbow onto the slick bar.

"Certainly," the man said. A theater smile, Demiana thought. A pretty good one, too. Practice makes perfect. "You are a guest of…"

"Horace Marigold," Demiana replied.

"I'm sorry, it's just that you entered the club alone."

"No need to apologize." Demiana looked around the courtyard. "Have you seen him?"

"I couldn't say." He pinched a lime over a glass of bubbles and ice, dropped in the rind and pushed the drink her way.

Demiana held up her glass and nodded. "I'm sure he'll turn up."

"Yes." The bartender looked up and to the right. He nodded, then returned his attention to Demiana. "He would like to see whomever he just bought a drink. You can meet him in the Marionette Room."

"And that's...?"

He glanced to the left.

"Excellent." She took her drink and went exploring.

The place still had plenty of art on the walls. Lots of color splashes, worms and noodles and strings. Not all were modern, but all were distinct and, as far as her untrained eye could tell, quite excellent.

She continued through another hall, stopping this time to check out the source of green light and thumping electronic music. Several people stood or sat around a table. A naked woman squatted on top, astride some kind of machine with pistons and rubber. Demiana moved on.

She passed some more people in various states of undress. A permanent cocktail party where she didn't know anyone, thank God. She hoped, anyway. She didn't want to know anyone here. Or anyone to know her.

The Marionette Room had no sign outside the entrance. It didn't need one. The chamber was large and high. There must have been 20 or 30 people milling about inside. The light was better. A yellowish spot illuminated the stage in the center, the naked people — a boy and girl, they looked so young — and all of the ropes. White and glistening. They crisscrossed up and down, each connecting to some appendage or part of the performers. Various audience members held the other ends of the ropes, presumably tugging and releasing as they pleased.

She took a long sip of her gin. No need to stare. Stick to the plan. Find Horace and get the Hell out of here. She had no idea what he looked like. She didn't fret. Security had obviously identified her. She'd stand and look cool until curiosity got to him.

A woman in a clingy white shift approached her, took her elbow and said, "This way."

Horace Marigold sat in a slim chair, legs crossed, dangling a rocks glass in one hand and the end of a rope in the other. He wore a silk suit that could've passed for pajamas. She expected some fat troll with greasy hair. As usual, she was wrong. The guy wasn't half-bad looking for his age — somewhere up above 60, she figured, but she couldn't tell. He had the most luscious blond hair that was at odds with his shallow wrinkles. He smiled like he might be happy to see her.

"Cute outfit," he said.

"Something I threw together," she returned.

"Glad I could buy you drink. We're very accommodating here."

"And then some."

His eyes scanned her, top to bottom. She rolled hers.

"I don't know what you've heard," he said. "But you're a bit old for me."

"I'm not a hobbyist."

"We all are, dear. Just a matter of meeting the price."

"Not me. I'm a real, live Catholic priest. Father Demiana DeFalco."

"A pleasure to meet you."

"I'm the one you tried to delete from the tragedy-of-the-commons mediation."

He looked to the woman on her left and held out the rope. "Don't let the boy ejaculate just yet."

The woman in the white shift glided around him and took the end of the rope. Horace looked passed Demiana, to the stage. He took a sip of his dark drink and Demiana wondered if he would get back to her anytime soon.

He stood and held out his hand. "Come."

Demiana took his hand. His skin felt like warm lotion. He led her closer to the stage. The bed, really. A very tall king-size, lit with cruelty. She wanted to be so cool. She wanted none of this to affect her. She wanted to turn and walk backwards like she did in grade school when the wind whipped hard. She could not look at the girl, pulled into an X. She was so thin, so undeveloped. She did not want to guess the age.

The boy swung above her. Whoever worked his strings now had him flying just above her, an incubus in training, pale and wiry. He should have had bat wings, too. Like that little boy in the painting she saw in the hallway. This boy's mouth pulled on itself. His eyes glistened. He didn't have the strength to hold his position much longer.

"You're killing him," Demiana said.

Horace said, "What would be the fun in that?"

Demiana looked at him through the corners of her eyes.

"What did you hope to accomplish by coming here?" he asked.

"I'm not going to stop."

He gave her hand a squeeze. "Exactly the kind of persistence that would make one want to have you removed from the proceedings, don't you think?"

The boy's chest heaved, straining to suck in air against the weight of his body. The girl squirmed as the ropes lifted her legs up and straight, in someone's attempt to envelop her partner.

"How old are they?" she blurted out. She hadn't intended to. Stick to the plan. Shit.

"They are fresh."

"Aren't they still in school?"

"Sweepers, or some such thing. Who knows. In need of a little extra money, I would think. Or they enjoy it."

Demiana watched a tear fall from the boy's left eye to the girl's right cheek. "In one second I'm going to jump up there and make a mess of your contraption."

Horace released her hand. He looked up at the far wall, snapped his fingers, and then made a parting motion in the air. The boy was lowered down onto the girl. They both huffed, cheek-to-cheek.

"See what I did there?" Horace asked. "I avoided catastrophe with subtlety. That's what I do, Father, though my accomplishments are not always apparent. In fact, I work hard to make that so. My methods occasionally belie my intentions. I work in mysterious ways. You, of all people, should understand that."

"There's not much mystery here," Demiana said. "Thanks for trying though."

She turned in the direction of the door.

"And for the drink."

She walked as slowly as she could stand.

— «» —

Neelesh sat on his stool, legs crossed. He chuckled a little, to himself. The kids were in a field before him, looking like corn stalks all bent and withered from the spent day. As the sun set, not one of them held their heads high. They flopped left or right on a fist. Some hung in a nest of fingers, others flung all the way back, mouths wide like they might catch rain drops.

"Capitalism won," Neelesh just about shouted. "Why?"

Three finished their yawns. Ten blinked. The others he assumed were now dead.

"Anyone remember what capitalism is? From first grade? Anyone? You learned it with your alphabet and which colors make which when you blend them? Anyone? Come on, toss me a cookie here. Capitalism is the foundation of our grand society."

A hand. Esprite. Neelesh pointed at her.

"It's a system of living that people built on business."

"Very good," Neelesh said. "More or less. Certainly when it comes down to the practical effects. The beauty of capitalism is its inherent fairness. Capital is stuff — money, property, machines, warehouses, cows, goats, cars — whatever. That stuff isn't a gift of nature or chance. It's purchased, earned, or manufactured. It's not muscle or birthright. Capital gives everyone a chance. Capitalism is everyone's chance."

"Birthright?" Sam Qui asked or stated or blurted. Neelesh couldn't tell.

"Yes, Sam. The kings and queens, emperors and czars handed their wealth and stature down family lines. Your rights, by birth, were to the family fortunes and seats of power."

"Like now."

Neelesh ran his tongue across his upper teeth. Never lie, he'd said to himself, many times, as he trained to be a teacher. You can't do this, stare into the faces of naive, trusting, impressionable little people all day and cough out the corporate phlegm. You can't. You'll go nuts. You'll become one of those prunes you hated so much in school. The ones that never looked you in the eye. The ones that ushered you through the stocks of the abattoir, silent as to what lay ahead.

"Not exactly," Neelesh said. "Monarchs had formal laws."

"They had laws about who could be king?" May asked.

"Some did. Sometimes it was more tradition."

"Like now," Sam reasserted.

"Not exactly."

"If my old man was a low grade," Sam said. "It wouldn't matter how I did on my tests. He'd get me a tower job having meetings all day. You never see a low grade kid turning a wrench. Never. They get set for life just like the king's kids back in the day."

"Sam," Neelesh said. "I've got to admire your grasp of the issues. You make a valid comparison between past societies and ours."

"That ain't going to be on the test, though, is it?"

Neelesh said out the left side of his mouth, "That could never be on the test." Then he stood. "You do express a complete understanding of the topic, though. That kind of thing is on the test. The part about the past."

Karen spoke as she raised her hand. "But you said the past was important because it taught about the present."

"Yes. Very glad you were listening. But it's the past you get tested on."

"Not the present."

"Not exactly."

"Could you be a little more exact sometimes?" Sam asked.

"You *are* our teacher," came a voice from the back. Neelesh wasn't sure who. The class chuckled in unison.

Never lie, Neelesh said to himself. Then, out loud, "I wish the tests were different. I wish there were no tests at all. I wish you could all spend the next four or five years stumbling about, trying to find your way, maybe finding things you never knew about, only to find they become your life's great love. It's messy, though. Impractical. The other side of capitalism is efficiency. A long, steady, incessant march towards efficiency. You will all learn more, and faster than I did. Your kids will outpace you. The price for improvement is discovery. At least at first. We've moved our times to explore until later in life. Maybe then, when you've got the time to pause and reflect, this class will become important and you'll be glad you had it and it won't matter what was on the test."

— «» —

"What kind of drawdowns have we seen?" McCallum asked.

"What's with the 'we'?" the image on the wall replied. Mid-50s, wide shoulders, very little fat or fatigue. His short gray hair shined proudly. Wayne Clement sat back, sinking into his office chair, wrinkling his blue oxford shirt. The camera on his desktop widened the view. A large blow-up of an old Captain Marvel comic book cover hung on the wall behind him.

"You are not listed as an investigating operative," Wayne said.

McCallum looked at him down his extended left leg, naked save for the mummy wrap around most of the foot and up the calf. He'd taken an easel and lowered it so he could put his foot on the cross bar.

"I am listed," he said.

Wayne's lip curled on one side. "Technically, yes. You are mentioned in the file."

"I was glad to hear you were the economist assigned to this case because I ain't too sure how to bill this call."

"We'll keep it quick then. There have been no expenses to this line item."

McCallum's head jerked three degrees to the right. He positioned his ear better, certain he must have heard wrong. "My case? An attack on an op?"

"Yep."

"They cut off funds?"

Wayne shook his head. "No. The company has not capped the expense account."

"Makes me feel all warm inside."

"That's why they do it. All ops should feel loved all the time. Isn't that what Andrea told you?"

"Right before she tucked me in. You wouldn't, by any chance, be working the associated case?"

"The doc who was murdered?"

"Yeah." *Doctor?* McCallum thought.

"In fact I am. The company thinks there are some economies of scale to be had. And there are, there are... Although you know I can't discuss any of that with you."

McCallum and Wayne stared at each other for a moment. McCallum knew it was time to change tactics.

"How's your wife?" McCallum asked.

The curl returned to Wayne's lips. "Fine."

"Any tests? You know, for her condition?"

"That feeling-empty thing? Because the last kid's off to college? They got tests for that?"

"DNA?"

"Nope. None ordered."

"Nothing?"

"Zip," Wayne said.

McCallum left his mouth partially open. He'd readied his breath and jaw muscles for questions that failed to arrive. Their impromptu secret code, if he understood it right, was failing to give him the answers he expected. No DNA tests? On his case? People dropped genetic samples everywhere they went, whether they wanted to or not. Blood, hair, skin, spit. Everyone left a trail.

"Any other expenses at all?"

"Funny." Wayne rested his head on his hand, elbow planted on his desk. "How many times have you come to me begging for more money to shore up a complaint? You knew you could take an asshole out of circulation with a couple hundred dollars spent on science and poof. I give you nothing. Now we have more money than we can spend and... nothing."

"That is funny," McCallum said. "You ever think of doing stand-up? You could crush with this stuff."

"No one wants jokes from their economist."

"Or their orthopedic surgeon. I can tell you that, too."

Chapter 8

McCallum fell into the rhythm his crutches demanded. Plant and swing, plant and swing. Getting from the apartment to the bus to the doctor's office took him three times longer than he'd planned. Getting from the doctor to the gym only twice as long. *Getting better at something I never wanted to do in the first place*, he said to himself, and failed to smile.

The full-sized action figure at the front desk gave him the 'get-outta-here' look. McCallum didn't blame him. He had crutches, a fresh black cast, and wore the grossest clothes he owned. Old gym shorts and a T-shirt he got in the sign-up package for a martial arts tournament twelve years ago. Getting here had made him look like he left before showering. He showed the man his cuff. He thought he might have to clink it to the desk, but the stuffed muscle recognized the real thing when he saw it.

Plant, swing. Plant, swing. McCallum made his way through the main chamber of the gym, looking side-to-side. He heard the familiar grunt before he saw her. Andrea worked a fly machine, crunching her arms together, dragging bars connected to pulleys carrying more weight than McCallum wanted to think about. She parted her arms slowly, baring her teeth… Wet clay over iron. He didn't work in the medium, but if he did…

"You out?" Andrea said as the weights clanked.

"You'll have to be more specific," McCallum said.

She hunched forward, dropping her arms to her knees, mouth open.

"You quit?" McCallum asked.

"I'm not chatty when I work out."

"No, I mean did you quit?"

Andrea closed her mouth. Her eyebrows pressed together, creating a moist pillow of flesh between her eyes. McCallum figured she'd been a detective long enough to know he wasn't talking about her workout routine. He stared at her.

"Yeah," she said.

Another veiled conversation. She understood. McCallum nodded.

Andrea continued. "I mean, I'm taking a break. I'll get back to it when the moment's right." She lowered her head and aimed her eyes. "The moment ain't right."

"Wish I could get back to it," McCallum said. "As you know, I've got this injury keeping me from my normal regimen. That hasn't happened to you, I take it."

"An injury?"

"An injury, a strain, all kinds of things can keep you from getting your thing done."

"Ah. The thing." Andrea reached for a water bottle on the floor next to her. She kept her eyes on McCallum as she drank. He kept his eyes on her.

She glanced left and right, gauging the distance of the nearest person. She tugged at her gold-bead cuff, moving it to let some air in between her sweaty skin and the band. She found McCallum's eyes again and nodded. "I've been able to keep up some of my program. Not everything. My trainer took me off the... ah... kettles. She didn't say why."

"Your trainer use a whip or a fish?"

"I take suggestions from this one either way. Work on other things, she said. So that's what I do."

"No idea, huh?"

"Don't expect I'll ever know exactly why."

"That kettlebell weight was pretty solid, I always thought. Good for the program."

"I would say central to my program."

"And you just quit it like nothing. Like it never did a thing for you."

"No," Andrea said. "Not like that. You know it's not like that. You been working out a long time."

"Longer than you."

"You know sometimes you give a station a rest. You work some other areas. Let that area heal up. Then you get back to it. You don't forget about it. You hit again and you hit it hard."

"It will be very tough to heft the kettlebell if you let it sit too long."

Andrea let her head hang. "I do truly know."

"It doesn't make any sense," McCallum said.

"Hardly ever does."

McCallum spun on his good leg and stuck his crutches up under his arms. "That must be some trainer."

"A trainer's trainer."

"Always is." McCallum started his pogo dance back through the gym.

"Rest up, Eddie."

He shot back over his shoulder, "You ain't my trainer."

— «» —

"You wanted to see me, Mr. Fhor?" Sam Qui hung in the doorway, clinging to the side, not willing to have anything but his voice enter unless absolutely necessary.

Neelesh sat back on his bamboo stool and looked the kid over. He wore the red shirt and khaki pants uniform that students at Ambyr Consolidated Schools wore all over the globe. A version, anyway. This one said 'School 64, Buffalo Catchment' over the left breast. Should Sam's parents get transferred, they'd buy another set of the same shirts, with a new name on the breast. Commerce must continue. Sam's black hair sat on his head like an old army helmet, drifting down over his eyes. Neelesh never knew if he had the boy's attention. Ever.

"Did I want to see you?" Neelesh asked. "Want is not quite the right word. I never want to call any students in after school. I want to get home just as much as you do."

"Should I go?"

"I need to see you, buddy. Come on in. Just for a second."

Sam swung in, took four steps and stopped before Neelesh, still perched on his stool.

"You didn't do so well on your last test," he said.

Sam's eyes aimed at the floor.

"We've got another coming up. What do you think about this one?"

Sam looked up. "What do you mean?"

"You think you're ready?"

"I guess."

"There's no time for guessing." Neelesh put his feet down and leaned forward. "Do you want to know a secret?"

"I guess—"

Neelesh shook an index finger. "No guessing. Listen. The company wants you to learn their version of history, but that's not why these tests are important. There's a whole 'nother level of evaluation. They want to know how well you can take in information, how you retain it, and if you can make valuable assertions from knowledge you've gained. History is as good of a test bed as anything. This whole class does double duty for them."

Sam's face was pointed at him. That's all Neelesh could tell for sure.

"These tests, Sam... I've seen boys do poorly and you know what, they don't go on. You know what I mean?"

Sam's mouth formed an egg shape. "You mean a digger or a sweeper? Is that what you mean? You think I'll be working next year. That's all I am?"

"No. That's why I wanted to talk to you. You're more than that."

"A sweeper." Sam's open mouth began to tremble. "A digger?"

"The tests don't always... you're not there in the tests. The real Sam. You're not there and I want you to be."

Sam licked his lips, then his mouth popped back open.

"Working?" he said in a whine approaching a cry.

Neelesh fought the urge to reach for the boy. You can't touch them. Ever. There were only two rules: no touching held second place after don't be alone with them.

"You come and see me after school tomorrow. We'll do a little extra work."

"I..." Sam sniffled. "I'll have to ask my Dad. I help him in his shop. We..."

"It's OK. I understand," Neelesh said. "Tell him to give me a call."

"OK."

"Come on, I'll walk out with you."

They strolled down the halls, now mostly quiet. School had only ended ten minutes ago. Kids, and teachers, left fast at midnights in the summer.

"You're smart," Neelesh said.

"That's what my Dad says," Sam returned. "That's why I can help him in..."

Neelesh smiled, bent down and whispered, "I'm not an op."

Sam narrowed his eyes and lowered his voice. "We fix scooters. To help people. Nothing in return, just so we're clear."

"Clear as day." They pushed through the doors and out into the night. The thick steam of blackness folded around them. Tiny insects swirled around the lights on either side of the door. They made Neelesh hold his breath until they were down the stairs. He glanced over at the car, then a little bit farther to the right. Movement.

"Hey," he shouted, hoping he picked the right volume. Not too scary, not too weak.

The small silhouette bent and twirled. Uniform red caught a sliver of light. Neelesh quickened his step. The figure walked towards him until he could tell for sure he'd been watching May Podlowski.

"Yes, Mr. Fhor?" she asked.

Neelesh huffed. His shoulders dropped. "Didn't you promise to walk with friends?"

"They all took off. I forgot my lunch box and then they were gone."

Neelesh bowed his head. Not again. He couldn't risk it again.

"Let's get you a new friend," he said. He turned and shouted, "Sammy!"

The boy stopped.

"Come here!"

The boy hesitated. Then he ran to them.

"Do you know May Podlowski?" Neelesh gestured to the girl.

"A… third grader?"

"Yes," Neelesh said. "And she needs an escort home."

"I… ah…"

"No, not Aida. I don't know any Aida. It's May."

"She's a third grader."

"I'll be fine," May said.

"I'm sure of it." Neelesh looked into bangs covering the area he assumed Sam's eyes resided. "We're all going to do our part and we're all going to be fine."

Neelesh walked towards his Saab. Maybe he'd drive with the door open again. It's cool, even with the bugs.

—— «» ——

Demiana danced. She couldn't help herself. Whenever that that guy played "Career opportunities," her and the whole pub bounced in unison, clapping, swinging, in sync the way humans rarely are, but strive to be. She knew why Jesus said prayers were best when sung. Music melted people, making them flow and blend into a single, higher being. From the many into one. She didn't know what God was exactly. She believed with abject certainty, though a definition sat outside her imagination, right where God belonged. Whatever God was, He-She was something like this moment.

The song ended and she found her beer. Karen found her.

"Did you see?" she asked.

Demiana said, "I couldn't see past that scrumptious chunk of man meat dancing with you."

"I know, I know. What the Hell is he doing with me?"

"I've got no idea what men want. Seriously."

Karen slapped Demiana's shoulder. "I was joking."

"So was I," Demiana said. "I totally know what guys want. Are you kidding me? It only takes a couple of days doing confessions to reshape your whole understanding of the male psyche. And let me tell you, it isn't pretty. If I hadn't already taken a vow of chastity, I'd be on my way now."

A guitar strummed in the back of the pub. The little band had done their shots, hit the restrooms, and clinked cuffs with whoever looked promising for later.

"Holy crap," Karen shouted above the rising music.

"Is that my new nickname?"

"Holy crap, as in I hope the Church doesn't put you on marriage counseling anytime soon."

Demiana raised her beer and bowed her head. "Amen, to that."

The band started, so Demiana pushed closer to her friend. "So where'd you meet him?"

"Task force," Karen said. "Production thought if datology got together with engineering and marketing more often their jobs would be easier."

"How's that working?" Demiana asked.

"Who cares," Karen said.

Demiana laughed. She took a sip and leaned in again. "Does it unbalance things? At work, I mean. A romance inside your little group?"

Karen shrugged. "Nah. We've got unwritten protocols for that kind of thing. Have to, you know? God, if you can't meet someone at work, would you ever meet anyone?"

"I wouldn't know."

"No," Karen said. "Besides, it's easier when you've got things in common."

"Makes sense," Demiana said. "Choose from your community."

"Community?" Karen repeated. "Is that one of those Catholic words?"

"I didn't think so, but I've been subverted. It means kind of a large, informal group."

"Like a task force," Karen said.

"That gives it a point. Communities don't usually have points. No end products."

"Doesn't sound like there's a point to the word."

Demiana laughed again. "Now I know it's Catholic. We're great at holding on to old stuff. Even the recently old."

"Come on," Karen said. "I want you to meet him."

"Sure." Demiana straighten up. I'd like to peek into your community, she thought. Or whatever you don't call it.

Whatever none of them call it. She pushed the idea through her head, the idea that something didn't exist just because you stopped giving it a name. Divisions, branches, units — circles in circles in circles. She loved peering into pools she'd never dipped into before. The reels and reels of people. The communities. What happened to that word? Why, in God's name, would Ambyr try to disappear that word like some old folk song?

Demiana hated knowing she had a lot to learn.

Chapter 9

Neelesh watched Miriam clink her cuff against the table plate. Scratched and murky, the flat slice of steel looked less and less like metal every time he came in here. It bounced light in funny directions. It needed to be polished — or at least cleaned — and that wouldn't happen until so much grime lay across the surface that signal conduction ceased. Which, Neelesh thought, might be any session now. He wished it were this one.

"How's the week been?" Miriam asked. Blond, 20 years his senior, he had no guess as to her height. He realized one day, talking to another teacher about how much they dreaded coaching periods, that he'd never seen her away from her desk. She could be legless for all he knew.

"No troubles," he said. He planned on saying that a lot.

"Let's see what we've got." She rested her head on a fist and stared up at the big screen on her wall. A set of bar graphs appeared, one for each of Neelesh's classes. The bars represented his students and their grade point averages.

"What gets measured, gets done," Miriam said. She said that a lot. "Your numbers are adequate. Overall, you're up two points from last month. That makes you my best teacher this week, who would've guessed?"

And the barbs begin. Miriam always made him pay for good news. "Not me." He tried to sound playful.

"Not that it's a competition." She enlarged one bar representing one class, looked at the details, then swiped it away and brought up the next. "If it were a contest, you'd be winning. Maybe it's good coaching."

"Yes," Neelesh said. "I'm certain."

"That makes all the difference in the world. Any issues you want to discuss?"

"Like I said, no troubles."

"You've got a note here, on your 10:15 PM Market History class. Sam Qui pending."

"I've withheld grades for the moment."

"Uncommon." Miriam continued to gaze into the charts. The reds and greens reflected feathery stripes on her pale, hammy face.

"I'm working with him."

With two flicks of her wrist, Sam Qui's biography blossomed onto the screen.

"Working with this kid, huh? Is there a point?"

"I think he needs more time."

"He's just about out of time."

"He's 13," Neelesh said.

"His scores are tepid."

"Not terrible."

"Not terrific, either. What are you hoping to accomplish?"

"He's bright. His analysis in class is strong. Orally he does much better than the tests show."

"Ah." Miriam turned her gaze to Neelesh for the first time. "You think you know better than the tests."

"Not exactly." He caught his smirk as it formed. Miriam wouldn't understand. His kids would. They said he needed to be more exact. "He exhibits mental prowess outside of the testing environment."

"You know we test for that."

"Even so, I'm observing skills and an understanding of the material that he has difficulty reproducing during timed exams. With a bit of work, I think I could help him better translate his intelligence in a testing environment."

Miriam produced a vague smile. No teeth. Just a line between two dimples. "What you are going through is very common among young teachers. It's not a bad thing. It's nothing to be ashamed of. We all want the students to be the best they can be. But by this stage, the children can't be changed."

"I'm not trying to change him. I'm trying to help him. He's better than his test scores indicate. With more training, with a better test-taking strategy, with more time—"

"And where does that time come from? The other students? See, this is exactly why you have a coach. You can't expend resources on this one student at the expense of the others."

"You can see by my scores that isn't happening."

"We're going to keep it that way," Miriam said. "Throwing time and energy at this child might help a little, in the short-term. In the long-term, a student with this kind of profile is going into hard labor fields."

"I'm not sure the profile is accurate."

"The system has been proven through millions and millions of subjects. The company has invested huge amounts of time and money studying the best way to sort us out."

"I'm a teacher," Neelesh said. "Not a sorter."

Miriam's dimples vanished. "None of us like that our fates show up in these numbers. The fact is, they do. For all of us."

No, they don't, Neelesh wanted to say. *I know for a fact they don't because that wasn't the case with me.*

Of course, he couldn't say that out loud. Ever. Silence was so often the price of position.

— «» —

"I don't feel good about this." A man named Mingo knelt before an apartment door, twisting thin metal prods in the keyhole of the door.

McCallum stood with his back to him, leaning on a single bamboo crutch. He watched the hall, listened for door creaks and footsteps, and hoped he had picked the right time of day. Nine in the morning. First shift people were at work, second shifters sleeping.

"I don't feel good about this at all," Mingo continued.

"Maybe you should take something," McCallum said.

"See? Taking something. That's the kind of word choice that makes me uncomfortable."

"Systems Security thanks you."

"Yeah." Mingo turned his tools in opposite directions. "That's why you came to see me in person. That's why you put a sock over the vid cam. Right. Where do I send my invoice again?"

"I'll owe you one."

Click.

Mingo withdrew his prods and returned them to a leather pouch on the floor. "You're in."

McCallum turned as Mingo stood and opened the door.

"See you around," McCallum said.

"Hope not."

McCallum entered the apartment. Large, cluttered, stuffy. Closed up tight, in August, with the AC turned off — the smell of age and dust boiled up and filled the space. He closed the front door and turned on a light. The curtains blocked nearly all of the morning sun.

The living room had two couches facing each other, both perpendicular to a large fireplace with an older-style monitor stuck to the sandy brick above it. McCallum catalogued his assumptions: The doctor hadn't spent much time in here. He rarely entertained. He had little use for a room this open and spacious. Browns and hunter's green. Masculine, but with knickknacks. McCallum walked to a table running along the inside wall. Mirror-topped, covered with statues of varying sizes and textures. Wood, soapstone, baked clay. The tallest was a good three feet. The smallest wasn't an inch. They varied in style, but all appeared to be handmade works of primitive art.

Penises were prominent. Almost every statue had one sticking out or up. Those that didn't were virtually penises in shape.

There were more totems on the mantel. The walls were plain. No paintings, masks, or other primitive artifacts.

McCallum hobbled back into the hallway, swinging his crutch in a small arc. The sweat bubbled on his forehead and streamed down his back. He couldn't risk opening a window. He couldn't risk staying much longer, either. It must have been more than 100 degrees in this place. Walking with one crutch proved harder than he'd anticipated.

Photos on the wall made him pause. The same man in three out of seven, posing with people native to places very, very far from the Buffalo Catchment. The man had to be the doctor. Thin, gangly, with floppy silver-gold hair. Dressed, always, in loose safari shirts. The man smiled on a grassy plain, with a giraffe in the background. He smiled with a toothless man in a jungle that filled in the background completely. In another, he sat in a mesh tree house, amidst a sea of leaves. The rainforest canopy, McCallum realized. He'd seen it in a movie once. Not in person. He never traveled. Who had the money? Or the time?

Other than this doctor.

The kitchen was hospital clean. McCallum moved down the hall. Two bedrooms, one for sleeping and one converted into a study. He stood in the doorway to take it all in. The oak wainscoting, the built-in shelves, the green leather coach, and bulbous oak desk. More figurines, a small collection of bones propped for display on black wires... the room had so much dark, wooden foreign stuff that it felt like a cave.

He walked behind the desk, parted the curtains enough for one eye, and peered into the courtyard. He could see where he'd fought the man in black. The blank. And where he'd lost the use of his foot. He let the curtain swing back and sat down in the deep leather chair. He swiveled and placed his hands flat on the desktop. This would be how the doctor saw things. His world, through his eyes, when he sat alone and pondered his mortality.

The desk had a palm-sized brass pad for tethering a cuff to the large screen hanging on the wall next to the door, a thick, green candle — one-third burned — and nothing else.

McCallum didn't have the doctor's cuff. No Systems Security access into the man's precious, private files. None of the rich electronic details of a life — expenses, travels, loves, hates, friends, family, frequent calls, and messages and records of what, exactly, he did day-to-day. McCallum had none of the data he turned to first in an investigation. Data that made up most or all of a case. He had nothing. A blank canvas.

No, another artist's work. McCallum had to pick out the finer points. He took it all in, the full picture before him.

The piece had depth and order. It had been constructed with care and attention to detail. It had a meaning, though the artist's intentions escaped him. He didn't understand all the figurines and the emphasis on sex organs. He liked the juxtaposition of the primitive with the manufactured, orthogonal shelves. It fit, in a way.

Accept for that piece of plastic. A card leaned against a terracotta statue of a man as tall as a beer bottle with a penis the size of his arms.

McCallum got up, walked over and picked up the card. White, rectangular, no bigger than his palm. It had a lanyard attached, so it could be worn around the neck. Thick as a pancake, it had no markings. Just a blue patch on one side. Rough to the touch.

McCallum slipped it into his pocket.

— ⟨⟩ —

Demiana held her coffee with both hands, sucking the warmth up through her arms and into her body. Not that she was cold. She couldn't remember being cold. This steamy, sticky summer started in May. No, the coffee felt calming, oddly enough. Comforting. Warm beverages should be mandatory at these things.

Norma came into the room, carrying a cold beverage of some kind. Figured. The woman's face pointed into her thin little mobile screen, the fan-type that people tethered to their cuffs when their eyes started to go. Poor thing. Norma kept her back straight and she maneuvered well. Demiana tried to smooth out the woman's wrinkles with her brain; to use her imagination to restore luster to her hair and elasticity to her skin. The woman didn't have an ounce of fat on her. She might have been attractive. Hell, she still could be if she'd stop the nonstop lamprey imitation.

"Morning," Demiana said.

"It is," Norma returned.

Demiana dragged her bracelet around her wrist like a tiny conveyor belt.

"Deal with it." Demiana heard George's voice as he approached the conference room. "Nobody gets to pick their roommate freshman year." George entered and stood behind his chair. "Nobody even tries. Nobody's willing to rock the boat because they are all so happy to be there — and not shoveling crap — that they simply deal with it."

He paused. Demiana tried to look distracted.

"Love you too," he said and tapped his cuff. "Sorry. Daughters. You know."

"Yes," Demiana said.

"How would you?" Norma did not look up from her screen.

"I am one. So were you, presumably."

Now Norma's head picked up. She turned her eyes on Demiana and opened her mouth. She might have said something if someone else hadn't beaten her to it.

"Excuse me," a man in the doorway said. "Is this the tragedy-of-the-commons mediation?"

Low grade. Demiana knew it instantly. Tall, probably sixty, with perfect silver hair and flawless skin. His dark copper suit fit him in the way achievable only by the best of tailors. The fabric alone would empty most bank accounts. He wore a caramel cotton shirt with a small broach at the neck. A family crest. No. An elaborate A with three other letters crossing the front. She couldn't make them out. Were her eyes going? See, she shouldn't have pitied Norma. Hubris. Which number sin was that again?

"Yes," George answered when he'd decided Demiana would not. "One of them, anyway. This one regards Albion."

"Then I'm in the right place." The man sat down between Demiana and George. "Wilson Fairbanks. Consul for Ambyr Consolidated." He held his hand out to Demiana.

She didn't take it. "No, you're not."

"I am, I assure you."

"What happened to Steve?"

Wilson smiled. "He was reassigned."

"Why wasn't I informed?"

"You will have to take that up with the Bishop."

Norma smiled. It made Demiana's cheeks and neck catch fire. She hoped her collar covered some of it. Her upper chest, not her cheeks. She should wear a veil like those nuns.

"Shall we, then." Wilson said. "We'd like to formally request an open airing of grievances."

"Oh, God," George said.

"More delays?" Norma said. "Is that what this is about?"

"No, No." Wilson waived his hands. "We need to all start from the same screen. Let us take some time to list out our specific disagreements and then address them properly. That is the procedure, is it not, Father?"

Demiana rolled her eyes. "What's the problem? George do you care to start?"

"Happy to," George said. "Ambyr Consolidated has constructed a nuclear power plant that BCCA/Hong Kong Holdings does not believe to be sufficiently safe for operation. We suspect the materials and quantity of said materials used are incapable of insuring radiation containment in an untoward event. In fact, we are not convinced it can contain a high rad leak even during normal production."

"That is based on—"

Demiana cut Wilson off with a flash of her palm. She turned to Norma.

"India Group concurs," Norma said. "Our cursory investigation has created grave doubts with regard to the integrity of the facility. And as an additional note, we have been disappointed in Ambyr's willingness to recognize our concerns."

"The black heart of the matter," Wilson said.

Demiana gave Wilson her attention.

Wilson said, "Both companies want a look at proprietary technology. That's all this is. Ambyr won't give them a peak behind the curtain and they feel snubbed."

George said, "Our doors are always open. Engineers from Ambyr have a standing invitation to visit any nuclear plant we have, anywhere on the planet."

"We've made similar overtures," Norma added.

"Our company is not obligated to share any advancements, techniques or methods with our friendly competition."

"We are not interested in sharing secrets," Norma said. "We are interested in the shared air and water table you're putting at risk."

Demiana tapped her cuff to the table pad and transferred a parcel of data. An aerial view of an industrial facility appeared. The buildings were the usual collection of concrete rectangles tossed into an open field, arranged by someone obsessed with 90-degree angles, and linked together with multicolored pipe. The only two features differentiating this monstrosity from all the others she ignored daily: a 200-foot tall pinched flowerpot with no flower — the iconic nuclear power plant cooling tower — and a high, fat wall reminding her of a medieval fort. It surrounded the boxes and tubes and tower, separating it from the verdant forest and a waterway.

"So that's it, huh." Demiana said.

"The Albion Medium Yield Nuclear Power Production Facility," Wilson announced. "In service, providing life-giving power to the Ambyr family for more than 25 years. Without incident. Not one. And so, per Article 4, sub-paragraph 7 of the Joint Articles of Mediation, I would like to move for termination of the mediation for lack of proof-of-standing."

"We've been through this," Norma said.

George shook his head. "We have pursued this issue for five years. We didn't call the Church to have it dismissed in less time than it takes to order lunch."

"We didn't even present evidence," Norma added. "We have engineering statements, power output estimates, and water, soil, and air samples."

"As do we. They all countermand each other rendering everything nil. The issue boils..." Wilson grinned, waiting to see if anyone laughed at his pun, "...down to this: This facility is outstanding. You want to know why and we won't tell you. Because we don't have to. This assembly is unnecessary and should be aborted immediately."

Wilson opened his arms, palms up, as if letting invisible kittens free on the table. He sat back, staring at Demiana. Demiana stared at the table, where the invisible kittens might have played, pawing each other, rolling around, being cuter than cute can be.

Kittens on a table. Scampering in different directions, bumping, tumbling — each with its own concern. Steven, the Bishop, now this guy, Norma, and George. Demiana smirked. She veered off, too. Nobody was on the same screen. Nobody had the same goals. She had no idea why Ambyr tried to bump her. She had no idea why the Bishop assigned her in the first place. Lack of experience did not seem like a compelling reason. The easiest thing to do, maybe the right thing to do, would be to issue a discontinuance. Wilson had a point. No one had shown any harm to the commons. And it would make Norma so mad. The Bishop had probably expected her to cave. She couldn't handle this. She should get back to her ministry. She could return to ensuring kids got their milk, that they grew up big and strong.

Or not. The whole thing bugged her too much.

Demiana inhaled. "Sit back, Wilson. We're gonna be here a while. I'd like to see all the evidence."

Not what she expected to come out of her mouth. It never was God da— Nope. Praise be the Lord.

Chapter 10

McCallum faced the canvas. Four lines, the start of his bridge. A flash of an idea that went nowhere. Great. His bridge to nowhere went nowhere. Just four light pencil lines on a big, white plain. Maybe he was done. Maybe that's all the painting could ever be. He saw it right, irony in simple perfection. He loved it this way. Unfinished on purpose. This could very well be the first work he ever finished.

He leaned forward, trying not to stress his bad leg. He took the canvas in both hands, picked it up from the easel and studied it. He set it aside and grabbed his sketchbook from where it had rested, upright against the foot of his couch. He took a pencil and drew an oval just above the centerline of the page. He hadn't drawn one quite like it in more than thirty years, he thought. This was how one started a comic book character. Ovals on ovals, in ovals, until they start to resemble muscle and bone. Tendons, like the Achilles, always protruding, straining, daring a villain to slice. McCallum drew in continuous circular motions, enclosing space, directing light, using the illusion of shadow to give the figure space, then form, then presence, and finally power.

When you're a kid with some ability to draw, you get asked for two things: caricatures and comic book guys — monsters, aliens, and busty women included. He did them all the time for his friends, rendering them goofy or heroic, menacing or outright disgusting. He liked the art of illustration, the flow, feel, and the impact of the art, and the smiles it produced. He put down the pencil when the company chose him for security work. When he picked it up again, years later, he wanted to produce different art. Smiles were not a consideration.

McCallum did, however, smile at his ovals. Perhaps because of the time involved in developing the skill, drawing a dramatically posed male figure was just like riding a bike.

Featureless. A hard, distinct physique filled out the seamless black body suit. The man stood in the first, basic fighting stance: left leg out, right back, with the foot slightly raised, elbows tucked to the ribs with hands up in front of the face. It looked like the faceless man might eat an invisible ham.

He drew the lanyard around the blank's neck. The white plastic card hung from it. This is not what he saw the night of the fight and yet seemed right. More right than his recollections. More right than what actually occurred. His picture said more with the card in it.

McCallum folded his arms across his chest and took in the drawing. He said to himself, "Art lies to get truth."

— «» —

Demiana sat slumped in her chair. The physicist had lowered the lights in the conference room. He must have thought it would make it easier for everyone to see his presentation on the big screen. She could see how a physicist might arrive at that conclusion. Reduce the interference from other light sources and all that, not realizing if he rambled on about "grays" and "Sieverts" with lights down low, the thickness of her eyelids would become a much bigger concern.

"…between seven and ten percent," the physicist said.

Demiana sat up, sucked in a big breath and re-focused. The topic mattered. They didn't pull this Japanese Maple of a man in here for no reason, right?

"I'm sorry," she said. "Could you repeat using slightly different language?"

The man's head moved like a chicken looking for more feed. When he stopped he said, "Due to resistance and other various factors, we lose about seven to ten percent of the electricity we produce to the, um, wires."

"Ah," Demiana said. "Moving power takes power."

"Precisely." The man seemed pleased. "We can reduce that loss by reducing the distance between energy generation and energy consumption. The Albion project was conceived as a test facility for more localized energy production. Small-scale plants like this one could be constructed in larger numbers, and in closure proximity to their clients. Neighborhood power plants, if you will."

"So you're walking down the street and there's a pub, a nail salon, a nuclear power plant, a candy store, a florist — that kind of thing."

"Um, yes, theoretically."

"Which is fine," Demiana said. "If they're safe."

"Exactly our point," Norma said. "Safety is one of the reasons big power plants are, in fact, big."

"And far," George added. "We don't put them downtown for a reason."

"Though not a good reason," the physicist said. "The risks do not escalate as a function of population."

Demiana smiled. "I guess that depends on who's measuring the risk. My proximity to a meltdown will figure into my risk calculation."

The physicist fluttered a bit. "I meant that the number of people living and working around an energy production facility does not alter the laws of physics. Whatever risk there is, and it is minimal, is the same if the reactor is in the heart of a city or a hundred miles out."

Demiana turned to Norma. "So is that what you don't like? The whole concept behind this thing? Albion? Are you concerned that Ambyr wants to start putting cooling towers on street corners?"

"Not at all," Norma said. "An increase in energy efficiency is laudable. We are concerned that they might do so in a reckless manner."

Wilson cleared his throat. "Ambyr Consolidated is no less concerned with our extended family than either of the other corporations is with theirs. This entire project is nothing but a profound outcome of that concern."

"Let's skip to the good parts, eh?" George said. "How come the walls of the containment units are so thin? We've been asking for years. Eight years, actually, and have never received a reply."

The physicist opened his mouth. Wilson put his hand in front of it.

"Ambyr does not recognize that inquiry."

Demiana's eyebrows rose. Her lips parted. She didn't want to say what she had in her mouth. She didn't. She was too young, too inexperienced, and so far from this corporate world of squeezing one place and watching a bubble bulge in another, she didn't want to say, "I don't understand."

But she did.

"Pardon me?" Wilson's head dipped to the side. She hadn't seen him surprised yet. She hadn't expected to ever. It made her feel a little bit better. Just a little.

She said, "I don't know what you mean when you say you don't recognize the inquiry."

"It is not a legitimate question."

"It is a question. It's been asked. I don't get it?"

Wilson smiled, as he might to explain the tooth fairy. "The gentleman from Hong Kong has no basis for the formulation of the question, therefore there is no question to be answered."

George said, "They won't admit we know the thickness of their containment vessels."

"And do you?" Demiana asked.

"With a reasonable amount of certainty."

"They have never been inside Albion," Wilson countered.

"That was not necessary," George replied. "You're running too thin and you know it."

"You've recorded radiation leaks? Really? May we see the reports?"

George pressed is lips, then opened them just enough to say, "There have not been any leaks. Yet. Our contention is that you cannot withstand an adverse event."

"Nor," Wilson said, "have there been any of those."

Demiana turned her gaze on the physicist. "Can Albion handle an accident?"

"Well—" he started.

Wilson cut him off. "I'm terribly sorry. I need to object to that question as well. There are no nuclear facilities impervious to catastrophe. Not in Hong Kong Holdings, nor the India Group. Asking the doctor to speculate will not reveal a fair and useful line of reasoning."

"Why don't you just let them in?" Demiana asked.

"We don't have to," Wilson answered.

"You don't have to *not* let them in, either. What's the big deal? It's a nuclear plant. They've been around for what? Like 100 years?"

"Closer to 150, but I understand your point. Still, there is no reason to open our doors."

"Because there are secrets?"

Wilson wiggled his fingers, "Mysteries."

Demiana leaned forward. "You realize I'm Catholic. I eat mysteries for lunch."

Wilson leaned forward to meet her. "Bon appetite."

— «» —

"My grandfather died in the Buy-Ups," Ting Ting explained to the class. "My grandmother said he got killed when they tried to take the family business. Did that happen a lot?"

Neelesh stared at the girl. Why couldn't she have asked where babies come from or how can two men have sex? An easy question. One he was, at least, permitted to answer.

"The Buy-Ups were a difficult time," Neelesh started. "Many terrible things happened."

"What kind of things?" came from the back of the room. Nothing like a little bloodshed to get the boys' attention.

"We don't actually have very good records of the period, because of all the turmoil. But remember, back then, everyone was armed. Because there were borders, everyone thought they had something to protect that was worth a life. These people weren't evil, just not as ... enlightened as we are now. When the borders — the invisible, nonsensical lines between nations — began to erode, sometimes people thought things were being taken from them, as opposed to being added into something bigger and stronger. That is not to say that Ting Ting's grandfather was wrongheaded. I don't know the circumstances. Many of the early, smaller companies were ruthless in their acquisitions. It was only after the parent companies, like Ambyr Consolidated, took control that all the fighting settled down."

"So there were a whole bunch of little companies, like my grandfather's?" Ting Ting asked. "Then Ambyr came along and bought them up?"

"It might not have been Ambyr directly," Neelesh answered. "There were precursors to the three. To Ambyr, Hong Kong and IG. Just like how there used to be thousands and thousands of companies. The difference between now and then is there were no big companies on top, stepping in to stop the silliness during the Buy-Ups. They were like children with no parents. Or teachers. What happens when I leave this class?"

Sideways glances, smiles, giggles.

Neelesh smiled along. "Some chatter? Low, at first. Then it builds the longer I'm away. What if I'm gone for 30 minutes? Are you all still at your desks? Reading studiously?"

Head shakes. A bit of laughing.

"Now imagine I'm gone for a few days. How much studying is going on then? I can't imagine. Chaos, I tell you. This class would descend into madness. There would be no learning. There may not even be much showing up. Everyone would scatter about and do their own thing. There would, essentially, be no class at all. Just a bunch of kids not progressing, not becoming smarter, wiser, better.

"Now imagine you're all little companies, out for your selves. Digging up what you want, cutting down what you want, busting up roads and not repairing them, stealing water, trading in secret, not paying your bills. Oh, and that's a big one. Nobody likes a deadbeat. How long do you think the world would function that way?"

The question sounded more rhetorical than it was, Neelesh thought. He really wondered what they thought. What their collective sense of time might be. Kids constantly surprised him with their internal clocks. They never ran evenly. Ten minutes of homework took forever. Ten minutes for a quiz wasn't nearly enough time.

"The answer is about 25 years," he announced. "The Second Dark Age, it's called sometimes. Though not by me.

I like to call it the Long Margin Call. It took about 25 years for the banks to divvy everything up, figure out who owned what, and bring the rest of the holdouts into the fold."

"Holdout," Ting Ting said. "That's what my father always called my grandfather. Sometimes he sings that song."

"I wouldn't know what song you were talking about," Neelesh replied as he made a curly smile.

Ting Ting started singing, "He was a holdout 'till the day he—"

Neelesh waved her off. Some of the students chuckled.

"It's OK," he said. "I *may* have heard it at some point. Your father must have been very proud of his dad."

"I think he died before he was born. I guess he never knew him."

"At least," Neelesh said, "he knew of him. He had a connection and he passed it on to you. It's valuable knowing about your past. It's the whole reason we're here, in this class, right? Because let me tell you, if you don't know much about where you came from…"

"What?" Someone asked.

He didn't have an answer. All he had were more questions, and he couldn't teach with those. Who? How much time had passed? Neelesh had let his thoughts ebb. He shook his head, fast and hard.

"Where were we," he said, not asking. "Citizens United. The American government declares corporations are people. Who wants to tell me why that's important?"

Chapter 11

The whirl of treadmills and clank of weights drifted in from around the gym. McCallum sat on a bench tightening the straps of the brace around his left ankle, a carbon fiber tongue that started under his foot and split to envelope his ankle and entwine his calf. The material weighed half of what he expected, and stored energy like a spring.

Andrea dropped her gym bag next to his. "Looks tough."

"Seems alright." McCallum stood. He hopped on the bad leg. "If I had one for the other leg, I think my vertical leap would be about six feet."

"Great for apple picking. What's that?" She pointed at the pad leaning against the bench.

"My sketch book." McCallum picked up the book, flipped a few pages and showed Andrea his drawing of the blank.

"Is that…" She let her voice trail off. "Cute."

McCallum tapped the tag he'd drawn around the blank's neck, watching Andrea's eyes. He handed her the pad and knelt down next to his gym bag. He drew out the white plastic card on a string he'd found in the doctor's apartment. He held it up to let Andrea see it. She studied it, eyes narrow, mouth in a neutral frown. She gave her head a little shake and looked at McCallum. He returned the tag to his bag.

"I like this one," she said. "Can I have it?"

"It's $4,000."

Andrea smirked. She held up her cuff, snapped a photo, and set the book down. "I'll get back to you. The price is ridiculous, but maybe I can come up with something."

McCallum nodded.

Andrea walked onto the mat and started stretching.

"It is nice of you to meet me here." McCallum followed her onto the mat.

"The only way I'll know if you're getting any better."

Andrea attacked from her stretching position, bringing a kick around wide, into McCallum's chest. He stumbled back onto his left leg, planted, bounced on the spring and fell flat onto his back. He lay there, like he might make a snow angel. Andrea brought her right foot around, placing the tip of her sneaker in the hollow of his neck.

"Huh," she said.

— «» —

Neelesh checked his cuff. 9:15 AM. He looked again at Sam. Sometimes the schedule got to him and couldn't remember the day or time. Happens to everyone, right? The cuff keeps you on track. And the cuff said *morning, second period*. Eighth-grade history for day students. Sam was a night student.

"Sam," he said. "What are you doing here?"

"Studying." Sam didn't look up. He kept his face so close to the desk, hair hanging down so low, that Neelesh only had about an 80 percent certainty it was Sam.

"Sam," he said with more volume. "This isn't your class."

"Studying harder."

The class continued its usual ripple of noise. It would continue until he made a bigger splash himself. Which he chose not to do. Sam's voice and posture gave off the wrong kind of energy. He walked down the aisle and knelt next to his desk.

"This wasn't what I meant," he said.

"Dad said." Sam clipped his voice.

"What?"

"More."

Neelesh realized the boy just barely held it together. He was going to have an aneurism before he let the other kids see him cry.

"Come on." Neelesh stood. "We're going to the nurse's office."

"No," Sam said. "It's OK. I'm fine."

"Please."

"I'm fine."

The girl in the next desk spun around, almost cracking Sam's head with her elbow. "Show him, Sammy."

Sam pressed his head closer to his desk.

"Show me what?" Neelesh asked.

"Show him."

"Come on," Neelesh put his hand on Sam's shoulder.

Sam's head rose and turned. The occipital bone surrounding his left eye had an eggplant tattoo. No. Too much yellow around the edges. The red eye floated in a vast purple bruise.

"Phoebe Ocala, you're in charge."

Neelesh moved his hand into Sam's armpit and lifted him from his chair. The boy bowed his head and led them out of the room.

Out in the hall, Neelesh whispered, "What is going on?"

"Nothing."

They walked down the silent, glossy hall.

"What are you doing here?"

"My father said if I wanted more learning, I'd best get to school. I'd best stay there until I learned everything I needed to know. I didn't have to help him in the shop anymore as long as I was at school."

"Did your father hit you?"

"He... he didn't mean it."

"He expects you to go to school 16 hours a day now."

"Pretty much."

They reached the nurse's office. Neelesh turned Sam until they were face to face.

"I will fix this," he said.

"You don't know my father."

"I'll get to know him."

— «» —

Demiana had loved the weeks off from the tragedy-of-the-commons arbitration. She went to mass every morning, volunteered at St. Ann's shelter for abused women and children, and spent two full days with her parents and sister. She loved summer's end, when the nights got cooler and leaves started to relive themselves of the monotonous green.

She knew very much what it was like to wear the same color every day and relished nature's diversity. She needed to make a suggestion to her order that they also change with the seasons, as God intended. They could still be austere and respectable in autumn shades. Browns and oranges. If the Buddhist monks could pull off saffron, she could certainly deal with a dash of gold. Her community could weather the change.

Community. Weather.

"Don't be an ass," Norma said

And Demiana was back. No more musings.

"This has nothing to do with shutting down the plant," Norma continued.

Vacation was totally over.

"Isn't that your ultimate goal?" Wilson said. "You think if we won't share our research, then damn it all, nobody should benefit from it?"

"Albion sits on the Erie Canal, which provides fresh water for millions of people. It is a shared asset. Our ultimate goal is protection of a common asset. You built a potential health hazard on a commons."

"Or," Wilson rose in his seat. "Are we confronting a much bigger problem, on a bigger commons? The hottest decade in human history was the last one. Producing energy sans the release of carbon into the atmosphere has become a top priority for all of us. I dare say it's our number two priority — right after safety for all concerned. Although, let's face it, the difference between the two grows smaller every year. Each unit of energy we pump into the atmosphere enhances instability and unpredictability. It raises sea levels and strengthens storms. It costs lives. The Buy-Up centuries did not leave us with much of an alternative beyond making our planet less of a greenhouse. Government-induced global warming created a safety issue that will take us decades to correct. Nuclear power is rich and clean — it can catapult us toward those goals. And this project, this Albion facility, it stands as the pinnacle of our achievements."

"Um, great," Demiana said. "You really make me want to see it."

Wilson's lips rippled. He tried, Demiana thought, to make a sudden scowl into a knowing smile. And failed. To recover, he said, "We firmly believe that outside critique would stifle innovation at this stage."

"This stage has lasted a quarter of a century." George blurted.

"But I wouldn't critique it," Demiana said. "And I'm certainly not going to steal any corporate secrets."

Wilson started, "I don't know—"

"I don't know either." Demiana cut him off. "I'm thinking I should. I'm thinking that if I'm going to sit through any more grandstanding about this place, I should stand there and see if it's grand. Ha. Get it?"

"Wouldn't that…" Wilson fumbled. "Wouldn't that amount to ex parte communication? Are we not forbidden from speaking with any of the parties involved unless all three are present?"

"I didn't know you were such a traditional guy?"

"I still open doors for the ladies."

"Good to hear," Demiana said. "That is exactly what I'm asking. I want to tour the Albion nuclear facility. You are right in suggesting that these proceedings should go down in the most open and transparent manner possible. That doesn't mean I have to do everything with the whole gang. Norma, do you have any objections to me taking a run over to Albion without you?"

"None at all," she said.

"How 'bout you, George? Does this injure your sensibilities?"

"I can't see a downside, myself."

"Me neither," Demiana said. "Set it up, Willy. We're taking a road trip! Woo-whoo!"

Demiana pumped her fists in the air.

The others did not.

Chapter 12

Neelesh knew sewers ran underground, carrying waste and slop. He knew they existed without ever seeing their black cavities, hearing their swish, or smelling the rot in the same way he knew of this neighborhood. It started less than a mile from his school. Half his kids lived in the crumbling, patchwork mess of ropes and cinderblocks and frosted glass. He never drove this way. This grid of roads never lay between him and any destination. No one's destination, he thought. From the map on the car's monitor he could see it sat between a highway and railroad tracks, a kind of dry-bounded island, which should've made it quaint and cozy instead of a pocket in your intestine catching the undigested and letting it fester.

Kids rode bikes and homemade skateboards, or walked slowly, inching their way towards nothing. The homes were small, most with detached garages behind the main houses. It made for long black or gray driveways, accentuating the rifts and erosions. Not all the homes were decrepit. Neelesh passed a few that had been painted this decade, roofs intact, and with some fairly diligent attempts at landscaping. The attention they had been given made the decay of the others more pronounced. He could tell that these were not bad places in a bad part of town. The lousy plots were simply uncared for.

Sam Qui's house had faded blue siding with white trim and gutters framing the front. Almond trim and gutters lined the side Neelesh could see as he approached. The lawn's grass came up to the ankles. The driveway had a Toyota pickup and four scooters, all of various ages, none new. He parked in front and walked towards the back. The garage door was open and he could hear music from inside.

"Mr. Qui?" he called out as he approached. "Mr. Qui?"

"Yeah," came a shout.

Neelesh reached the threshold of the garage. A bright orange scooter stood propped on a couple of car tires, most of its parts strewn about on a tarp. A man sat at a bench along the back, he'd turned to face the entrance, soldering iron in his hand. He wore jeans and a thick, khaki shirt. It had all kinds of extra straps and pockets and loops for what, Neelesh couldn't tell.

"Are you Mr. Qui?"

"Who the fuck told you to ask for Mr. Qui?

"I wasn't told to ask for anyone."

The man's eyes went to Neelesh's wrist. He studied Neelesh's stainless steel bracelet. His eyes jerked back up to Neelesh's face.

"Who are you?" he asked.

"Neelesh Fhor."

"What you need?"

"To speak with you. Are you Mr. Qui?"

"Yeah. Jack Qui. Everyone calls me Jack Qui. Anyone come looking for a little friendly help with their scooter — a bit of advice or some kindly assistance with nothing asked for in exchange — do you have me? Nothing is requested in return. These people always say ask for Jack Qui. Go see Jack Qui, they say. Except for you. You say Mr. Qui."

"I don't have a scooter," Neelesh said. "I'm Sam's history teacher."

Jack Qui set down the tool, completed his turn, crossed his arms and titled his head back a few degrees. "I'll ask again. What you need?"

Neelesh stepped into the garage. The man had a good 30 pounds on him, and who knew what kind of experience. He obviously worked his hands a lot. Neelesh ran for exercise. Not that this would get physical, he told himself. That was for the dumb or desperate. Neelesh reminded himself that he was neither.

"Your son is very bright," he said.

"Yep. A real firework, that one."

"I think if he were to apply himself he could be doing much better at school."

"Thank you for the data."

Jack Qui said nothing else. He didn't move. He didn't even appear to breathe.

"These kids are like a family to me, Mr. Qui," Neelesh said. "I look out for my family."

"You thinking I don't?"

"It's a shared responsibility. You aren't expected to know what goes on at school so I made an extra effort to come out here and inform you that Sam's grades do not adequately reflect his abilities."

"Come all the way out here, huh? Not over here. Out here, like it's a fucking different world from yours. Let me thank you again for making the dangerous journey. Now you can be on your way back to your lovely land."

"We both want what's best for Sam."

"What's best is Sammy learnin' a moonlight like motor repair. That way, whatever God damned hole the company throws him into he's got a chance of surviving. No one's gonna trade him a cord of wood for what he knows about history. You have me?"

The way Jack Qui's head cocked back, Neelesh could see right up the man's nostrils. Lightless shafts. Like sewers, he thought. Whatever he said would flush up there.

"Glad I don't have a poorly performing scooter," Neelesh said. "As the only thing I'd have to trade for it is a history lesson and you don't seem interested in that. Which is a shame. Some recent history can be quite useful, like the development of anti-barter policies. Being caught trading can leave a real black eye on your record. No one wants a black eye. I know I hope to never, and I mean never, see one again."

"You threatening me?" Jack Qui almost laughed. "Me?"

Neelesh turned and strolled away. "Yep," he tossed back over his shoulder.

— ⟪⟫ —

Demiana double-stepped and adjusted her gate. She laughed to herself, waiting for the other shoe to drop. How funny. She ran on the black path through the park, through leaves in the midst of turning, passed grass still vibrant, under a sky losing its luster. Monsignor Bujold ran next to her. He had never before asked her to join him on a run.

The Monsignor pounded at the ground at a speed she found difficult to match. Too slow for a run, too fast for a walk. She found herself skipping on occasion to re-set her pace. Skipping would be perfect, she thought, aside from the fact there was no way her direct superior could find it anything but insulting. The pace could have had a benefit. She could, if she wanted, gab away which was a preferred component of any workout. Of course, that would mean chatting with the Monsignor. That was a whole different kind of exercise.

"I heard you are planning a trip," the man said in a surprisingly even voice. Middle-aged, with a couple of extra pounds everywhere, she'd made the mistake of thinking he'd be huffing hard by the first mile marker. Maybe this workout wasn't all that stressful for him, either?

"Albion Catchment," she replied. "Couple of hours away."

"Did the Bishop?" He paused and took a breath. "How should I ask this? Did the Bishop suggest your expedition?"

There it was. The other shoe. Thank God she didn't have to wait much longer.

"No," she announced. "The road trip was all my idea."

"You can't... ah... make a decision on this mediation without it, huh?"

"No," Demiana repeated. "That's what led to the idea. I need a deeper understanding of the issues. First-hand understanding."

"You couldn't," he took an extra breath. "You couldn't review video or stills of the facility?"

"I could. I have, actually. Quite a bit. I've been trying to get a sense of the place. Trying to figure out what's got the Kongers and the Groupies so spooked or intrigued or whatever."

"This will lengthen the proceedings."

Demiana made a couple of exaggerated breaths, pretending she needed a moment before she could speak.

Because while it was her natural inclination to talk and talk and talk, she also wanted more information. Ha. Wasn't that the story of her current life?

The Monsignor said, "I was hoping this could be wrapped up soon."

"I'm very sorry," Demiana replied. "I didn't know we had a time issue."

"It's just... how should I say this?"

"Time is always an issue?" *Agh! Shut up, Demmi,* she said in her head.

"No, actually," the Monsignor said. "The... energy is a commodity we trade. One we would like to continue trading."

"Yes. Sure."

"We could potentially be trading even more out of this dioceses."

Demiana blew out some air as if this hop, skip, and a run taxed her physically. If you've got to move your mouth, she said to herself, don't use words.

"Is there a chance you might find in favor of the complainants?" the Monsignor asked.

"Let the Kongers and Groupies into the power plant?"

"No." He chugged along, facing straight ahead. "Shut the facility down."

"Can I do that?"

"If it were in the best interest of the shared commons, of course."

"Of course," Demiana said. Fu— She stopped her thought. *Fudge,* she said in her head. *Flying fudge.*

"There are number of people who think that might be in everyone's best interests."

"Everyone's," Demiana repeated.

"Everyone's," he said again. "Alright, then." He slapped his hands together. "Let's finish this off."

The Monsignor took off at twice the pace.

Demiana skipped, bent forward and caught up, staying a half-stride behind and to the man's left. *It would seem,* she thought, *that the tough part of the workout had ended. Now it would be just sweat and pain.*

— «» —

The guy didn't look that tough, McCallum thought as he stretched on the mat. He worked his leg in the brace. It still didn't feel natural. He had logged too many years without it for the device to blend in after a month. He still limped. So, even though this guy didn't look that tough, McCallum figured he, himself, probably looked even less so.

"Detective," the man knelt next to a large gym bag. "I'm Master John."

"Great."

He took a slick, black cane out of his bag and stood. He twirled it through his fingers, flipped it behind his back, grabbed it with the other hand and tossed it to McCallum. McCallum caught it. Barely. Master John's actions were fast and unexpected.

Master John said, "You are authorized to carry a cane. I'm going to teach you how to use it."

McCallum spun the cane over the back of his hand. He turned his wrist and balanced the rod on the edge of his outstretched hand. It was heavy and evenly constructed. He found the fulcrum point without a search. This was not a crutch. This was a weapon.

"Your medical deferral sites a cane specifically." The man returned to his gym bag. "Which is not a bo or jo."

"I have baton training."

"That was in your file. Yes. Baton training is derived from keijojutsu techniques, which have been adapted from the Shinto Muso-ryu. Shinto Muso-ryu also provides the foundation for what we want to do here."

Master John drew a cane from his bag, white with black dashes up and down the length of it.

"Once upon a time in the Tokyo Catchment, the government set policy against the carrying of swords. Walking sticks became fashionable and, as usually happens, a set of techniques emerged putting those sticks to use. Uchida-ryu comprises twelve techniques for defense with a stick similar to what you and I have here."

McCallum swished his cane quickly in small arcs. "It's twice as long as a security baton. And twice as slow."

"It hits twice as hard," Master John said. "It also extends your reach. The real difference is—" he dropped his cane onto his outstretched arm, catching it in the crook. He spun it. "is the hook."

Master John caught his spinning cane at the tip, with his other arm, and brought the handle around entrapping McCallum's left ankle. He stopped and grinned.

"The bent end of the cane can be used to ensnare." He pushed the cane back, brought it back and up and made a slow jab, handle-first, into McCallum's stomach. "It also blunts the force of an attack and makes it easier for your opponent to get a grip and disarm you."

McCallum grabbed the handle of the cane, thumb fitting into the hook. He slowly rotated, using his hand, and the weight of his body, to pull the cane from Master John's hands. He finished his rotation facing the master, holding a cane in each hand.

"I have refined the Uchida-ryu techniques to downplay the weapon's weaknesses and amplify the strengths."

"Sounds like fun."

Master John held out an open hand. "It will not be."

McCallum tossed him the white cane. "You don't know what I find fun."

Chapter 13

Demiana sat in the Bishop's chambers again, in the red leather chair facing his desk that could have its own catchment. Bishop's Desk Catchment, population: one. Which would work out best for everyone, seeing as how it had its own time stream and all. She couldn't quite make out the math, but it seemed like every 30 minutes in her life counted for one minute in his. Not that she minded the wait. The chambers were beautiful and cozy — in a power-mad librarian kind of way. The time let her read. She brought a book-sized screen this time, in anticipation of the wait.

Anticipation. That's what bugged her. Not waiting, but waiting for the great unknown. The proper channel for communication between a priest and a bishop was through the Monsignor, her direct superior. For the second time now in two months, she sat, as ordered, anxious, and feeling what? A slight sense of betrayal? Was that it? She was doing something behind Monsignor Bujold's back?

She tried to read the skinny piece of glass she'd tethered to her cuff:

> *Control rods are made of a material that absorbs neutrons, thereby limiting or preventing fission. Removing or inserting the control rods in the uranium array regulates the rate of the reaction. Removing the rods allows more neutron interaction with the fuel, increasing heat. Inserting control rods reduces the neutron interaction, reducing heat.*

No. It wasn't a slight sense of betrayal. It was fat glob of betrayal percolating in the back of her skull. The Monsignor wanted the Albion Nuclear Facility shuttered. The Bishop wanted to cut the Monsignor out of the proceedings. So that meant... who knew. She wondered if the Bishop knew. He certainly had the station to simply give her an order and sit back knowing it would be fulfilled. Subterfuge, circumlocution, innuendo — not only was it unnecessary, it was fearfully inefficient.

The door behind her opened. She heard shoes on the hardwood. She should have turned or stood and curtsied — instead, she touched her screen, placed a bookmark into the *So You Want to Build a Nuclear Reactor* document she'd been trying to read.

"Father DeFalco," the Bishop said as he skirted the desk.

"Your eminence."

"Your field trip has been approved."

"Thank you."

"I sensed some hesitance from Monsignor Bujold." The Bishop sat in his tall-backed chair. He settled his forearms on the arms of the chair and dropped his hands over the ends. "Did you sense any hesitance on his part?"

"About the trip? To Albion?"

"Yes."

"Not, well, exactly... in words that would leave me with, you know... hesitation as a resulting finality."

The Bishop looked at her. She didn't try to extract too much meaning from the intense but placid gaze. She had too little to go on. Much too little.

"I also have a sense," the Bishop started, "that after you have visited the power plant you may come away with a full and complete understanding of its importance. We are shepherds, you and I. We have a flock to tend, whether they be believers or those still on the path to believing. Tending a flock can take many forms.

"For I was hungry and you gave me food, I was thirsty and you gave me something to drink, I was a stranger and you welcomed me, I was naked and you gave me clothing."

"Matthew." Demiana nodded.

"Matthew:25," the Bishop added. "Jesus delineates fairly clearly our mission in this world."

"He never gets to nuclear power on that list of his."

"He didn't have to. All of man's excursions are but corollaries. How we address our basic needs changes, but not the needs themselves."

"There is nothing new under the sun."

The Bishop nodded. "If caring for our flock means the warmth of uranium, then so be it. If it means preventing a radioactive plague, then that is the path. Go to Albion and see all that you should see. Take as much time as you need."

"Ecclesiastes," Demiana said.

"Pardon me?"

"Nothing new. The quote. Sometimes people attribute it to Shakespeare, but it's from Ecclesiastes."

"Yes."

"I just wanted you to know where I was coming from," Demiana said.

"Your erudition is not in dispute."

"I wasn't showing off. I just really like that passage. About the wind going round and round, the sun rising and falling and rising again. There is no remembrance of men. I think we are more than shepherds. We are caretakers, keeping the flock *and* the fields in decent shape for the next guy."

The Bishop narrowed his eyes and deep wrinkles sprayed from the outside corners. "Well then, Father DeFalco. I suggest you take care."

— «» —

McCallum raised his cane, hands spaced to the ends. Master John's cane cracked down on the middle. McCallum took the force with his legs, bending at the knees, absorbing the energy, using it to start his own spin. He moved to hook the Master's cane with the crook of his own. The Master ran his cane in the same direction, outrunning McCallum's snare. Master John drew his white cane back, like a baseball bat, and lunged with the point of his elbow, striking McCallum in the chest, mid-twist.

McCallum fell to his back, arms spread. Master John stepped to the side, placing his right foot on McCallum's cane and the tip of his own on McCallum's throat.

"Do not focus on the stick," Master John said. "The stick is part of you, not all of you." He stepped back and offered his free hand. McCallum took it and rose.

"When you fight without the stick," Master John continued, "you use your arms and legs. When you fight with the stick, you use only the stick."

"It feels natural." McCallum bowed. "I'm a stick person."

"Natural is good, but you must bring your whole self to the melee if you want to overcome your opponent. I brought a stick to the conflict and beat you with my elbow."

McCallum bent down and picked up his black cane. "Don't suppose we're done for the day."

"I'm not leaving until you are much harder to kill."

A woman's voice from the side of the mat said, "I don't have time for that."

McCallum and Master John turned and watched Andrea approach. She swung a lanyard around her finger, spinning something white into a blur.

"How's he doing, Master John?"

"I would qualify him for night security at a nursing home."

"A tough nursing home," McCallum added.

"Good enough." Andrea stopped. "I only need him for a milk run."

She caught the tethered, whirling white card. The piece of plastic he'd given her last month. No, he thought. The corners were more rounded. Dangling from her hand was something *like* that card. She held it out to him and he walked over.

"Welcome back to duty, Detective," Andrea said. "Limited duty, anyway."

McCallum took the piece of white plastic and the black cotton ribbon long enough to let you wear it like it was a medal.

"This is a radiation badge," Andrea explained.

"Like they wear in the mines."

"In power plants. Systems Security has been asked to provide an escort for someone who wants to visit a nuclear power plant out in Albion. I said I knew just the man for the job."

"Thanks, I guess."

"I know it's not detective work, but for you this should be low-impact work. Let you get your legs back. Besides, I had a feeling you might find it interesting." Andrea winked.

McCallum nodded. Then he squinted and asked, "Who needs a security escort to a power plant?"

"Some priest," Andrea said. "If you can't handle it, I'll put you on… What did you say, Master John?"

"Night security at a nursing home," he called out.

"Yeah," Andrea said. "That."

— «» —

Sukhbir Fhor set out dinner. Neelesh inhaled, taking in as much of the onion-cumin-cinnamon scent as possible. She'd found fresh spices and used them to maximum effect, toasting them before mixing in the chicken and chickpeas, building the curry properly to enthrall all five senses, even sound. This dish made a pleasant clunk on the table. It had weight and presence. The scent, the sight — it would help the dinner along. He knew his mood — and the conversation sizzling inside him — would not. He took his first bite and proved himself right. The texture, the savory-sweet flavor — this dish had a rich complexity rivaled only, he realized, by its chef.

Neelesh smiled at his mother. "I went to my new doctor yesterday."

"How nice," Sukhbir replied. "Is the chicken too tough?"

"It's perfect and you know it's perfect."

"I would not want to assume."

"The doctor visit was a bit embarrassing."

"Really? How so?"

"After they took some blood, I asked where to next. They said home. I said there must be some mistake. I hadn't had the half battery, let alone the full battery of tests. They looked at me like I was some ollie down from the hills."

"Hmmm." Sukhbir slipped a fork full of rice and glistening chicken into her mouth.

Neelesh set his fork down. "I've had them twice a year, every year, since I can remember — and I can remember a lot. I remember crying, not wanting to go into that big humming tube without you when I was, what? Four years old? I wasn't in kindergarten yet. It's one of those traumas you don't forget. To this day, my nightmares involve big white cylindrical machines emitting a steady tone so low I sometimes think I'm imagining it."

"I am sorry, dear."

"My new doctor tells me there's no need. There is nothing in my records indicating any reason ever to put me through a series of costly, invasive, time-consuming tests. Of course, the tests weren't even in my records. At first, they didn't believe I'd had them. The accounts I provided were detailed enough to convince them, for what it was worth. Because they still had no reason. No birth defect or secret malady in my past that my doctor and her staff could see. So, I've got to ask. What am I missing? Why all the tests?"

Without hesitation, Sukhbir said, "It was for the best."

"Was it? That's what I don't get. You always said it was important. You always insisted that my health depended on all those tests. The marrow draws, the fMRI, the EKG and those nodes they put on my head. I hated it, but I thought everybody did it, right? I had that idea because that is what I'd been told. By my mother."

"I wasn't wrong."

"They looked at me like I was a nut. Nobody has all those tests twice a year. Not someone healthy, like me. The company would never pay for it. Bone density tests, cardio stress tests, the fasting, the enemas — I think my new doctor was on the verge of ordering a deep psych exam because of my confusion."

Sukhbir chewed and stared at him. Neelesh could see the rush of activity behind her eyes. Clever and insightful — she had a myriad of thoughts, he knew for sure, all kinds of ideas failing to produce a single utterance.

"How about you, mother?" Neelesh said. "When's the last time you had a barium enema?"

"I don't keep track."

"They're kind of unforgettable. I had my last in April. The new doctor said I will not need another for ten years. If I ever need one."

"Your curry is getting cold."

"Like when you're lying dead still in a big, bright tunnel? Freezing, skin aching for an itch? When did you have your last fMRI?"

Sukhbir looked up to the chandelier, hands on either side of her plate. She seemed, to Neelesh, to be praying or communing with spirits or ancestors or anyone who might send her a way out of this conversation. After a moment, she closed her eyes and bowed her head, in thanks for whatever it was she might have received. Neelesh decided he would dislike whatever it was she had to say in advance of her saying it.

"We are all different, aren't we," Sukhbir said. "Dr. Cohen was very, very thorough with you. Maybe too thorough. In the end, what does it matter? You are here, healthy as a professional athlete, and all the traumas are behind you."

"But that's just it. They're not."

"Don't look back. It's inefficient."

"The tests are still with me. They created a question. Why? Why was Dr. Cohen so thorough with me? Was he like that with everyone? Because I have a hard time believing the company would let him run thousands of dollars of useless tests on all of his patients. I can't actually believe he could run them on me, if they were actually useless. Were they useless, mother? Were they?"

Sukhbir lifted her head and narrowed her mouth. "You are the healthiest man in the Great Lakes region. Before that, you were the healthiest boy on the Atlantic seaboard. I found fresh cumin and real cinnamon and took special care to open them for the base of the best curry I have made in years. Not eating it would be insulting to me and foolish for you."

"I—"

"Eat." Sukhbir sliced her hand over the table. "And don't talk with your mouth full."

Chapter 14

The car looked like some kind of origami box with the sides pinched in. Demiana snickered at herself for being disappointed — it shouldn't matter what kind of conveyance they'd sent for her, right? Yet she secretly hoped for a right, proper op car. One of those twenty-wheeled wedges so black you're not sure you've actually seen it. That's how she wanted to roll into the power plant. This black box, well the only way she knew it was an op car at all was the red 'SYSTEMS SECURITY' scrolled down the side, stretched into a stripe. She'd never warm up to this toaster. Unless it actually made toast while they drove. That would improve matters.

As she approached, the driver's door opened and a tall strap of beef jerky got out. Velcro hair, fading from whole wheat to silver as it approached the ears, a full array of creases from too much squinting and scowling. And yet, he had draw. She couldn't tell what exactly — his stance, movement, confident poise, an inscrutable combination of features… something made her want to look at him.

Inscrutable, she thought. And here I thought I'd get some reading done on the ride out.

"Father Demiana DeFalco," he said more than asked.

"And you are… what? I'm sorry. I really don't know. Agent? Operative? Is sir OK?"

"Ed McCallum." He maneuvered ahead of her, with a hint of a limp. He opened the passenger door. "You can call me Ed."

"In that case, you can call me the Mighty D. Or D-squared. How 'bout…" she got in the car. "Fa-Dee, you know, like short for Father DeFalco. No, sounds too much like Fatty. Who wants that? I'm all done dating and still don't want that."

McCallum rounded the car and inserted himself into the driver's seat. "You going to talk all the way there?"

"Pretty much."

"Guess that means I don't have to."

"I don't know about that," Demiana said. "I have questions. Lots of questions."

"So do I," McCallum replied. "I keep them to myself."

"Not my MO, op. Is that how you'd say it. MO?"

"Modus operandi is Latin and therefore not recognized by Ambyr Consolidated. We tend to say 'pattern' or 'behavior' nowadays. You've been watching some old movies." McCallum clinked his cuff to a pad in the car's dashboard. The dash lit up.

"Not old movies," Demiana said. "I hear too much Latin. The Church is lousy with it."

McCallum pulled the car out onto the street and headed for the highway out of the city. "I thought priests were supposed to be good listeners."

"I thought all ops were self-centered bullies … until you opened the car door for me. So maybe we'll both get enlightened on our little trip."

"That would be refreshing."

"We're going to get along famously," Demiana said. "Which switch is for the lights and which is for the siren?"

—— ⟨⟩ ——

Neelesh stood in front of his white board. His students gazed out the window, at the back of someone else's head, their desks, an index finger, some point in space above and to his left — one had his eyes closed and one student looked right at him, though the girl's eyes looked too wide to be focusing.

He tapped his cuff. UNIT REVIEW: PRE-BUY-UPS appeared on the screen. "This is the stuff that's going to be on the test, people, OK? I seriously want everyone to do well. Seriously. That's why we're going to do this the hard way. Out loud. With maximum embarrassment."

That last word got them. Embarrassment had a value unlike anything else with kids this age. Money came from their parents and time was still mostly their own. Social standing, though — that had some leverage.

Neelesh tapped his cuff again. THREE FREEDOMS.

"Who wants to name the Three Freedoms?" Neelesh asked.

Several hands went up. He ignored them.

"Who wants to name the Tree Freedoms and has a name beginning with Nule?"

The class chuckled. Hands fell. Nule Avantende looked side-to-side so quickly his up-turned bowl of hair flailed out, letting Neelesh see his eyes for the first time that semester.

"Aaah…" he said.

"The Three Freedoms, Nule. You've been hearing them since pre-school."

"A, yeah," the boy said. "Um. The freedom to move."

"Good," Neelesh said.

"The freedom to think."

"One more."

"The freedom to dream."

"Excellent."

"Ting Ting!" Neelesh wadded out into the small sea of children. "What do these freedoms have to do with the pre-Buy-Up world?"

"They made it?"

"Yes. You're right. Now say it like a statement."

"They made it."

"The lack of the Three Freedoms brought about a world in which we have the Three Freedoms. Very good." Neelesh reached the back of the room. "Jo Ann, this is a tough one. What did the old world have that the new one does not have that denied us a freedom of movement?"

The girl sat, staring forward. Neelesh hated calling on her. Her pulse rate tripled if he just looked at her. Sweat burst onto her brow with every question. He gave her a moment to compose herself. She made fists with both hands and a muffled noise.

"Pardon me?" Neelesh asked.

"———" Jo Ann said.

"A little louder."

"Borders," she said.

"Excellent. Two stars or three points or whatever we're giving out today."

"Wait!" Trai exclaimed. "There's extra credit for this?"

"Not extra, young sir," Neelesh replied. "Forgive my figure of speech. There is simply credit for class participation. In my final report."

"Because I knew the Three Freedoms since I was like three."

"I knew that. So it would be hardly sporting to ask you. I'm here to push you. Test you. Make you a stronger, smarter young man. In the spirit, tell me, Trai, what was different about the old world that denied people the freedom to think?"

The boy turned in his desk. He put out a hand, gesturing for everyone to wait, then he lowered it. "OK, OK, in the old days they had laws."

"Perfect." Neelesh nodded. "Laws that told you whom you could love, who could go to school and learn, what you could and could not wear."

Neelesh walked back towards the front of the room. "Sam Qui, what about the old world prevented humans from fulfilling their dreams?" He stopped next to Sam and looked down.

The boy titled his head back and looked Neelesh in the eyes. "Class systems that kept the poor poor and the rich rich."

Neelesh smiled. "Nicely done." He continued his walk.

"Though I can't really say why that's only the old world," Sam added.

Neelesh stopped and spun slowly on his toes.

"It's no different now," Sam continued. "So I'm not sure why it should count as a reason for the Buy-Ups. I mean, you were asking about differences, right?"

"Things are different now."

"Once in a while you hear of some poor kid getting rich, but you never hear it the other way. That doesn't seem too different, then."

"There are no structural barriers of upward economic mobility."

"I have no idea what you just said."

"Going with Sammy on that, Mr. Fhor." Trai added.

"The answer, for the test," Neelesh said. "Is that the companies eliminated class and caste systems. That's what you need to answer to pass. You can doubt the answer. You can debate the answer with me or amongst yourselves. You can even believe it's total crap served warm. You cannot, however, answer any other way on your exam. The companies gave us all the freedom to aspire, to hope, and to dream."

"Sure," Sam said. "We can dream all day and night. But there's dreaming and there's getting. Now that's a difference."

— «» —

Once on the highway, McCallum told the car to take them to Albion Catchment. He didn't name the nuclear power plant. He liked to drive a bit himself once he got near more populated areas. The Priest pushed her seat back to its limit, giving her room for a person twice her size. She curled her legs up underneath her, making her look even tinier. He wanted to paint her as Tinkerbelle all in black, maybe clinging to a spire of a dilapidated church, looking out over the dark urban landscape, a city that no longer chanted "I believe." A fantasy. It would probably sell. Which wasn't the point, so he'd never do the painting. Her face was too perfect to paint. That expression, like she was going to burst out laughing any second at a joke you didn't get, that would be so impossible to capture and so amazing if you did.

"You ever kill anyone?" Demiana asked.

"Yes," McCallum answered. "That's a solid first question. Coming at your subject from the side, throwing him off-balance. You a trained interrogator?"

"Not in so many words. Similar techniques, different agendas. Did the Company tell you to watch me?"

"Watch you or watch out for you. They didn't specify."

"Ha," Demiana said. "They don't know. Did they tell you to question me? Report back?"

"No and no."

"Would you lie if they had?"

"If instructed to do so."

"Otherwise, no. Huh."

"Not big on lying," McCallum said. "I look for truth. Truth is usually the best tool for that."

"So, seeker-of-truth, does that mean you're not the normal op out there busting up rogue farmers markets?"

"I'm a detective," McCallum said. "I find the markets." He stretched and crossed his legs. "Then I bust them up."

"How come we're not driving faster than everyone else? Isn't that one of the best things about being an op?"

"Not really. Start rocketing down the road and supervision calls and wants to know why you flipped off the governor and you've got to tell them something. Now you're lying and you already know how I feel about that."

Demiana turned in her seat, putting an arm up on the back and tucking her chin into her elbow. McCallum had an odd feeling. She studied him not like he was a suspect or up for review, but more like a piece of art, as if her scrutiny came not from purpose but from interest. A plain, honest curiosity.

"You're not a thug or a speed demon. You're a gentlemen, with a sense of humor and pleasing to the eye — so how is it you've got no wedding ring?"

"I should be asking you that."

"I'm thinking you cotton to girls, not boys. You gave me the quick check. You're not bi. You pick something and stick with it."

"You know all that already? Maybe I'm just feeding you all this to get on you're good side. A ruse to build trust."

"Oooo. An air of mystery. There must be oodles of boys or girls in your outer-circle wanting to jump in. Yum. What's with the limp?"

McCallum checked the read-outs on the dash. They had an hour and a half left to go. He stretched his arms and re-crossed his legs, trying to find a new level of comfort in the little car they'd given him. A baggie, the ops called it. An electric car designed for high efficiency and nothing else. Systems Security only used them for very light duty. Most ops found a way to elevate their tasks — might run into trouble, could need to go off-road, can't carry any recovered contraband — enough to warrant a better vehicle. McCallum knew he didn't have that option. Anything tougher than this babysitting gig would have required a tougher op. He snickered inside. He was a baggie.

"Injury," he said.

"Job related?"

"Lost a fight."

"I find that hard to believe."

"You been to Albion Nuclear before?"

"Oh it's your turn now, is it?"

"Doesn't the Bible say something about sharing?"

"Not a word. You're thinking of pre-school."

McCallum smirked. "They should've told me to watch out for you."

"I'm an untested variable."

"So what is our mission, exactly?"

"Exactly?"

McCallum watched her eyes roam up and over him, then return to his.

"There's no exactly, exactly," she said. "I'm going to the power plant to look around."

"A tour?"

"Sure."

"The Church is interested in nuclear power?"

"The Church is interested in everything."

"The Company is being awfully accommodating."

"I'll say. A detective as an escort. Like mixing your Mai Tai with a cement truck."

"Not exactly," McCallum said. "Don't want to burst your metaphor, but I am on light duty. Due to the limp and all."

"Ah," she said. "So they wanted somebody smart but they weren't worried about any butt kicking."

"I could still kick your butt, if needed."

"That shouldn't be an issue."

McCallum adjusted his legs again. The left one got stiff more quickly than he'd expected. "The Church has its own security detail. How come you're not using one of those?"

"The Swiss Guard? They stay mostly in Rome. I've only ever seen an agent once. Doesn't the nuclear plant have its own watchdogs?"

"Seems not."

Demiana said, "Life's full of mysteries, but who am I telling, right? Mysteries are your stock-in-trade."

"Yours, too," McCallum said.

"Different kind."

"There's only one kind."

Chapter 15

Ms. Vera Voloshama — "please, call me Vera" — from the Albion Medium Yield Nuclear Power Production Facility, Division of Ambyr Consolidated, Department of Corporate Relations handed Demiana and McCallum white tags on lanyards long enough to drape over their necks.

McCallum held it close to his eyes. The little white card was identical to the one he'd found in Dr. Cohen's apartment. He was glad he had kept the one Andrea gave him in his pocket. He much preferred this one.

"It is an extreme precaution," Vera said with a wide, glistening smile. McCallum placed her in her late-twenties and 120 pounds. Pale skin with curly red hair, she had the poise of someone used to spending a lot of time standing in high-heels and made him want to hide his cane.

"They will change color if you are exposed to more radiation than normal," she said. "I say more than normal, because we are exposed to radiation every day. We are showered in it from electronic devices, the things we eat, even the sun."

"White's fine with me." The Priest looped her tag over her head. "Goes with the outfit."

McCallum tossed his tag over his head. He turned and panned the buildings. A couple of boxes, a fat silo-looking thing and a 200-foot tall cylinder pinched in the middle. Not a shape you saw too often. He didn't know its name. All the structures shared the same sandy-white color. Only a few of the pipes and ducts broke the monochrome. Yellow, orange, and green, probably coded for function. He didn't care. The walls — not fences —and guard towers pulled his attention. The walls stood three-times his height. The towers sat at each corner, over the entrance, and in the center. It would be hard to find a place not visible from above. This place felt like a castle first and a power plant second.

"If you'll walk this way—"

"We'll be headed for that observation tower?" The Priest cut Vera off. McCallum brought his attention back around to the ladies.

"Not directly."

"Let's try directly, then," Demiana said. "I know you've got this and that planned out, which is very kind, really. I just don't want to waste your time on things that are, you know, a waste of time. Can we get up in that center tower?"

"It is not normally on the tour."

"This is not a tour."

"My understanding differs." Vera smiled again, this time straining.

"I came to look around," Demiana said. "That thing was designed for looking around."

"There are security concerns."

Both women looked at McCallum. He shrugged his shoulders.

"Access is limited." Vera glanced at McCallum's cane.

"I'll manage," he said.

Demiana smiled with tension, imitating their tour guide. McCallum hid his smirk.

They walked through the front office building, moving faster than McCallum would've thought possible with Vera in those shoes. The lady had talent. Whether she used the talent to get through this whole thing faster or to maximize his discomfort, he couldn't say. He tried to pay attention to her talk while giving things a good look-see of his own.

"...basically a steam engine," Vera continued. "The heat of the fission reaction turns the water into steam which spins the turbine, generating electricity. It's a simple design that's been in use for nearly two centuries."

McCallum peered through every door and window they passed. He couldn't catch sight of anyone. He had the feeling people worked around the corners or behind the frosty doors, but he saw no one.

"…water cools the steam returning it to its liquid form, which is then pumped back into the reactor."

They entered an elevator. He glanced at Demiana, hands clasped behind her back, rocking on the balls of her feet.

"Construction began on the facility 32 years ago this month," Vera said. "Our 30th anniversary of going online will be this spring."

"Thirty," Demiana pondered out loud, "Is that gold or silver?"

"Uranium," McCallum said.

Demiana glanced at him, a smile curling up the left corner of her mouth. The door opened and Vera started walking, never looking back to see if her guests remained in tow. She tapped her cuff and whispered three words McCallum couldn't hear.

They followed their guide down a long corridor. At the end, she turned and raised her hand. As they got closer, McCallum made out a steep and narrow rising stairwell. The uniform sandy tile made all the steps and risers blend to the point of optical illusion.

"Systems Security is expecting you," Vera said.

Demiana and McCallum stopped and looked at each other.

"We didn't think there were any ops stationed here," Demiana said.

Vera gave a condescending smile. "You were misinformed."

"After you," McCallum motioned to Demiana.

"I knew I shouldn't have gone with the skirt."

"Don't worry." McCallum tapped his cane. "I'll be keeping my head down."

He did not watch the Priest as she climbed the stairs. After what he figured to be a good head start, he set his cane on the first step and began his climb. Stairs or rungs? The access fell somewhere between a stairway and ladder. He heard Demiana make her entrance, then hurried up and finished his climb. He emerged into an octagonal gazebo, enclosed in panes of thick glass. There were scuffed bamboo chairs and a thin shelf ran all the way around for elbows and coffee mugs. Two men in red and black jumpsuits stood facing Demiana, but not completely diverting their attentions from their duties.

"And this is Detective McCallum," the Priest said as he planted his feet and cane. "Detective, this is Brick and Van."

The op closest to him — Van, was it? — froze up, failing to complete his hello, arm stuck in a queer partial reach for a handshake. The man was 5'9", well-muscled with dark hair and features, in his late 20s, and, in McCallum profession estimation, looking at a ghost. It gave McCallum a not-so-professional chill. He was not now, and never had been, dead.

"Welcome to tower one," the other operative said. Same age, same build, but the opposite demeanor. He seemed happy to have visitors, and quite unfazed. Brick. The name fit.

"Thanks," McCallum said. "Don't let us take you from your duties."

"No," Van managed.

"The view is wonderful." Demiana rushed to the window facing the water. A thin river, running close to the plant. "That must be the canal."

"The Erie Canal," Brick said.

"What brings you here?" Van asked McCallum, his tone flat and stressed.

"She does." McCallum nodded towards Demiana, not taking his eyes off the guy.

"Is this some kind of inspection?"

"Have you been briefed on us?"

"No," Van said.

"What makes you think *I'm* going to brief you?"

The op's lips tightened. He said, "Professional courtesy" without moving his jaw.

McCallum laughed. He glanced around — Demiana moved from pane to pane, the other op following so closely that he couldn't have realized what the lady did for a living — then returned his eyes to the closer op. Van stared at him. Whatever surprise he'd suffered fell away, leaving a pissed-off kid, angry he'd been startled.

"What's the point of this place?" Demiana asked. "I mean, don't you have a quarter of a million cameras and sensors all over the plant? Why do you need two fully functional males perched up here like hawks?"

"That's kind of the purpose, ma'am," Brick answered. "Never quite thought of it that way, but we are kind of like hawks, ready to drop down on the mice."

Demiana gave the op an extra-exaggerated quizzical look. "Mice?"

"Rapid Deployment, ma'am."

"And do you deploy rapidly often?"

McCallum caught the creepy op eyeing his cane. "You authorized to carry that?" Van asked.

"You been out in the sticks too long," McCallum answered. "I'm sorry, but I need to you see your ambulatory device authorization, sir. That's how you ask that question, if you were ever going to ask a senior op again, which I wouldn't advise."

"We keep things cool," Brick told the Priest. He glanced at McCallum and then at his partner. "Right?"

"Yes," Van said. "Keepin' it cool. How'd you get injured?"

"Ballet."

"Great." Demiana stepped between McCallum and Van. "I've seen enough. Up here anyway. Let's continue our grand tour."

— ‹› —

Neelesh sat down to lunch with a bowl of biryani and a reader tethered to his cuff. He called up a search program and sent it out looking for information on his old doctor and mentor, Dr. Chesterfield Cohen.

"Hi." Margie Laporte sat down. A spritely third-grade teacher, roughly his age, she kept her hair short, which a lot of teachers did for easy maintenance — but on Margie, the cut showed off her long, supple neck.

"Hi," he replied.

"What are you eating? It smells delicious."

"Leftovers." Neelesh put down his screen.

"I don't even know what I've got here. Some kind of enhanced yogurt supplement thing."

"Sounds healthy."

"I'm trying. You know, respect the temple and all."

"Room for one more?" Damar Cu appeared out of nowhere, as usual. Neelesh stifled his large, internal groan. If Margie showed up, wait three minutes and Damar would walk by, surprised and happy to stop.

"Were you attracted by the scent, too?" Margie asked.

"I'm not sharing," Neelesh said.

Margie smiled and titled her head, showing off that lovely neck. Neelesh smiled back. Damar sat down and proceeded to open his lunchbox. The pale, curly-haired test tube of a man-child talked. Neelesh didn't process the words. He picked up his reader. The search results were equally uninteresting. He brushed his finger on the surface to drill deeper.

"What kind of music?" Margie asked.

Neelesh looked up. He assumed she had responded to something he'd just ignored. Damar looked side-to-side as if someone in the room might be straining to hear his answer. As if anyone wanted to hear his answer.

Damar lowered his head and his voice. "Let's just say the kind of tunes that don't get broadcast. These blokes were toasty. Very toasty."

Neelesh returned to his reader. A link near the bottom read: Medical practice of Dr. Chesterfield Cohen sale complete. He tapped it.

"You ever go out to hear bands?" Margie asked.

Neelesh read about the sale of his previous doctor's practice to a holdings group. He hadn't contemplated, until that moment, that Dr. Cohen had a private practice. He had heard of such things, just as he'd heard of other dimensions, never figuring he'd been to one. Dr. Cohen had his own little division of the great Ambyr Consolidated and Neelesh had never given it a thought. He added this to his on-going mental list of things he didn't pay enough attention to in his youth. Attention!

"Oh, sorry, what?" he asked Margie.

"Bands. You ever go out to hear live music."

"That's on my list, too," he replied. "Of things I should've paid more attention to in my youth."

"I've seen everybody," Damar said.

"You're not terribly far from your youth now," Margie said.

"No," Neelesh said. "Certainly. But that's not how it feels sometimes. These kids can make you much older than your age."

"Repeat, repeat." Margie nodded. "Every day I get here feeling 18 and leave feeling 80."

"So anyway," Damar cut back in. "A bunch of us are going when the band is back in town next Friday night."

"Who's in the bunch?" Margie asked.

"Well, you and me would be a good start."

"I," Neelesh said. "You and I would be a good start."

Damar looked at him and spread a thin, toothless smile across his face. He held it until it was clear the smile was fake from the start. Then he turned his attentions back to Margie.

Neelesh returned his attentions to his reader. He delved into the company that had purchased the Cohen practice. Baskell-Brooke Holdings, division of Comar West Atlantic Group, division of Cellprog, Division of Ambyr Medical. Neelesh tapped on Cellprog and his nerves fired off. It seemed like all of them. Did he blush? Could they see that?

"Sounds like fun," Margie said. "What do you think, Neel?"

"Ah… yep." He tried to recall what parcels of conversation went into his ears. He'd been sitting right there. He heard them, even if he didn't process the language.

"Great." Margie smiled.

"Great." Damar did not smile. He ripped into his sandwich like a vulture at a fresh corpse.

"Great." Neelesh had no idea what he agreed to, but if it pissed off Damar Cu, he was fine with it. He went back to his screen.

Cellprog. Advanced Biomedical Research. They specialized in clinical studies on active human candidates. Their profile didn't say knowing or willing.

— «» —

The restaurant seemed fine. Cute and calico, just the type of thing Demiana expected to find in a town of twelve hundred. She had passed being picky about three hours ago. Anything with a seat would be precious now.

"How's your leg holding out?" she asked McCallum. "Not that you're crumbling under the task. I'm not saying that. It's just, I'm played out and I've never had a mysterious leg injury, so it occurred to me that you might, you know, be feeling it."

"It's OK," McCallum said.

"That was a lot of walking on a lot of hard surfaces. It would wear out a pro athlete."

"It's OK, Father. Did you see what you wanted to see?" The Detective picked up a plastic menu. Demiana looked at her own lying there on the table and left it. They were the only people in the place, which didn't surprise her. The last of the lunch crowd had gone and the dinner rush wouldn't start for another hour, if it started at all.

"I didn't see much," she said. "And not for lack of trying. We saw everything. And nothing."

"What were you expecting?"

"No idea. I thought some great truth might appear, some kind of radioactive bush burning in a hallway explaining the weirdness of the place to me. I went on faith."

"You do that a lot?"

Demiana popped her eyebrows up and down. Let him figure it out. She would have to eat something. Get some more sugar in her blood and up to her head.

The Detective scanned his menu, as if he couldn't have read about the five sandwiches by now. "There is a painting by Caravaggio — Supper at Emmaus — which is beautifully detailed when it comes to Jesus and the disciples and the table they're at. The background is blank. It's one of the things I find so fascinating about the work. You can see the spots on the fruit but the background? Nothing. Caravaggio went out of his way to show that nothing."

Demiana popped her eyebrows again. "So what I didn't see was what I needed to see?"

McCallum flipped the plastic page to view the selection of fried things on the back. The waitress appeared. A thin teenager in a white dress and green apron, trying to grin her way through the outfit's effect. Demiana gave her the 'sorry, honey' slump–and–smile. Then she tried to correct it. Maybe she liked the country girl look. Whatever works, right? The waitress said some friendly things. The Detective smiled and talked. Demiana ordered the meatloaf and scalloped potatoes because she couldn't remember ever having such things before and they sounded homey. Not her home. The homes around here, in someone's outsized imagination.

"People," Demiana said as the waitress left. "I expected to see a lot more people. Who did we see? A mouthpiece and two ASS ops? Sorry. Ambyr Systems Security operatives."

"It's OK. I take no offence. And yes. That was it."

"Do you think maybe it takes more folks than that to run a nuclear power plant?"

"Yep."

"Do you think we maybe should have seen a soul or two wandering around? I know we didn't get inside the hot areas — who would want to — but seriously? Nobody needed to change a light bulb today? Or walk down a hall to a meeting? What are the chances that we didn't see anybody at all?"

"Zero."

"Zero," Demiana repeated. "What the Hell does that mean?"

"I don't know."

Demiana gave the Detective her serious look, all brooding brow and pouty mouth. She knew she didn't look all that scary. She also knew when to shut up. She'd learned that in the mediation classes the Church gave. If you want people to talk, you can't be talking. Detective McCallum stared back at her, his mouth starting to look like it was painted on. He must have been taught the same things. Shut up and listen, they'd both been told. Well, this dinner just bottomed out. They were going to freakin' look at each other for the rest of the night, like the freakin' worst first date ever.

"So why didn't you just say you didn't see enough people?" Demiana asked. "What's with the Caravaggio and leading me around by riddles? Do you think the Company sent you down the wrong chute and you should've been a professor?"

"Artist," McCallum said. "A painter, really."

"Oh, well. That's different."

"Thought you might appreciate the symbolism in the painting."

"'Cuz I'm a priest?"

"Excuse my prejudice. I didn't mean to—"

"I'm kidding." Demiana waved the thought away. "It's mostly true. I'm a little more plainspoken than my brethren, as they so often remind me. Jesus taught with parables and symbols, which was part of his genius. Good stories live, adapt, and survive. Good art stays relevant when it's the perfect cocktail of concept and ethereal relevance. So you're right. I've seen several Caravaggios and they stick with you longer than lectures."

"Several?"

The Detective's face changed. She hadn't seen the look before and certainly never imagined seeing it ever. His eyes softened around the corners, making the crow's feet droop. His mouth parted, like he wanted to say a bunch of things all at once and they got stuck and he forgot, for a moment, that the strong silent type shouldn't say any of them at all.

"I visited the Vatican before being assigned to the Buffalo Diocese," Demiana said. "It was an honor. Some priests live out their whole lives never making it to Rome. My father used some juice and got me there so I could spin around with them, my parents, for a while, before being air dropped into whatever. I had never heard of Buffalo, as a place. I'm familiar with the great furry cow hunted to near extinction by governments. Anyway, the Vatican has a herd of Caravaggios and I tried to see them all."

"You have an interest in art."

"No," Demiana said. "I'm interested in humans and we express ourselves more openly and truthfully in art than anything else. Even the trashy stuff has an emotional base. 'Oh baby, baby dance with me all night.' It's garbage, right? But it stands in for basic human needs. The good art, the lasting stuff, that's where you really see the crux of humanity. That's why art and faith are so thoroughly intertwined. The Bible's all about singing and storytelling. Then the Church gets into architecture, painting, and sculpture. You need the sublime to represent the sublime. Art, truth, faith — they're all branches of the same tree. Cut from the same mold. Wait. What was my metaphor? Calves from the same mother. How's that?"

"Well…"

"Yeah." Demiana shook her head. "You snagged my meaning anyway."

"Faith is an art form."

"Exactly. It's the intangible that really matters to people. No matter how much we covet Porsches or Tag Heuers or anything from Chanel — mmmm, Chanel — they're only stand-ins for pride, power, love. Expressing the intangible is messy business. You say a stroke on a canvas represents beauty. I say God's love does. It's faith, either way."

"Makes you an artist."

Demiana felt her first big, genuine smile of the day. "Never thought of it that way before. Huh. My, you're an interesting Detective. Not what I expected, though I should know better. I'm fifty-fifty when it comes to pre-judging, which one is not supposed to do in the first place, but I can't help it."

"No one can," McCallum said. "Human nature. Got to process the signals fast."

"So you do that, too?"

"It's a necessity. And a danger. You been an op for as long as I've been, you can rely too much on your quick read."

"You like to go a little deeper."

"I try."

"Is that what you were doing with that op up in the tower?"

"Who wasn't supposed to be there?"

"Bureaucracy?"

"Possibly."

Demiana leaned over the table. "You were grinding him."

"Maybe a bit."

"Did you get any deeper?" she asked. "Did you learn anything by the way he reacted to you?"

"You've got no fear when it comes to questions. Is that from being a priest?" McCallum sliced his hand back and forth about head high. "You up here, above the melee?"

"That's a danger in my profession," she replied. "Thinking you're on the shore, when all of us are in the stream. The same da— The same stream. But you find me haughty. How disappointing."

"No," McCallum said. "Not at all. I didn't mean you're uppity. I wondered if you didn't have a better view."

The waitress returned with their entrees. Demiana looked at the Detective's big salad and scrunched her lips. That's what she should've ordered. She looked down at her pile of meatloaf, under a deluge of dark gravy, nestled against potato disks drowning in buttery goo and the guilt melted away.

"You didn't answer my question," she said. "You thought I'd forget under the weight of this incredibly robust food. And you are right. I will probably nap all the way back to the city, so answer now. What's the digest on that creepy op? Van was his name."

McCallum said, "Don't know."

"But?"

McCallum looked her in the eyes. She could see him doing his mental calculations. Is it worth it to stall her when you know she's just going to keep asking again and again, through dinner and all the way home? She knew her annoyance level and while she had trouble turning it down sometimes, cranking it up was a whole different deal. She could do that in her sleep. She put that message in her eyes.

"The picture wasn't perfect," McCallum said. "Why didn't my station know they had ops? Why have a surveillance tower manned like that? Why have one at all? And if you've got a tower, why in the middle when I would've thought the company's big concern was keeping folks out? The only reason you have a manned operations tower like that is to keep folks in."

Chapter 16

McCallum held the door for the Priest. The air had a minty coolness. Fall had just set in: the sun no longer beat the air long enough to give it a full baking, yet the colors warmed. Inverse, he thought. As the temperature dropped, the light seemed more fiery.

"You must love this," Demiana said.

"What?" They walked towards the car in the lot next to the restaurant.

"Trench coat weather. You look so at home in that thing, I can't imagine what you do in the summer."

McCallum noticed dangling wire on the eve of the building next door, where a camera should be.

"I pray for rain." McCallum scooped his arm around the Priest's waist and passed behind her, putting her street-side as they walked.

No one else was walking, three cars rolling down the street. Twilight. Bad for the eyes. He maneuvered the Priest through a wide swing into the parking lot, putting extra distance between them and side of the restaurant. There was a white, egg-shaped utility truck backed into its parking spot, his baggie, and four other small, family model cars.

The creepy op from the tower, Van, leaned back against McCallum's car, arms crossed, legs crossed, like he was waiting for a ride home.

"Hey," Van said.

McCallum crouched to his knees, spun to the left and jammed his cane onto the cement. His hand slid to the mid-point. A leg cleared his left shoulder. Good kick, had it landed. McCallum sprang upward, ramming the curvy handle of his cane into the jaw of his attacker, the nice op from the tower. Brick's head snapped back and McCallum pulled the cane in, grasped it with both hands, and hooked the op's left ankle. He turned as he yanked, dropping Brick to his back.

"Run," he said to the Priest. No idea if she listened. Van charged. *He'll try a leaping kick,* McCallum thought, so he bent his body just as the op's foot cleared where his head had been. Van landed and took a traditional Thai Krav stance while his partner began to lift himself, hand on the back of his head. Not much time.

McCallum swung his cane down like an ax, aimed at chopping Van in two. The op's arms made an X; he caught and pushed McCallum's cane to the side. McCallum advanced, stomping with his lead foot, sliding the other. He brought his cane up and around again. Brick rose and hopped into a classic battle stance. The Van blocked again, forcing the cane to his left. This time McCallum expected it. He rammed the cane, using their combined force to strike Brick's face, plowing him back to the ground.

Bad leave, McCallum said to himself. He had left himself open. A kick to his stomach forced out all of McCallum's air. He doubled over, red pain webbing his eyes. A punch to the head set his ear on fire. Return to position one! Return to one!

"Enough!" A female voice screamed. The Priest.

McCallum brought the cane up on a guess. It swished through nothing, but forced Van back a step. They both regrouped, taking fighting poses, eyeing each other. The asshole's bounce looked familiar. A tight tuck, elbows right to the hips, hands like claws. Lots of ops used the technique. Something else...

"I'm calling the ops," Demiana said.

"We are the ops," Van replied.

"I'll call more."

Hop and kick. McCallum blocked it with his cane.

Punch, punch, punch. McCallum batted them away, feeling his carbon fiber tool rattle the boy's bones. Van bent and darted for a grapple. Clever. It forced McCallum to change footing, duck to the left. He took his cane in both hands, held it cross-wise, and smacked the op in the shoulder. No damage. Too little force on too much muscle.

"I want to report a fight," Demiana said.

The op turned, separating his arms, like he was pretending to have a staff of his own. McCallum saw an opening. He rushed him, no time to change grips. He planned to hit him edgewise again, across the face.

The cane split in two. McCallum stumbled, his arms splayed, each hand now holding half a stick. He planted a leg to cease his momentum, catching himself as he caught a glimmer of light. A gossamer thread three inches from his face. It extended from the op's raised right fist, to his left wrist.

The wire had sliced through his carbon fiber cane like a hand through air.

Van lunged. Wire is death. McCallum dodged right, got low. Keep away from the wire. Van lunged again. McCallum dodged left, pumped his leg up and down, plunging it into the side of Van's leg, near the knee. The asshole crumpled with the blow. McCallum rammed the bottom half of his cane into Van's temple. He threw the other half into Brick's forehead, knocking him down a third time.

Just maybe, he thought. *I might live—*

"Look out!" the Priest shouted, pointing over his shoulder. McCallum spun in place.

An old guy in a jumpsuit. With a cattle—

— «» —

Like squeezing blood from a stone, Neelesh thought. He almost said it out loud. Some days he could find a way to rev up interest in the class. Other days, like today... he couldn't even fake it himself.

"Factors leading up to the dissolution of nations," he said, to no effect. First period of the evening shift — it could be rough. Unlike the morning kids who crawl to school and wake up in his presence, most of these kids have been doing something for the last few hours. They used this class as a rest period. He took this as fact because he wanted to rest too, every day. He wanted to sit back, put his legs up, and digest his dinner while reading a mystery.

"Why not," he did say out loud. He climbed on to his desk, wove his fingers into a little hammock, set his head in it, and laid down, eyes on the ceiling. "I don't care about this stuff, either."

"What?" someone asked. He couldn't quite tell which girl.

"The nations dissolving," he replied. "They fell apart because not enough people cared anymore. It is tough to teach about things people don't care about. Of course, I could teach about what people do care about. It's not like people stopped caring. Never thought about it that way, the Buy-Ups as a kind of care transference. Huh."

He heard rustling. Some students would take advantage of his position and the lack of a direct line-of-sight. He'd have to fix that, but he was so comfortable.

"So," Neelesh said with force. "Anyone know what a nation was so we can get back to not caring?"

"Lines on a map," another girl said.

Neelesh sat up. "Yes. Borders. Bravo. The nations were defined by lines on a map. Imaginary barriers that the ruling governments agreed upon. Except when they didn't. Before the Buy-Ups, the land on the other side of the Niagara River was called Canada. Same air, same trees, same water — but if you wanted to go over there, you had to pass through a checkpoint staffed with security personnel. Because this side was a different nation."

"The United States," a boy up front shouted.

"Good." Neelesh clapped his hands. "Now. In what I just told you is a clue to one of the reasons the nations lost their charm. Anyone?"

"Because they were dumb." Annabeth Green said. She loved answering questions if the answer involved things being dumb, stupid, or grossly inadequate. For that reason, she did well in his class. Neelesh often wondered how well she fared in Math.

"Dumb," he said. "Can you elaborate? What is dumb about the nations?"

"You said the borders were imaginary. But they had guards. That is dumb."

"Annabeth is right, in her own way. Saying this side of the river is different than the other side when in fact it is not was silly. Paying guards to reinforce that idea was wasteful. Borders were pretty easy to dissolve in the end, because nobody — say it with me now — nobody ca…"

"Cared," the class said in unison. Neelesh took it as a minor victory.

"But nations had been around for thousands of years. What happened in the 21st century to make people finally give them up?"

"The Buy-Ups?"

"No, this leads to the Buy-Ups. Remember, I said people did care about borders so much because they began to care about something else. Something to replace the borders."

They didn't get it. He knew they knew their history, but the boat, it would seem, was still too far from the peer.

"Nations existed in one form or another for thousands of years because people got something from the structure. They saw a benefit in it. People learned early on that working together made work easier. They had big family farms, then villages, then towns, then cities — groups that worked like companies, with each person doing what he or she did best for the good of the whole group. Collections of cities became nations. Bigger is always better, right?… Right."

"No," Annabeth said.

"Yes," Neelesh replied. "I mean, correct. There is a right size for everything, and some of the nations got too big. Huge borders made no sense. People were grouped together who didn't want to be grouped together. They had no common cause or purpose. Even worse, some groups of people were split up, separating them from their common cause or purpose. Hunger, anger, and general unhappiness meant a perpetual state of war. Anyway, back to the question. What replaced nations?"

"Companies?" Robert Wojak offered.

"Always the right answer. By the 20th century, companies had abandoned borders. Multinational corporations largely ignored borders because they were, as Annabeth so aptly put it, dumb. In truth, companies were only one factor. We've had businesses for thousands of years, but people didn't wake up in the year 2000 and decide to start tossing out governments. Still, Robert, you get up on the board."

Neelesh tapped his cuff. 'Companies' appeared on the white screen behind him.

"Anyone want to guess at the next factor?"

He paused. Two-thirds were actually focused on him. Awesome. He continued to make this a bit of a game.

"Again, this is something you care about. You. We stopped caring about imaginary borders because we started to care about..."

He held his arm up and shook his bracelet.

"Our cuffs?" someone said-asked.

"Yes." He lowered his arm. "In a way, anyway. We started to care more about each other now that we had the easy, economical means of reaching out to, and staying in touch with, other people — regardless of where they lived. Our lives were no longer confined to villages or cities or nations. We could be friends with anyone, anywhere, and at any time. We formed our own connections. Our own groups of people with common cause and purpose, regardless of location. The phony groups gave way to the phone. Ha. Get it?"

No one laughed. Neelesh tapped his cuff and 'Telecommunication' appeared on the big white board.

"Telecommunication entails more than phones," Neelesh said. "Anyone want to give me something else that falls into that category?"

"Television," came from the back.

"Yes."

"Telepathy," came from the middle.

"No," Neelesh said. "That's not an actual thing. I wish it were. I would beam this all into your brains while I sat here eating pie."

Now the kids laughed.

"I would've also accepted radio, computers, or the internet. The telegraph started it all, but it's boring. Oh, and telekinesis."

They looked at him, puzzled.

Neelesh laughed. "That's not a thing either. You can tell, because pie's not floating into my mouth right now. OK. Factors leading to the dissolution of nations. Telecommunications makes nations less important and companies provide many things nations provide, making them a reasonable alternative. Now we come to the hardest concept I have to teach seventh-graders. Anyone thinks he or she knows the third factor?"

"Debt," Hamlish d'Jango called out.

"Oh. Well." Neelesh let his face go long and wide. "You know about debt."

"Lots," came another voice.

"Why wouldn't we?" came another.

"Last year's class..." Neelesh let his voice trail off. Last year ran in a different direction. The company changed the order of classes, giving these kids a whole different base of knowledge. "You all learned about debt."

"In Business Fundamentals," Annabeth said. She gave him an indignant face with obvious pleasure.

"Hamlish," Neelesh said. "Can you tell me what debt is?"

"When you owe somebody something. Like we owe the company for our education and health maintenance."

"Perfect. Annabeth, how does this apply to nations?"

"Nations owed the company."

"That is in the neighborhood of correct. I'll take it." Neelesh slapped his finger across his cuff and 'Debt' appeared on the board. "Nations borrowed trillions and trillions of dollars from whomever would lend it. Banks, companies, individuals. They paid back the loans, with interest, about as fast as the money came in from taxes, duties, fees, and sales of assets. Then the money slowed. Nations weren't taking it in as fast as it needed to go out. Economists realized assets were no longer capable of offsetting debt, so the lenders of the world decided to what?"

"Buy-Ups?" Robert answered.

"We're nearly there. Before the world tumbled into chaos and war, the companies forgave all the debt. People agreed that nations had mismanaged society, so the companies took charge. And here we are: strong, healthy, and safe thanks to corporations, phones, and debt."

"Really?" Robert asked. "They just agreed?"

"Yes."

"Weren't there like tons of companies?"

"They all agreed to do what they do best and work as teams. Just like soccer. You put your fast guys here, your big guys there, and your quickest and bravest in goal."

"Bravest?" someone called.

"What position did you play, Mr. Fhor?

"An extra point on the next test to anyone who can guess."

"Goalie" they all shouted.

"Score!" he shouted back.

—— «» ——

Demiana watched the Detective lock up and crash, his body so stiff she thought he might shatter like porcelain. The man standing there, with the black metal poker, looked familiar. She couldn't place him. Not bad looking, wavy blond hair but bad context. Really awful context with that yellow jumpsuit. What the Hell kind of color was that for a man in his 60s.

Van knelt at the top of the Detective's head. He looked like the might cradle it. No. He had a thread in his hands, she guessed — she couldn't really see it — and he was about to slice the Detective's head clean off.

"No," she said, taking a step forward.

Van lowered the wire to the Detective's throat.

"More trouble than it's worth," Demiana said.

The icky op looked up at the old guy. The other op — the nice one — Brick, got to his feet. Through the corner of her eye, she saw him wipe blood from his face. The front of her eyes fixed on the old guy. Handsome, almost distinguished. Who was he? Her bracelet would remember. She brought it up and told it to start videoing, wide angle, off-the-cuff storage.

"He identified you?" the man asked.

"I'm assuming."

"You know what they say about assume," Demiana added.

"We can't have this kind of trouble." The man looked Demiana up and down. He lifted the metal bar and checked a small light near the grip.

"I can't believe killing an op and a Catholic priest is going to further your cause. You're talking disposition of two high-yield earners. There will be investigations on two fronts. Maybe you can adjourn the ASS ops. Maybe you adjourn the Swiss Guard. But both? Simultaneously? Hell, if you've got the juice to do that, you don't need to dispose of us in the first place."

The man stared at her. She thought he had a mild look of amusement on his face. She didn't know him well enough to know for sure. She did know him, though.

"He's permanent trouble," Van said. "He requires a permanent solution."

"What kind of pull are we talking?" Demiana walked towards the man in the yellow jumpsuit. "How deep do your strings go? Junior here is sweating this, but you look like this is another day at the office."

"She's stalling," Van said. "She called in the altercation."

"I'll call it off." Demiana raised her wrist. "It'll give us all some time to think."

"I don't feel so good," Brick said. She could see the nausea curling around inside him. The Detective must've really walloped him.

"Everything's fine," Demiana said into her bracelet. "Little bar business. Boys being boys… certainly. And thanks again."

"They're scanning the area," Van said. "Standard operating procedure."

"Let them," the man replied. He collapsed the poker like an old telescope and dropped it into a side pocket. He put his hand out. "Father, if you wouldn't mind accompanying me back to the plant."

"What about this guy?" Van asked.

"Leave him be."

"But—"

"Leave him."

Demiana took the man's outstretched hand. Soft, warm, but with fragile skin. As dapper as he was, skin never lied. It had seen better days.

The man said, "We have what we came for."

He led her to the egg-shaped truck.

Chapter 17

Neelesh listened to Miriam clink her cuff against the table plate. He didn't look at the plate. The grime and crosshatch bothered him. Normally such things did not. He had no overwhelming aversion to germs or mess. His apartment had as much clutter as any other unattached, not-dating bachelor he knew. Miriam's desk was a not a bachelor pad. It should not wear a coat of yuck built from decades of its owner not caring enough to swipe a cloth across it, even once.

"Your numbers are good," she said. She always said that. Neelesh always had great numbers. He knew his kids did well. He paid attention.

"Numbers aren't everything." Miriam faced him, arms planted in the shape of a volcano, her interwoven fists holding back the magma.

He had no understanding of what she had just said. "What?"

"Numbers are only part of the story," she continued.

"I…" Neelesh changed the tone of his voice. "I come in here every two weeks to talk about my numbers."

"I apologize if it appears that way. You come here to discuss teaching methods and practices. The numbers are a guide."

"And mine are good."

"*A* guide," Miriam said. "Not the only guide."

She tapped her cuff and brought up video of Neelesh lying on his desk. From that angle — taken from the camera in the corner, by the door — he could see the whole class from above, with him prone in the lower right part of the screen.

"What are you doing here?" Miriam asked.

"Lecturing," Neelesh answered.

"From your back?"

"I do my best work on my back." Neelesh tried to use his smile to pry one out of her.

It failed. "This is not your best work. This is not teaching the way the company needs children to be taught. Yes, your students are doing well. In fact, your metrics are in the top quintile across the spectrum — when it comes to retention, anyway. Retention of historical facts is not the main thrust of your class."

"I teach history."

"That is the material. What you're actually teaching is a communication model that the students are going to need to follow for the rest of their lives."

"I'm familiar with messaging protocols."

"Really?" She pointed to the screen. "Because this is not showing that."

"I got the kids' attention. I engaged them."

"You diminished your authority. Your clownish antics make you less of an authority figure."

The back of his neck heated. He beat down the urge to fling his arms about and shout.

"It is rare that I have to have this conversation with teachers. I can't say as I'm surprised, though. You're young. You still think you're one of them. That you're on their side and they are on yours. You're not their friend, Neelesh."

"I'm not here to make friends."

Miriam pondered the thought for a moment, then, in a moment Neelesh never expected or wanted, and found hard to believe, she smiled and leaned forward. The middle-aged blond woman changed. After six years of basic office pleasantness, she iced over.

"No," she said in a voice low and acidic. "Though I'm not fully sure you understand exactly what you are here for. Do you think you belong here, Neelesh?"

His blood chilled. Did she know? Did whatever pressure Dr. Cohen applied years ago let up with his death and now she knew? The whole company knew he had no business being a teacher?

"The question was not rhetorical," Miriam continued.

"Of course I belong," he said, quite certain his face didn't match his words.

"Then show it. Show the company it wasn't wrong when it invested in your education, when it decided you were worthy of one of the most precious tasks in the whole company — preparing others to join. Show us we were right."

But you were wrong, Neelesh blew through his head. *I don't belong. I don't belong. I don't belong.* Sweat bubbled at his hairline. The pores on his palms opened and issued the hot vapor he felt inside.

"The company wants you to teach these young people how to take direction. Teach them how to pay attention and accept whatever they need to be told, not regardless of how boring, but in spite of it. You are not to engage them. You are not to make this fun time. You are to teach them to properly respond to authority. That means, first and foremost, retaining your authority."

"I'm a good teacher," Neelesh said.

"We'll see."

— «» —

McCallum's wrist tingled. He jolted, flailing. Where was he? Dark, cold. Dark? Nighttime? His throat stung. He'd been breathing with his mouth open as wide as a beer pitcher. The girl. The woman, really. The Priest. He sat up on the concrete, butt not so numb that he couldn't feel the cold. They took her. How long ago? How long had he been out? His cuff tickled him again and he looked at the face. 6:23. Early dinner. They took her and left him alive? That wasn't right. Why did they attack? Who was that angry op with the wire?

Too much to process. Stop, sort, score. That's the training. Highest score goes to the girl — no, woman. No, the Priest. Yes. Demiana DeFalco ranked as his primary concern. He jabbed his finger into his cuff and said, "Priority, Andrea Kim. Now." Two more cars rolled by, tires scuffing the black asphalt. He wondered how many people noticed him lying there like an olli out of wine. How many?

"McCallum." His supervisor's voice jumped in his ear.

"Andrea, I need back up."

"Why?"

"Assault. Three parties. They took the Priest I was escorting."

"Yeah," Andrea said. "She told us. I sent a local to find you. I'm gathering he hasn't just yet."

"She told you what?"

"There was a misunderstanding between you and another op. You ended up on the jazz end of a cattle prod."

"They took her," McCallum said. "She is reporting under duress."

"That could be," Andrea returned. "Not our problem. She said she decided to stay at the nuke plant for a while and would no longer require a sitter. Did you know there was Systems Security assigned to the facility?"

"They're the ones that jumped me!"

"I don't doubt you, but the Priest is off my to-do list now. There is no longer a budget line for her protection. How are you? Can you move?"

"I don't..." He looked around for his cane. "Yes. I can move as much as I need to, anyway."

"You stay at square one till a local gets there? Got it?"

"I think this girl's in real trouble."

"There's lots of girls in lots of trouble. You sit there."

"How long ago did you call the locals?" McCallum asked.

"I don't know," Andrea answered. "When the Priest's call came in. Around five, I'm thinking."

McCallum dragged himself upwards. It did not go smoothly without the use of his mobility device, which, he now remembered, would no longer be of much use.

He said, "You also thinking the local might be busy?"

"That would not have been my guess."

"How 'bout maybe they don't give a shit about a city op?"

"That would be unprofessional."

McCallum rubbed the back of his neck. "There is a lot of that going around."

"See me in the morning." Andrea ended the call.

McCallum checked the message that woke him in the first place.

PanHealth wrote: *Good workout today, but your heart needs to be elevated for a full twenty minutes to count. Come on, Ed. Give yourself 10 more. You can do it!*

McCallum did want to repeat the workout. Real soon. With a new cane, and maybe a stun stick of his own.

Stop, sort, score.

No, he didn't have a budget — or authorization — to help the girl. The Catholic Church used the Swiss Guard for security. He didn't know anybody in that outfit. The Church made it a habit of staying out of trouble. He tapped his bracelet and brought up the dossier he had on Father Demiana DeFalco. He found the name of her supervisor.

"Priority. Monsignor Bujold,"

A pick-up truck ambled into the parking lot, electric motors barely pushing a sound. Black with red stripes, a light-bar on top, and the words 'Ambyr Systems Security' on the side. The window lowered and an old, round uniformed op stuck his elbow across the cab door.

"You Ed McCallum?"

A man's voice sounded in McCallum's ear. "Yes?"

McCallum flapped his hand at the op and turned away from him. "Monsignor, sorry to disturb you, but I have some concerns about Father DeFalco."

"Hey!" the old op coughed. "You McCallum?"

"Is she all right?" the Monsignor asked.

"I can't say."

"Buddy!" the old op hollered. "You McCallum?"

McCallum turned to him and nodded, as he said, "She's reported her whereabouts as the Albion Nuclear Plant."

"Oh," the Monsignor said. "I see."

"I'm talking to you." The op pointed.

McCallum raised his index finger. He held it up to the man, hoping to illustrate that he needed one more second or minute or moment. "Have you heard from her?" he asked.

"I have not," the Monsignor replied.

"She is no longer officially under my protection, but I still have concerns."

"I understand. Thank you for your, uh, diligence. I'll look into the matter."

The op yelled, "Tell your girlfriend you'll call her back."

The Monsignor ended the call. Too abruptly, McCallum thought. If it were one of his direct reports they'd been talking about, he'd have more questions. There were so many unanswered questions. A big, spotty canvas worth — none of the lines coming together, none of the hues making a shape. He walked towards the pick-up truck. The old op sat in the cab, arm dangling out the window, glaring. Not getting enough respect. Not happy that a Buffalo operative came to play in his yard, and downright pissed he had to put down his third pork chop because of it.

McCallum stopped. Nice truck. Nicer than the baggie he had sat in for two hours to get out here to the fringe of the grid. He pointed at the op, then he pointed to the left. The op looked at him, one eyebrow up to the rim of his cap, the other closing down. McCallum held out his hand and flicked two fingers back and forth, urging the man out of the truck. Then, again, McCallum pointed to the left, up near the edge of the one-story slab of a building. The old op pushed open the truck door and plopped out. McCallum turned, put his hands on his hips and looked left, gazing at the blank wall as if there were something to see.

The op took a stance next to him, put his hands on his plush hips, and tried his best to see whatever the big city detective found interesting.

McCallum slid behind the man, up into the truck cab and closed the door.

"What the—" The op thought about moving, or at least making of show of it.

McCallum waved. He clanked his cuff against the dash and said, "Priority override."

"You think that's funny, boy?"

"No," he replied. "Me napping on the concrete for an hour, now that was funny."

He put the truck in reverse, backed up out into the street, and slammed the shifter into drive.

— «» —

Demiana sat back in the booth, legs up and crossed across the black leather bench seat. She didn't want anyone even attempting to sit down next to her. She'd ordered a Martinez to test the bartender. The exquisite result made her order another, which the nasty op should be bringing any second. What was his name again? Van Gogh? Van Dyke? Vaninath. Van, for short.

He wore jeans and a black t-shirt now. Great body. Great hair. She would've found him attractive if he weren't repulsive in every other way. Narrow, darting eyes. Ghostly silence. He seemed to be in a permanent muscle flex. She watched him walk towards the booth with a drink in each hand and she knew he'd deliver plutonium to a core in the same fashion. He had no 'casual' setting on his internal dial. He sat down and passed Demiana her cocktail.

"What did you get?" she asked.

"As I said, I'm not allowed to speak with you," Van replied.

Demiana stuck her finger in his drink, pulled it out, and popped it in her mouth.

"What is that? Ginger ale?"

He glared at her.

"Just ginger ale?"

She took a sip of the Martinez, admired the balance of the sweet vermouth against the gin, and scanned the rest of the bar. It reminded her of a hotel bar she'd visited in the London catchment. Not room for 25 people, only four at the little circular bar. More of a stop-off than a gathering place. The whole building had a hotel/dormitory feel. Two men sat at the next booth over. They were also fit and, by her estimate, in their late-twenties. Like her and Vaninath.

"I see why they call you Van. Vaninath is too much for my tongue. Not the kind of work out I like to give it."

He gave her the same, unfaltering stare. The gaze of an exam proctor or an X-ray tech. A trained lack of affect. It made her want to jump around, make goofy faces, poke fun at him — anything that might ripple the flatness of his dark, shadowy face. Not brooding. No, brooding would've been a freakin' thing. He put out nothing.

"How long am I going to have to sit here?" she asked. "Why does a nuclear power plant have a bar in the first place? Do you people do this often? Grab visitors off the street and force them into your queer hotel bar? I'm thinking you do, because the bartender's no hobbyist. The guy's got high technique. Not that you'd know, nursing a ginger ale like you're out to dinner with your parents. Maybe I'll get you a Shirley Temple next round. That might become your signature drink. I mean, everything about you screams simple syrup."

The man with the cattle prod entered the bar — sans cattle prod, thank God. He'd freshened up, she could tell. He was now wearing a decent shirt and slacks. He waived to the bartender, then to the other couple. His smile seemed sincere and just the right size. He ran fingers through his golden mane. She knew this man. Where? An older guy but with younger hair? She never got a good look at him in the truck on the way here and then he had disappeared. Now that she did get a good look, she had a tingling. They'd met, but somewhere different — though that would have to be true. She'd never been to a club inside a nuclear reactor before. She had to get her cuff up and run a check. Or keep mining her memory, hard and unrewarding as that may be.

"Oh good," the man said from the end of the table. "Vaninath got you a drink."

"Two," Demiana replied. "You're a round behind."

"I catch up quickly." He sat.

She twisted her wrist as if checking the time, "It's impolite to keep a lady waiting." She tapped the function tab. "Of course, I guess that pales next to kidnapping."

The cuff whispered in her ear: Horace Marigold, Consignment Director, Cellprog, Division of Ambyr Medical, Ambyr Consolidated.

"Horace?" It didn't sound right even as she said it. Communication links didn't lie, though. Except when they did. But, now? No. She recalled the hair — different but similar. Horace, the gooey suave sex club patron. The one who tried to get her pulled from this assignment.

"Horace is my brother," the man said. "My twin, so don't fault yourself. My name is Phanes. Phanes Larkspur. It is a pleasure to make your acquaintance."

"The parking lot didn't count?" she asked.

"I was working."

"And now?"

He chuckled. "Still working. It never stops here. But this is certainly more convivial."

"What's the plan, Phanes? I called the SS and the Bishop. No one's looking for me. So now what?"

"I do appreciate your cooperation."

"I appreciate you not having anyone put to death. What I don't appreciate is not knowing how I'm going to get home."

"It might be best if we delay that for the time being."

The bartender appeared with a short, brown drink for Phanes. He nodded thank-you and pulled the tiny plastic sword from the edge. It skewered a brilliant red cherry.

"Delay as in an hour or two?" Demiana asked.

"Our current predicament may require a longer stay. In my absence, I took the liberty of arranging a room for you. If you'd authorize access for my associate here, he could stop by your apartment and collect a few things."

Demiana brought her drink up. She wanted to get something in her mouth before something else got out. Words that would sound slick and crazy and come out like a scream.

Please, Lord, she prayed. Give me the strength to endure these yahoos. "What are we talking here? A toothbrush and swimsuit?"

"I'm afraid you may want to plan for a longer stay. 24 days, to be exact."

Chapter 18

Demiana laughed when she saw her quarters. Double the size of her apartment at the rectory, this had a small living room, its own kitchen, a bedroom with a bed twice the size of the one she'd left. The beige and bamboo had the austerity of the Church, so the whole set-up reminded her of home — only better.

"What's this place for?" she asked Van as they entered.

"Living?"

"People live here? On site at a nuclear power plant?"

"Yes." He stopped not more than a foot inside.

Demiana darted around, poking at things, pulling open drawers, flicking lights. "This one happens to be free at the moment?" she asked.

"Yes."

"What happened to the last resident? Please tell me you didn't kick them out because they developed a glow that kept everyone up all night."

"No."

"No — you won't tell me that? Even though that's what happened?"

"No," Van said. "The woman who lived here has been transferred."

Demiana sat on the arm of the couch. The furniture faced a large wall screen, but she wanted to face Van, who stayed put in the doorway. She couldn't decide if he was timid or polite. Neither seemed likely.

"Now you're going to get my things," she stated.

"Yes."

"You have any experience collecting a woman's sundries?"

"Sundries?"

Finally, Demiana cheered in her head. *An expression.*

"Girl stuff," she continued. "Unmentionables."

"Can you give me a list?" Van suddenly jerked himself straight and tapped his big, double-strapped cuff. "Go."

Demiana could tell he'd started talking to someone else. She looked around some more. A cute place. It had holes in the wall above the four-seat kitchenette. Someone had lived here long enough to decorate, at least a little. She backed up her train of thought, *Someone lived here? Behind mammoth walls, in stumbling distance from a cooling tower and fission reactor. Not someone... someones. Enough to keep a pub in service.*

"I'll be right there," Van spat. He jabbed his cuff and brought his attention to Demiana. "Send me access and a list of necessities. I'll head out to the city as soon as I take care of another issue."

"Trouble?"

Van spun and left with precision. Every position looked like it came from a list. Timed and tried. Practiced. Even common things like turning. 'Trouble' put him back in his arena, she realized. Taking a lady priest to her room was really weird. He had nothing on his list for that. The phone call, a security issue, he had the response for that in a well-rehearsed repertoire. She looked at her own cuff, checked the time, got up and closed the door. She pressed the bracelet's main function key and said, "Call Detective Edwin McCallum."

She had a hunch what the trouble might be.

— ‹›› —

Neelesh ran. He didn't particularly like running. He didn't particularly like any other form of exercise any better. Running cost next to nothing and he fit it into his day or night, somehow. He thought about visiting the school gym before school started. That meant getting up and out even earlier. Midnight, after his last class, was not much better. There were days when he wanted to sleep in the teachers' lounge. The only alternative was day break. He could try to shove a workout in after any shopping or chores, before dinner with mother. That might be the worst. So he ran at night.

He jogged up the long driveway next to his apartment building and ran into the rear parking lot. All sweaty and huffing, he preferred to use the backdoor. The driveway worked as a cool down. He dropped his speed by two thirds and clomped on the pavement, next to the brick and sandstone, past the puddle by the back drain spout.

He walked past his Saab Sonnet. A deep sapphire blue, with hints of yellow in the trim. A scrumptious, sexy two-seater. Exactly the kind of car a wickedly available bachelor should have. It hadn't been cheap. Of course, he had nothing else to spend his money on. His schedule didn't leave him time to do much else besides drive to school and mom's and school and back. You might as well do it in something you loved. He loved the curve of it, the fluid continuous shape. And the way it handled on the track—

He stopped. The lip of the read deck lid rose up like it wanted to blow a kiss. He got closer. The paint on the edge had been broken. White primer and even a little aluminum showed through. The bend had no other scratches around it, as he might have expected from an accident. This couldn't have been an accident. He jiggled the lid. It had too much play. It was as if he'd popped the release from inside. His stomach turned. He inserted two fingers and pushed the release. The deck lid jumped up an inch. Someone had pried the lid up enough to reach the release. Someone had wanted access to his motor.

Neelesh lifted the curved slat and positioned the prop-rod that would keep the deck lid open. He'd never looked at the motor before. He had no familiarity with anything powering the car and yet he knew, without putting it into words, that he might find something.

Wires had been cut up and down the side of the long black box that made up the center spine of the car. All the snips were clean. The work was thorough. There did not appear to be a wire left intact. One cord had a long piece of white tape stuck to the end, like a pennant. The writing didn't look very official, so he took it and stretched it out.

It read: Know any good motor repairmen?

— «» —

McCallum sat in the pickup truck, facing the main gate of the Albion Medium Yield Nuclear Power Production Facility. The truck weighed 2,900 pounds, had a 71-percent battery charge and read 'full function' for each of the four motors — one for each wheel and an individual maximum output of 208 kW. He could, by pressing his foot an inch closer to the floor, flatten the gate. In the process, he'd strain those two uniform ops through the chain link like applesauce. They stood at attention, looking into his tinted window, wondering what kind of rattle-case had his foot on the pedal. He stared back at them, waiting for them to reposition. Just two more feet apart and they'd be able to escape the crashing steel. If they'd just inch over, just a bit. He thought about using the public address system and commanding them to step aside, but that would reveal his secret. They might not know the only thing keeping him out was his reluctance to run them over. If they stayed ignorant they might drift away on their own, or get tired, or some fool might reposition them. So he waited in steady silence.

He heard organ music in his ear. He checked is cuff.

"Father DeFalco?" he answered.

"You wouldn't, by any chance, be waiting outside for me?" the Priest said through the communication link.

"As a matter of fact, I am," McCallum returned.

"You're very sweet, but you can go home."

"I'd like to check on you, if it's all the same."

"You probably think they've got a cattle prod to my neck and they're making me say all these things, but I assure you. I'm fine."

"Then no one should mind me checking."

"Almost no one," the Priest said. "You and Van did not hit it off. Just hit, mostly. And for some reason, he wants to hit you again."

"That doesn't change things."

"It should. Things need to change. I don't know your history with Van. I have been in enough bars after enough beers to gather a reasonably clear understanding of the future. You two are going to whack on each other until one of you can't whack ever again. Maybe you're in the right. In fact, I'm pretty sure you are — but those are not judgments I can make. I don't want to be a part of it and right now I'm feeling like the cause, the casus belli if you were, and I'm none too happy about it."

"No offense," McCallum said. "This goes a bit beyond you now."

"Nope. You're right. I wholly understand this is out of my gravitational pull. I'm not the center of the universe. I just feel responsible for bringing you two together today and now I want to fix that by driving you two apart."

"How much longer before he gets here, you think?"

"You get no tactical update from me," the Priest said. "Listen. There's something flippin' wonkers about this place. It's not right. It's a mystery and I need a detective. You are the only detective I know, and if you're reassigned due to insubordination, you're no good to me and this place goes on being its walloping weird-ass self. The guy I work for turns the other cheek. Do you know what that means? Someone slaps him on one side, he turns and offers the other. Not because he's weak. No, no. He can call down floods and firestorms if he wants. No, he does it because it's the stronger, harder, tougher play. He wins in the end, always. A slap don't mean shi— I'm trying hard not to curse."

"You're doin' alright."

"It gets harder when I get tired or excited and right now I've got a heaping dose of both. Go home, Detective."

"It would go against my better judgment."

The ops on the other side of the gate talked. They stiffened and adjusted their stances. They never took their eyes off his front windshield.

"We've got something in common, you and I," the Priest said. "I don't lie. It's not even a priest thing, although we do try to uphold the truth and whatnot. I'm just not good at it, either. Fibbing. So when I tell you I'm fine, I really mean it."

"You want to stay there."

"Yep."

"Can you tell me why?"

"Call me later. I know you'll have a pair of hours to kill and I'm betting you hate every song on the radio."

McCallum just about smiled.

"Alright," he said. "Turning the cheek." He spun the truck in a hard circle. Wheels on the left side going backwards, wheels on the right rolling ahead; the most fun thing you can do with true four-wheel drive. He'd never been much of a gear-head, but the spin felt good. He pushed both transmission levers forward and flatted the accelerator.

He looked in his rearview mirror. A black shape oozed from the side, crossing in front of the gate. His instincts made his foot twitch. He wanted to jam on the breaks. He thought better of it, though. Whatever fight he had left in him came from fleeting chemicals — hormones and natural stimulants. Not from his tired bones and electro-shocked muscles. Next time he fought, it would not be to survive. It would be for the win.

Chapter 19

"This way," Margie Laporte said. She led Neelesh through a door with a picture of broom on it. She held the door as he passed through. He couldn't manage it without brushing against her. She insisted on standing with her arms outstretched, breasts jutting forward, a pleasant obstacle in his course. She looked down the hall to see if anyone noticed, stretching her lovely neck, face on the verge of giggling. Neelesh stopped in the middle of the large closet, surrounded by mops and spray bottles and stacks of rough brown paper products. The air smelled of oranges, mint, and chlorine. Certain they weren't followed, Margie shut the door, brushed by Neelesh, oblivious to — or welcoming of — their touching (he wished to God he knew which), and through another doorway. She flicked on a light. A beat-to-death couch, a bamboo-and-duct tape chair, and a coffee table that had once been a cabinet door filled the tiny room.

"Welcome to the secret lounge," she said.

"I had no idea."

Margie dropped her lunch box on the table and dropped herself to the couch. "Those of us who know try not to spread it around."

"I'm honored, then."

"Lars Sans Lui brought me here when I started. Thought he could fuck me on lunch."

"Lars?" Neelesh laughed. "He's like 80."

"Tell me about it. I don't think he could've pulled it off if I let him have a go."

"I don't know." Neelesh set down his lunch box and sat. "He gets around pretty well. So this is another favor I'm going to owe you."

"Don't think I'm that nice." Margie pulled a plastic container about of her lunch box. "I wanted to hear about your car and figured you wouldn't talk much with the rest of staff around."

"And they are always around, aren't they."

"Constantly," Margie said. "I feel like this place is more zoo than school. And I'm on display. Teachers, kids, coaches, staff—"

"Damar." Neelesh cut in.

Margie chuckled. "He's like a puppy, isn't he? Or like one of those birds that imprints on the first thing he sees after cracking out of shell. Why the fuck did it have to be me?"

Neelesh laughed.

"Tell me about your car trouble," Margie said.

"There's not much to say, really."

"You used the word 'sabotage' when you called."

"I did." Neelesh pulled out his own container. He'd planned to warm the rice dish, but the secret lounge didn't seem to have a microwave. He'd eat it cold. He'd rather sit here, alone with Margie, than any other option coming to mind.

"Sooo...?" she dragged out.

"I have no proof," Neelesh said.

"This is serious harm. Who'd you piss off so much that they'd want to do this? A scorned woman, I bet. No, no. A jealous husband."

"I'm not that interesting. There's only one person I can think of. It's the parent of one of my kids."

"Oooo. Nasty. You give the kid a bad grade?"

"The opposite."

"Is this parent some kind of caveman?"

"Ha," Neelesh laughed. "He is kind of a caveman."

"Are you going to call the ops?"

"I haven't decided."

"What happened to get this parent so frothed?"

"I'm not sure, really."

"You don't have to tell me." Margie popped the lid on her salad and picked up a fork. "I'm prying. It's rude."

"No," Neelesh returned. "You gave me a ride in without asking a question. You're certainly entitled to your curiosity. The worst part is I'm going miss my track day."

"What's that?" Margie asked.

"Two or three times as year I take my Saab to a race track. It's… liberating."

"Driving fast? Sounds delicious."

"As to who wrecked my car, I honestly don't understand it. I tried to help a student and the father took offense."

"Big offense."

Neelesh nodded. He sat still, eyes locked on the florescent glint coming off the edge of his orange plastic bowl.

"There is a lot of stuff I just don't get," Neelesh said.

Margie rolled her eyes. "That's the truth."

They both took bites of their lunches.

"Have you given any more thought to Friday night?" Margie asked.

Neelesh froze mid-chew. They'd talked about this. Something. Damar, the creep. Music. "Is that this Friday?"

Margie swirled her spoon in her plastic container. "It's OK if you don't go. I get it."

"No, no," Neelesh protested. That expression on her face, the letdown. He didn't care for it at all. "I've just been, you know, distracted by the car and all."

"Yep," Margie said. "Men and their cars."

— «» —

McCallum walked into Detective Supervisor Andrea Kim's office without being called. She'd done him the service of not calling — not creating an electronic circuit leading from her to him with lower management waiting to see the loop completed. McCallum would do her the service of showing up and answering her questions before she had to ask. She would have to, in the end. After all, he had commandeered another cost-center's asset. That type of thing didn't stay off the spreadsheets.

"Your limp's better," she said from her chair behind her desk. "How are you feeling?"

"Spry," he replied. "Thanks for asking. I'm still wearing the brace."

"You getting around poorly otherwise? That baggie we gave you too cramped for your leg? You need something bigger to drive?"

McCallum moved his head side-to-side. Not his eyes. "I want to report a car-jacking."

Andrea made a long, slow blink. When she opened her eyes they bulged out of their sockets.

"I was forced to reassign Albion Division's light truck last night while under direct threat of bodily harm."

"Somebody forced you to steal a truck?"

"Yes."

"That's what you're going with?"

"Yes sir."

"How many guys it take to over-power you?"

"One."

Andrea looked up and huffed. "I'm looking for something a little more attuned to your record, Detective. Maybe three guys? You think this jacker had some buddies?"

"Did the Albion op report more than one?"

She lowered her head. He expected her to say 'are you fucking kidding me' but that wasn't necessary. Her look said it better.

"One assailant forced me to acquire the Albion vehicle and transport him into the Buffalo catchment."

"Alright then." Andrea threw up her hands. "Let's go with that. What happened after you got to the city?"

"The party in question disappeared."

"You decided not report this policy transgression until now?"

"I was sleepy."

"Sure." Andrea nodded. "Who wouldn't be? The op — the Chief by the way — whose truck you took, he failed to mention seeing anyone else at the scene."

"The assailant was very sneaky. That's how he overpowered me."

"How many intra-office martial arts competitions have you won again?"

"I'm currently on light duty assignments as per my injury."

"Oh. Right. How could I forget." Andrea sat back in her chair. "How come you didn't trigger a priority alert?"

"The assailant prevented me from doing so."

"Of course."

"He knew enough to prevent me from requesting assistance."

"So what's he like an op?"

"An ASS op."

"Whoa, whoa, whoa. Maybe we should go with head injury. This is getting way out of—"

"I've got a photo." McCallum held up his wrist.

Andrea's face rippled in disbelief, annoyance, disbelief, annoyance — she tapped her cuff and held it out. McCallum clinked his against hers, transferring the file.

"You can see by the time-stamp that I took this last night, during the first of our altercations."

Andrea lowered her bracelet to the contact pad on the desk. She dragged her finger around the screen and flicked the photo up to the large monitor on the wall.

The nasty op from nuclear facility appeared on the wall, posed in fighting position three, Ambyr Systems Security uniform distinctive despite the dim light and blur of the shot.

"I need to identify and locate this man," McCallum said. "He is an active danger to corporate operations."

— «» —

Demiana had to admit, it didn't much feel like prison. Systems Security permitted her to wander anywhere she wanted. So much so, that she decided to test the length of her leash. She walked to the reactor.

She had read more than enough to recognize the cooling tower, most of the ancillary buildings, and the nuclear reactor's dome-topped containment silo. Her radiation badge flopped on her stomach as she walked. Twice she took it and held it up to her eyes. Yes, nuclear facilities were safer than airships or automobiles. Those were statistics. She didn't want to be a statistic. She didn't want to visit the core, either, but when in Rome and all that. If they wanted her to be here for a month, she would be here. Fully and everywhere.

She'd been to clubs that were tougher to get into than the main reactor. A lot tougher. She blew into the jumbo Thermos like it was coffee shop. The inside featured spotless polyurethane-glazed bamboo flooring, ceiling, and sides, through the entrance and down either bending hall. She stopped and knelt. They'd cut stalks lengthwise and ran them concave-side up where the floors and walls met. Curved seams. This building had no 90 degree angles. No corners to collect dust.

It kind of creeped her out. She understood why they'd want to keep the place extra clean and checked her badge again. She decided the Lord wanted her here, now, and that being creeped out was beneath her. Or behind her. Or whatever. She picked a direction and walked.

No smell, but the place had a dull hum, just under her hearing. It threatened to creep her out again, but she'd been through that with herself. She had a mission, poorly defined as it might be. She came to the first of several air locks. Again, no locks to stop her. She entered the central work area of the reactor tower.

The high ceiling made the humming and tapping sounds echo together, creating a dull cotton of noise. The monitors, cables, pipes, work stations, more pipes, and thick twisting ducts gave her no place to focus, until she turned slightly to her left and saw the center of it all. A cocoon. A two-story, icy-white, woven, imperfect cocoon, set on its end as if plucked from a giant tree branch and stuck in the center of a factory.

"May I help you?" The voice came from farther to her left.

She turned, not bothering to close her gaping mouth. A man stood by a stack of electronics she knew nothing about. He had a white lab coat and a patch of brown hair.

"You're not 27," she said.

He smiled. "Not in quite some time."

"Sorry, it's just..."

"It's all right," he filled in. "I get that a lot. This place has a very young crew."

"Except for you," Demiana said.

"Oh no. There are a few of us ... mature workers. More every day." The man pointed to the far end of the chamber. An older woman stood next to a man in his late-twenties. They both watched the same desktop monitor.

"More mature workers?" she asked.

"The opposite, I know. You'd think it would go the other way around. The seniors up-training the juniors. Not here, though. Welcome to opposite land. Excuse me." The man glanced at a piece of the machinery in his stack.

Demiana glanced back at the cocoon. Hoses and pipes coiled and entered the top through what looked like a frayed puncture. She could not see the bottom. Too much equipment. While far from an expert, she had done extensive research. That should be the location of the reactor core, where the control rods dip into, and emerge from, a pool of water, mitigating the reaction of the uranium which heated water to steam, spinning the turbine she could hear in the next building, and starting a flow of electrons that would power lights and monitors and microwave ovens all over town and beyond.

She said, "The butterfly that crawls out of that thing is going to be the size of a jet plane."

"Spider." The man continued to tinker. "That there is a web."

Chapter 20

"What are you doing there?" McCallum dipped his brush in glistening black paint and brought the tip up to the canvas. He followed the pencil lines loosely. They were guides, not rules. Not company policies.

"Whatever I want." Father Demiana DeFalco's voice came through his cuff, into his earpiece, and down his ear canal. "I haven't had this much freedom since high school."

"So you're liking it? Living at a nuclear power plant?"

"My Lord, no," the Priest replied. "You think I joined the priesthood because I like freedom?"

"So what are you doing, then?" McCallum continued to fill in shading, line after line after line. Some parts of a painting could be monotonous. Sometimes he liked that.

"This is part of my continuing education program."

"You need to live there to learn?"

"Isn't this how you do things, Detective? I can't imagine you do your job sitting at a desk."

"My job's doesn't involve showing people the road to salvation."

"But you are more than just the job, aren't you."

McCallum dipped and brushed. "This is not coming together for me."

"Which part?"

"Yours," McCallum said. "Even if you want to stay put, why do they want you there?"

"Now you get it. That's why I'm staying. I can't for the life of me figure out why anyone would want me around. I'm going to stay here until I figure it out."

McCallum chuckled. He worked the brush more, laying in the series of skinny lines.

"You think it's a stall tactic?" McCallum asked. "A slowdown for that tragedy of a mediation?"

Now he heard a chuckle in his ear.

"Tragedy-of-the-commons mediation," the Priest said. "We do them more than baptisms now."

"Is a couple of weeks going to make a difference?"

"Hardly. The companies have been chewing on this one for going on 30 years. What does a couple of weeks do?"

"You tell me."

"The dispute is all long-term stuff," the Priest said. "The tragedy of the commons is a big picture, view from a thousand feet type of thing, you know?"

"I don't."

"OK, so 300 years ago—"

"You're killing me," McCallum said. "You got to go back 300 years?"

The Priest made a piffle sound. "What else have you got to do tonight? If you had a date, you'd be on it. And why don't you have date? You're not terrible to look at. I mean, I haven't seen you since the fight, but you weren't all mucked up just after. Besides, you've got that look that would work with new scars. They'd fit right in. There are dames that go for that."

"Dames, huh."

"I've been reading a lot of detective books with my newfound time, trying to teach myself how to look for clues. Anyway, 300 years ago some guy wrote a piece about a big field that three farmers used to graze their cows. The field wasn't owned by anyone."

"A big field and no one owns it?" McCallum continued to paint.

"I know. The old days were full of heterodox crap like that. You could buy and sell people, but a plot of land could just sit there being open to everyone. They were called commons. Like that area in the middle of a round-about. It doesn't really belong to anyone."

"Shared space," McCallum put in. "That's what ops call it."

"Shared space," the Priest continued. "So about the cows. One farmer realizes if he adds a cow, he gets more milk. The grass is costing him nothing, because it's from the commons. Then another farmer catches on and he adds one. By the time the third farmer ups his heard, all the grass is gone and the cows die and everyone's out of business. A tragedy."

"OK." McCallum moved his brush in short, sweeping motions, trying to lay paint like light.

"The companies are still like that. They didn't get to build this world from scratch. They inherited a lot of capital. Sidewalks, sewers, roads—"

"Bridges," McCallum cut in.

"Solid example," the Priest returned. "Glad you're still listening."

"It's almost interesting."

"I can tell."

"Don't see how a nuclear plant is a commons."

"It's not," the Priest stated. "It's everything else. The land, air, and, most importantly in this case, the water. All three companies share the Erie Canal. The water way that runs by here. If this place bonks out and irradiates the water supply, a whole bunch of assets go the way of those cows."

"Making you sit there puts a stop to the mediation."

"For a little while."

"Until Ambyr gets it right." McCallum stood up straight. "They've got to balance out their shading."

"Are you high now? Is that why you can listen to me go on about cows and commons?"

"No," McCallum said. "I'm evening out the shading in a painting. I'm making it right and it takes time. I won't let anyone look at my work until it is perfect."

"Oh," the Priest said. McCallum waited. Then she caught up. "So if I wanted to bring over art critics from the Hong Kong Holdings and India Group, you might not answer the door."

He stepped back to get a look at the painting. It had some shape. He very nearly liked it. "I might go as far as to kidnap a priest if I thought that would keep them from seeing my unfinished work."

"You wouldn't make the mistake," the Priest said, "of snatching the wrong priest."

— ⟪⟩ —

Neelesh leaned back on a small bamboo table in the back of the classroom. On occasion, he liked to talk from behind the students. They didn't know where he was or what he might be doing, so they paid more attention. Slightly more. A little more. Possibly.

"Vocabulary will be on the test," Neelesh announced. "This is not a spelling test, although that is always important. I'm talking about meanings. Let's go over them." He dabbed his finger on his cuff. The big screen at the front of the room faded from white to black and the first word appears. Individualism.

"Anna," Neelsh said. "You want to give it a try?"

Anna sat in the third seat, second row. She made smacking sounds with her mouth. Neelesh would have preferred the more common 'um' or stretched out 'sooooo'.

"Individualism," she said. "That is putting the individual first."

"And what does that mean. Really."

"That I'm the most important thing in the world."

"Yes you are, Anna. Great." Neelesh poked his cuff again. "Collectivism, Gerry."

"Yeah," Gerry replied, hands folded on his desk. "That's the opposite of individualism."

"And…"

"And it's people who make the collective more important than the individual."

"Not bad," Neelesh said. "Not bad. You are not as important as your group. The collective — your group — is the most important thing in the world. More important than your individual needs or desires." Neelesh brought up the next word and called on Karen.

"Corporatism," she read off the screen. "That's what we have now."

"More or less," Neelesh said. "What does it mean, though?"

"It's when the companies are in charge."

"Yes, but, isn't a corporation a set of employees — individuals — trying to make the best life they can?"

"Ummmm…" Karen trailed off and he let her.

"If that were true all of us would be on our own, right? No one would help us stay warm, healthy, or get an education."

Silence.

"Or is the corporation a collective. Everyone must subjugate their will to the will of the company?"

Heads nodded to clenched hands, fell to little fisted mounds on the pale wood desktops, or simply sagged foreword, too burdened with boredom to keep upright and alert.

"If that were true, every employee would simply do their job. No moonlighting, no outside investments, no inventions, inversions, or independent thought. Everything from the company, everything for the company."

A sauna of silence. Neelesh only knew they were still alive by the intermittent rustles of adjustment, the natural twitchiness of even the most torpid child.

"The answer is 'none of the above' for those still with me. Corporatism is the best of both donor 'isms'. It is a collective environment that allows the individual to be free. The company is a vessel on which we all sail, doing what we have to in order to keep it afloat, and doing what we want when our responsibilities have been met. We get the power of the group and the satisfaction of self-determinism at the same time. It is the perfect world and you have had the great fortune of being born into it. The million-year war between the soldier and the army, between the citizen and citizenship, between the bee and the hive — that war is over and it is a tie."

"A tie has no winners," Sam Qui said. Neelesh almost jumped. He'd forgotten, for a moment, that anyone else shared the room.

"No losers, either," Neelesh replied.

"I don't know. That doesn't sound right."

"What do you mean?"

"It's that a tie kind of means there was an end. There's never an end. Not to this kind of stuff. I think you're thinking of a stalemate."

"And that's different than a tie?"

"In chess it is."

"You play chess."

"All the time," Sam said. "You don't have to read real good to play chess."

"What's a stalemate?"

"You can have two kings moving around forever and they call that a stalemate. It's not really an end, it's that we can't do anything else."

Can't do anything. Can't do anything. It echoed in Neelesh's head. "That's kind of pathetic," he said out loud.

"Maybe we should call this patheticism," Sam said.

Trai up in the first row made a muffled laugh into the crux of his arm.

Eh, Neelesh thought. At least he was listening.

Chapter 21

McCallum reclined in the sauna, spreading his limbs as far from each other as possible. A white towel lay across his lap. He had thought about tossing it twice now, but balked out of modesty or laziness, he didn't know. His leg felt better. All his muscles did. After the cold swim, the warmth loosened his body, steaming the ache away. He didn't know the other two ops melting on the teak benches, which suited him fine. He had no need for chitchat. He just wanted to breathe and soak heat.

He should've knocked on wood. The room had plenty.

Detective Supervisor Andrea Kim opened the glass door, wearing a towel and nothing else. Not even her cuff. She stepped in, glanced at the two ops on either side of McCallum and referenced the door with a quick jerk of her head. They looked at McCallum, each other, Andrea, cinched up their white towels and scampered out.

"Captain," McCallum said. "I normally stand when a lady enters the room."

"And?" She sat down.

"My leg."

"It's all right. I didn't come for a show." Andrea extended her legs, crossing them at the ankle. "Think those two are getting the gossip gin spinning?"

"It would be the most interesting thing said about me in years," McCallum said.

"Not even," Andrea replied. "You've generated a lot of interest lately." She glanced at his left wrist. McCallum understood. She wanted to make sure he'd left his cuff in the locker room, too. No code talking. It would be somewhat relaxing.

"I'm starting to think you didn't come in here for a quickie," McCallum said.

"Keep the dream alive."

"You got a hit on that image?"

"Yep," Andrea said. "Took a while. I called the squids, thinking the machine caught a bug. They said no. Just a slow search. Whatever. I didn't care after I got the results. A teacher in the Riverside area."

McCallum bolted up. "That doesn't fit."

"Not with your story, no." Andrea sat, arms out, sweat beading on her forehead. "You given that story any more thought? This heat clear your head?"

"You saw the uniform. You saw how he carried himself. That wasn't a teacher."

"Don't know what I saw. You and I both know images are down there at the bottom of the reliability bin. Right next to people's memories."

"If you're thinking I crafted that image—"

Andrea waved a limp hand. "The thought did cross my mind. You probably got the talent."

"I'm not that kind of artist."

"And I've never benched 225. Maybe I could, if I had to. Not the point. I was about to call you when I got a call from a division director at Ecron Energy. He wanted to know what I was working on."

"What did you tell him?"

"What I wanted to tell him was 'thanks for removing what tiny little doubt I was having about a fine detective.' What I ended up saying was fuck you."

"That's nice."

"Which part?"

"The fine detective part."

"Yeah." Andrea put her hands behind her head. "Don't know what you got going on, but it's ASS business and not even Energy gets to tell me otherwise."

"I appreciate that," McCallum said.

"We'll see if that lasts. Best thing for both of us would be dropping this mater into a hole and sodding it over. Best thing for our branch of this wonderful company is maintaining our authority. Nobody fucks with the ops, Ed."

"Nobody," McCallum echoed.

"Nobody," Andrea repeated. "Mother of God it's hot in here."

"I like it."

— «» —

"I'm not supposed to talk to you," the man said.

Demiana decided the man, Gene, wasn't all that old. Fifty plus, but not a big plus. He seemed older when she met him, in the middle of the nuclear reactor, because the others she'd met were 50 minus 20. Now that he'd freshened up, put on a modern pair of jeans and a dress shirt, smoothed out his thin but still walnut hair, and shaved, he didn't look so spent, like a fuel rod, all cracked and tired, on its way to a retirement home a mile beneath the Smoky Mountains. He looked like he had a smidgeon of life still in him.

"I've heard that before," Demiana said. "What did Phanes say, exactly?"

"Keep it to pleasantries," Gene answered.

"This is pleasant." Demiana forced a lilt into her voice. Upbeat. It wasn't a false lilt, really. She had a nice cocktail in front of her and they sat in her favorite of the pub's three booths.

"We'll keep this pleasant," she said across the table, "We'll talk about you. Surely Phanes won't care about that. Have you spent your whole life in nuclear power?"

"Afraid so," he replied.

That made sense. She almost asked if his hobbies made sure he stayed indoors for all of his time, work and free, but she caught herself. She didn't need the answer to come out of his mouth, as it came out more than enough other places. Skin tone, color, all-body slump. She certainly didn't want the answer. Spending the next ten minutes hearing about bird taxidermy or handmade action figures or mineral collections would drain her.

"The company said I had high attention to detail," Gene continued. "Detail is much praised in the nuclear business. It is a business of checking things in distinct order."

"Do you think Phanes is listening?" Demiana gave Gene her devilish look.

"Someone, perhaps."

"Or not," Demiana said. "You're probably a knock-out employee, which is why they brought you in to teach these youngsters."

"Not exactly." Gene looked away.

Demiana figured she got close to a boundary between the personal and the corporate. Was there a boundary? No. She'd got him veering out where Phanes inferred he shouldn't go.

"How long have you been here?" Demiana took a sip of her cocktail. A Sazerac. Amazing what you can get in this little nuke pub.

"About ten months." Gene came back to her. His life was a fair topic.

"Because someone younger transferred out?"

"I would guess, although that is not my specialty, guessing. I'm not a guesser. Like I said."

"You said this was opposite land."

"Yes." He grinned. "Albion is backwards. Not a hick town, I don't mean that."

"Though it is, a little."

Gene's grin widened. "A little. What I meant was the seasoned crew replaced the newer folks. Although even that isn't entirely true. Most of the young people I have dealt with were — are — seasoned, despite their ages. They have all been very accomplished."

"They, as in a lot?"

Gene nodded. "Since I've been here, we have had two or three birthday–slash-going-away parties a week, every week."

"Birthday–slash-going-away parties?"

"Everyone who's left has done so right after their 30th birthday."

"That's weird. Even after adjusting my weird gauge so I can sleep on this compound, that is really Edgar Allan weird. And you've been to like 80 of these things?"

Gene looked up for a moment. Doing math in his head, Demiana assumed. Then he looked back at her and said, "Yes. That would be about right. Give or take a few."

Demiana watched Gene sip his beer and look around. There were a few others at the bar. Two guys around the age of thirty, talked to by a woman pushing 70.

"When did she get here?" Demiana thumbed in the direction of the woman at the bar.

Gene followed the point of the thumb and said, "Last month."

"Is she a seasoned pro, too?"

"In fact she is," Gene said. "She has a great deal of experience. Her specialty is shutdowns."

"Shutdowns, as in reboots?" Demiana asked. "When you're upgrading software or making repairs?"

Gene shook his head. "In the near future, Albion will be going offline. For good."

— ⟨⟩ —

Neelesh got on the bus. His cuff took the fare out of his bank account. He didn't have to hesitate, just board and sit. The company made it so easy to burn though money. The cuff, the bank, the company. You barely needed to consent. Sometimes he wasn't completely certain he consented at all.

Five other people rode the bus. He walked towards the back, where the bus operator sat, gazing into a reader. An ancient guy in a blue uniform two sizes too big. He looked up, nodded through the start of a smile he didn't bother finishing, and went back to his reading.

Midnight, Friday night. A group of teachers headed out to some bar to listen to some folk band play disappeared music. He couldn't do it. He couldn't go and compete with Damar for Margie Laporte's attentions. Not without his car.

Sleek, cool, fast — all the attributes he wanted to project. The car helped. Right? It made him daring and successful and someone a woman like Margie would want to date. To kiss. Everything. The car that couldn't move. No power. No potency. The car that was no longer sleek or cool or fast. It might still look that way. People who knew a little about Saab Sonnets might assume it, but they would be wrong. His particular sports car was a fraud. It could do nothing but sit around faking it.

Can't do anything. Can't do anything. What had Sam Qui called it? Patheticism. Brilliant. The boy who couldn't pass a History test to save his life (very closely literally) summed up his and everyone's existence. Brilliant.

What a bright boy to have such a dull, dull dad.

Neelesh watched the shadows of the city brighten and fade through the bus window. The alternating lights and dark spaces, halos and Hells. He saw Sam Qui in the flashes and Jack Qui in the black and he thought about all the things he'd like to do to him.

Chapter 22

Demiana tried to call Phanes. The directory had no such person. That never happened. She'd seen it in movies — the hero trying to call someone only to have the cuff say 'entry not recognized,' which usually meant the person in question was either a spy from a rival company or a ghost. She walked across the crispy lawn from the reactor to the central tower, hoping the guy was a ghost, hoping all of these people had died in a nuclear explosion 25 years ago. Well, not really 'hoping' because that was mean, but it certainly would make her life easier. Ghosts would make the most sense.

She'd chosen black boots, black pants, a black t-shirt, and a black leather jacket. It showed off the white square of her collar. She'd found the outfit to be effective in the past. And great for her range-of-motion, for things like climbing super-steep stair/ladders.

No one stopped her from reaching the top of the central guard tower. No one ever stopped her from doing anything here. She should have loved it. No lattice of evermore pious superiors telling her where to be and when. Of course, she never would have become a priest if freedom ranked in her top five personal necessities. Day one: Give yourself over to the Lord.

All freedom is relative.

Van and Brick waited for her at the top of the stairs. Brick smiled like he was glad she showed up. Van had a shadow across his face. Lying on his back in the Sahara at noon, he'd have a shadow across his face, she decided. She hadn't quite mastered his landscape yet. She'd work on it, though. Starting now.

"What's the skinny on Phanes?" she said as she reached the top. "I can't phone him."

"I, uh…" Brick started.

"He maintains a low level of conspicuity," Van finished.

"What is he, like a Grade 1? Nobody gets out of the Church directory. I mean, nobody."

"Is there a message you would like me to convey to him?"

"No, Van. There is a message he's supposed to be conveying to me and I've become impatient for it." She turned to the other op. "Brick?"

"Father?"

"Did the company re-name you when you turned 18 because it fit so well?"

"No. I… uh…"

"You look about the same age as Van." Demiana stepped into the tower, stopping next to Brick.

"Four months apart."

"We are not supposed to perpetuate conversation with the priest," Van said.

Brick looked at him, face kinking up on one side. "What? My birthday some company secret?"

"The policy doesn't invite examination," Van returned.

Demiana looked at Van. "Shouldn't you be calling Phanes?" She turned back to Brick. "When is your birthday?"

"I turn 30 next week." His smile widened.

"A lot of people around here seem to on the cusp of the big three-O."

"All the originals," Brick said.

"Enough!" Van shouted.

"What?" Brick shouted back, arms raising, palms up.

"The director was clear."

"You think she hasn't noticed half the people here turn 30 this month."

"I said enough."

"Shit, Van. She was sent to observe things. I'm excellently sure she's observed some. So, I'm just being polite. I think the director also said to be polite."

Van stepped between Brick and Demiana. "He didn't."

Demiana backed up an inch, careful not to fall off into the stairwell, which was very much like a well. A hole in the floor. She decided the room didn't have enough room for this kind of excitement.

"Van," Demiana said. "You get any nice gifts for your 30th birthday?"

Van repositioned. Demiana smiled now that she could see his face again.

"How'd you know I had a birthday?"

She laughed lightly. "You had to, silly. We all do, every year."

"Did you down my bio?"

Demiana shook her head. "Brick said you were within four months of each other. Your birthday could be four months from now, but I'm betting it's past. I'm playing the odds. Phanes said I might be here shy of a month, so I'm betting more than a month from now is too late. You'll all have turned 30 by then, am I right? Phanes wants me to stay here until all the — what did you call them? Originals. Right. I'm here until all the originals have turned 30."

Van glanced at Brick.

Brick said, "See? She's massively smart, just like Phanes said."

Demiana said, "Call Phanes. Tell him I'm up here in the tower with my flying jacket on because I don't want to catch a chill when the Swiss Guard airship fetches me. He's got 27 minutes. Then I unleash Hell."

— «» —

Neelesh wriggled in the chair. Another favor. He had to ask yet another favor of another person. His whole life seemed to be an endless series of favors he asked for and never repaid. Maybe everyone felt the same, he didn't know. Maybe everyone needed a hand up. There was no ladder to climb, just a continuous chain of people reaching down and grabbing hold and hefting. The people rising had friends or relatives to reach out to, or they could promise a reciprocal lift in return when they rose. All of society grabbed and tugged and winked. Which kind of made Sam Qui's comments dead on right — and almost, not quite, but almost made Jack Qui's sabotage, if not justified, at least understandable. Here he sat, after all, stretching out his hand to the kind of person Jack Qui probably couldn't.

"You don't have to do this," Neelesh said, nestled into the plush chair.

"It's fine." His mother tapped away on her desk. She had three monitors on her desk, all turned from anyone sitting on the other side, comfy in the plushness.

"I know it's not exactly the kind of thing you do."

"You know that?" she answered. "For sure?"

He had no answer. He hadn't been to her office in years. She seemed happy when he said he wanted to stop by. She introduced him to 15 people on the way in, smiling, laughing, making them stop their work, whatever it might be in all those partially formed animal pens, so unlike her big, fully walled and windowed office with all of its color and warmth. Soft and silky. His mother's office was hers, he realized. Personal. Gold lamps and a painting of a temple on the wall facing her. Neelesh had only ever been a teacher, but he knew space like this meant low station. He realized she must be more important than he had considered.

"I'm not going to give you the report," Sukhbir Fhor said. "That would be unseemly. I will tell you that the Qui household uses a lot of power on Sunday mornings, usually right through mid-afternoon. During your track time, I'm sorry to say. Do those data have any utility?"

"Utility?" he repeated. What a cold word.

"You want to know when someone is home without their knowing."

"Yes," he nodded. "How did you…"

"Please," Sukhbir said. "I hope you're having an affair. That would mean you had a social life of a sort."

"I'm not that intriguing," Neelesh said.

"Pity. Still, it must be very important for you to come all the way downtown on one of your only days off."

"Unfortunately, it is," Neelesh said. "I wish I could stay."

"I wouldn't hear of it." Sukhbir went back to her typing and peering into the monitors. "Is there anything I should know?"

"I don't think so."

"You would know best."

Neelesh understood that she did not mean, at all, what she said.

— «» —

McCallum stood with his hands behind his back, pulling his jacket tight. He had to look like an artist tonight. Jeans, a Tattersall shirt, and the dreaded tweed sports coat. A negative of a blueprint screened onto a mirror. He liked the mechanized detail laced with hints of your own face. On the surface, the work expressed pride in our ability to build. Under the surface, McCallum saw a question. Did the great structures of our environment really reflect us? The builders? Did we live to create or create to live?

"I didn't recognize you," the voice said from behind.

McCallum turned. "I'm undercover."

Emory — no, Walter Whelan now — stopped next to him. Just barely 30, in shape, perfect haircut, skin, and teeth. The dark, mustardy suit came into style about ten minutes ago, not even long enough for the tailor to achieve that fit on him. He had his left hand in his pocket, so McCallum couldn't see the cuff. His right hand held a tall glass of champagne like he did it every day. Maybe he did, now.

"Barely recognized you," McCallum said.

"It's easier going down than up," Walter said. "That's a law of physics and everything else, it would seem."

"Down how many grades?" McCallum asked.

"Too many." Walter rolled his eyes. "To be honest, there's a reason the company does not leap levels very often. It can be difficult to adjust."

"You seem to be doing just fine. Wealth looks good on you."

Walter smirked. "Still feels like I'm undercover."

"Wish I could say it gets easier."

"You do this a lot?" Walter asked. "Pretending to be someone you're not?"

"Every day." McCallum returned to the art on the plain, white wall.

"I've never been to this gallery before." Walter focused on the blueprint mirror. "It's nice."

"Aga does a wonderful job," McCallum said.

"I got a message inviting me to the special showing. They said there would be an Eddie McCallum. You can imagine my surprise."

"I can imagine. Bet you couldn't wait for Saturday night."

"I'm a fan of the arts," Walter said. "So where is your piece?"

"This way." McCallum backed up and turned to the right, motioning for Walter to follow.

The gallery consisted of just four rooms, each about the size of a standard hotel room. A garden in the back gave the space a more open feel than the space should have allowed. Aga told McCallum there would be wine and cheese tonight, so she expected a healthy crowd. McCallum counted about 30 people at the moment. She had been right. Whether they were buyers or not, he couldn't say. Nor did he care. He'd come for the crowd noise.

The next room had a series of vibrant paintings McCallum admired for their use of color. They skewered the eyes, with their bolts of lime and lighting blue. He couldn't do that, himself. He couldn't attack the viewer that way. He had respect for an artist that could.

He stopped and pointed to the large black and white oil on canvas. An old, iron bridge, arches riveted, pavement worn, leading one's eyes to a vanishing point in the center, but never getting there. The middle had nothing.

Walter waited until two women in front of him moved on and stepped up to the optimal viewing range. About five feet from the wall, he decided. He took in a bit of his champagne. McCallum stood next to him, glancing around.

"Oh," Walter said. "A self-portrait."

"Thought you might get a kick out of it."

"Hell, I might buy it."

"It's very expensive."

"Lillian and I don't know what do with half our money anyway."

"That's a nice position to be in," McCallum said.

"One would think," Walter replied. "But if your game's not trying to impress others, it gets a little useless."

"So what is your game these days?"

"I don't play games, Detective. How about you? Did you put me on the gallery's call list because you want to make a sale? Or did you just want to catch up?"

"Who Aga calls is her own business," McCallum said with part of a smile. "Seems you've gotten successful enough to catch her attention. So how is Human Assets? Keeping you busy?"

"There's a lot to learn," Walter said.

"I had this case recently that you might find interesting."

"Ah." Walter made the biggest nod he could. "A case."

"Yeah," McCallum continued. "I came across this guy working off the books as an ASS operative, but the company's got him assigned to a grammar school. Says he's a history teacher."

Walter's eyes narrowed. "You think he can't be both things."

"He had the skills of an op. Tough to fake."

"You think he's undercover at the school?"

"ASS has no records of that. Or this guy at all."

"So you think he's faking one these identities, huh."

"The thought occurred to me."

"And it's lucky that you ran into an expert on faking it?" Walter looked around.

"I'm just happy to have run into a low-level Human Assets executive. I imagine you've seen a lot of shaky things in your career. For instance, what do you think the hardest part of faking an identity might be? Where's the weak spot?"

Walter's narrow eyes closed all together. He took a breath. McCallum kept his eyes on him. When Walter got around to opening his, McCallum wanted him to see the brunt of his stare.

Walter exhaled, swallowed and said, "There are lots of ways a phony can screw up. Hundreds every day. Old friends, family, guys from college that should be living hundreds of miles away but happen to be at the same restaurant as you at the same time. That's not what you're looking for, though. You want other facets of a person's life that have to be meticulously traced and altered. School records are tough, but manageable. Medical records are the worst. A person can change from a man to a woman to something else altogether, but their teeth stay the same. Their fingerprints, iris patterns, DNA… if you've got a weak heart or a bum pancreas, nothing you do will cover that up. Did you know every human ear is different? Like snowflakes. The company could be using ear-prints to track employees. They don't, as a practice. As a fall back, if that is all you have to confirm identity, it is infallible. And there aren't too many surgeons moonlighting with ear replacements."

Walter turned back to the painting and slugged down the last of the drink. "Does any of that help?"

"It's a start." McCallum looked around for one of the wait staff. He didn't normally like to drink Aga's free booze, but he felt he stumbled into an exception.

"I'm sorry, Walter," McCallum said.

"Eh," he replied. "We're all sorry in our own ways, right? I mean, look at that painting. The detail, the shading, then the big, bright nothing. I'm no art expert, but that is talent. The kind that might feel wasted on security work."

"It's all for the good of the company," McCallum said. "How 'bout we get another round?"

McCallum eased through the knot of people, into the yard behind. The gallery sat in the north end of the city. Other than an ancient Catholic church, nothing reached higher than three stories for miles. It was mostly split-level homes, with split-level shops like this one on the main streets. It made the garden more a cove of brick and planking and gutters, than a setting for tea. The night air had an edge to it, hinting at the changes about to come. No call for hats or sweaters, though. Not yet.

They found a waiter in the back, a teenager who probably hoped to turn his drawing into escape someday. McCallum asked him if he could scare up a beer and the kid hopped off.

"Make it two," Walter added.

"After champagne?" McCallum commented. "Shouldn't mix like that."

"I shouldn't mix like this." Walter ran his eyes over the yard. A couple in the far corner passed a tube back and forth, giggling. McCallum guessed it was filled with some form of cannabis. Another couple chatted real close. First date or affair, he couldn't tell from this distance in the dark. The fairy lights along the back edge of the building didn't throw a lot of light. Aga and her patrons liked it that way. A rest from the white walls and gallery bulbs.

"So you and Lillian." McCallum tried to fake surprise.

"We got married last month," Walter said. "I'm going to formally adopt her little girl."

"Swell."

"Everything worked out wonderfully."

"Until I called," McCallum said.

"Always knew there would come a time."

"I do appreciate it," McCallum said. He hoped he sounded like he meant it. "This case... usually I can see things. This one's like a bad restoration. Like there is a painting under the one I'm seeing and that is the one that has all the meaning."

The teenager returned with two bottles of Molson Golden. "Aga said to keep 'em out here," the kid said. "Sirs," he added, realizing it might be expected.

"Won't go back in there," McCallum said. "Promise."

McCallum and Walter clinked the long necks on the bottles.

"As long as we're on the subject," McCallum said.

"God," Walter cut in. "How many shoes are going to drop here."

"Do you ever look into employee health records?"

"No." Walter shook his head. "If we have to, if there is a genuine company benefit to digging into a person's most personal stuff, then yes, we do it. I have people for that."

"Neelesh Fhor. Buffalo Catchment. Just a quick look."

Walter didn't want to. McCallum could tell by his eyes, his lack of movement, his unheard sigh. He wouldn't have wanted to do it, either. Hell, he wasn't going to look. People outside security were sniffing around this case and Walter had a real, solid aversion to the inquisitive. For very good reasons.

To the man's credit, he took a big swig of his Molson, handed the beer to McCallum and brought up his left forearm. McCallum had been right. A shiny new cuff, platinum and exotic. He couldn't tell the make. Walter tapped the face. He said a couple of things only he and his com link could hear, and tapped some more. McCallum watched people look at art, holding their chins, grimacing, rarely smiling. Not even at that crazy florescent work, so obviously made to zap a smile out of you.

Walter took back his beer. "I see why you're so happy to run into me."

"I'd be happy no matter what, Walt. I'm a super friendly guy."

"Mr. Fhor's records are unavailable at this time. I've never seen that before."

"Can't say as I'm surprised."

"At which part?"

"Nothing goes right with this guy. Nothing."

"It seems his records haven't been fully transferred from his old doctor to his new one."

"And you can't get his records from his old doc?"

"He's no longer practicing."

McCallum stepped in real close to Walter, angling his head to see Walter's cuff when he raised it — which he would, when McCallum asked, "What's the doc's name?"

Walter brought up his left arm and read "Dr. Chesterfield Cohen."

McCallum stepped back and raised his beer. "He is certainly not practicing any longer."

"You know the guy?"

"He's dead." McCallum tipped the bottle way, way back. "Had his throat slit to the spine."

Chapter 23

Neelesh waved to the tow truck driver as he pulled away. He gazed upon his Saab, blue metallic paint sparkling in the sun. Poor little car, he thought. You shouldn't have gotten mixed up in this mess. The end of the driveway had a new assortment of scooters in various states of repair. Most were banged and bruised. A hum came from the detached garage. He walked to the entrance and stopped. Jack Qui stood inside, watching an electric motor that was fastened to a bench, its center shaft spinning. The noise came from the wobble. The shaft looked fuzzy.

"Got another when you're through," Neelesh shouted.

Jack Qui looked over his shoulder, arms crossed, mouth dipping. He looked back at the unbalanced motor.

"You ever work on a Saab?" Neelesh continued. "I'm certain you have."

Jack turned again, adding a smirk.

"Well, I got another one for you out front. You can probably diagnose the problem without even looking."

Jack leaned forward and killed the motor. He turned and planted his feet wide. He flexed his whole upper body, straining the grease-striped T-shirt. He didn't have to say 'I use my muscles for a living' or 'I've won more fights than you've even had.'

"I'll fix it," he said, "But it'll cost you."

"I don't think so," Neelesh replied.

"Pay upfront and we'll get you back on the road in no time."

"I. Don't. Think. So."

Jack raised a single index finger. "I said stay out of my business."

"And you made sure I had to come back."

"There's lots of motor repair shops."

Neelesh said, "Not with your intimate knowledge of my difficulty. I was supposed to be at the track today."

Jack laughed. Once. His face mean. "You've caused me some difficulties."

"So you thought eye-for-an-eye, huh."

"The boy's giving me sass. The wife's pissing on me. All 'cuz you're trying to feel better about yourself."

Neelesh re-straightened. "I am trying to help your son."

"Really?" Jack said. "You helping by disconnecting him from his father. Getting his folks to scream-fight."

"It's about his future."

"For a teacher, you don't know shit." Jack turned back to the bench and flicked on the motor.

Neelesh entered the shop. He stomped over to the man and touched his shoulder. Jack grabbed Neelesh's wrist and yanked him hard, over his shoulder. Neelesh was lifted off his feet, then dumped onto the bench. Neelesh screamed, face snarling, his chest pressing into the edge, face hovering over the countertop, near the spinning shaft at the center of the unbalanced motor. Jack extended Neelesh's arm by the hand, bending it down at the wrist, a bit farther than it was supposed to go.

"You come into my shop like this?" Jack Qui said. "My shop?" Jack pressed his weight into Neelesh's back and put his left hand on the side of Neelesh's head, fingers splayed. "It ain't safe in my shop."

"Whoa," Neelesh said. "Whoa, man. This is not the way."

Jack pushed Neelesh's head closer to the shaft. "I always tell people to stay out my business because it's soooo dangerous."

"You fucking kidding me?" Neelesh shouted.

"Sooo dangerous." He pushed more.

Neelesh squirmed underneath him. The motor thumped and whined, dancing in a fuzzy, elliptical path. Not a smooth circle. The edge spun faster than he could see.

He jammed his eyes closed. "I was trying to help!"

Jack pushed farther. Neelesh felt the wind of the motor on his eyes lids. Panic roiled inside him, bursting his lungs. He would not howl. No howling. NO. He forced himself to loosen, struggling for any micron of give, digging for momentum. One more lurch against the monster.

The weight left his back.

Neelesh flew sideways away from the motor, scraping the edge of the bench across his chest. He tumbled off the end, arms flailing, trying not to fall.

"LFTTESHM!" He heard from Jack. Neelesh caught the wall of the shop, steadied himself and opened his eyes.

Jack Qui stood hyperextended, feet threatening to leave the floor. A man grappled with him from behind, raising him by use of his arm under Jack's chin, across his neck. The man twisted Jack's left arm behind him. Jack's right arm swung around searching for something, anything. Finding nothing.

"FHESM!" Jack couldn't move his jaw enough to speak.

"I'm going to let you go," the man said with a patient drawl. "Snort once if this isn't going to be a problem for me."

Jack tried to wrangle free. He had no leverage. His face got redder and fatter.

"If you pass out," the man said, "I know you won't be a problem."

Neelesh stood. He didn't know what to do. He'd just started breathing again. He watched. He had no other plan.

"Fmnt!" Jack Qui blew out his nose.

"I'll take that as a yes." The man dropped him and took one step back.

Jack bent at the hip, sucking air like a jet.

"You OK?" The man asked Neelesh. He was poised for more fighting. His eyes zoomed back and forth between the two of them.

"Uh huh," Neelesh managed.

The man had painfully short hair. Not a grossly big build, but solid. Even through the trench coat, Neelesh could tell the guy's hardened grit. His cuff peaked out from under the coat sleeve. He had the thick, black kind that you saw on ASS ops.

"I wasn't going to do it," Jack said.

"You think I'm a mind reader?" the man asked.

"Thanks," Neelesh said.

"Stay right where you are," the man said to Neelesh. "Don't even twitch." He turned to Jack. "You, grease-ball, turn that thing off."

Jack stepped towards the bench, one hand rubbing his neck. He used the other to switch off the motor.

"Stay facing the bench," the man added. "Grab your skull like it might be coming apart."

Neelesh moved away from Jack.

"I said don't move!"

Neelesh looked up. The man seemed like he might charge him.

Jack looked at Neelesh, confused. "You bring extra muscle?"

"Why would he be needing extra muscle?" The man would not relax.

Neelesh didn't think of trying to hide his own confusion. The man held one of those poses you see ops take when there's going to be a fight. If he was an op. The trench coat covered what might be a second band on his cuff, or might not.

"Who are you?" Neelesh asked.

"I asked a question," the man stated. "Don't care who answers."

"I…" Neelesh started. "I just wanted my car fixed."

"You won't be needing it," the man said. "Turn around and put your hands behind your back."

Neelesh let his face show a full and total lack of understanding. What did this man say? Turn around? Who'd been attacked?

"Pivot, Mr. Fhor." The man's voice rose. "Now."

"There's a misunderstanding," he said.

"Tell me about it," Jack added.

Neelesh faced the wall of the shop and laid his knuckles against his butt.

Something hard and plastic encircled his wrists with an unpleasant zip.

— «» —

"I didn't take you as one for making threats," Phanes said.

"You were right," Demiana replied. "I don't make threats."

They sat in a control room, of sorts. She didn't have the slightest idea what it might control. The monitor on the wall spanned 24 feet easy, though measuring lengths and girths and such never interested her much and didn't figure into her work. The room had a high, curving ceiling with the kind of lights you couldn't see. Phanes sat at a long bench with his back to her, which she didn't like at all. She liked seeing people's faces when she spoke to them. Especially when it involved the extraction of information. She sat in a small armless chair, which she also disliked. No arms meant no slumping.

"I do a lot of things on faith," Demiana said. "Staying here any longer is not going to be one of them. I agreed to stay the other night because it seemed to keep that detective from going all John the Baptist. Now that he's safe, with his head tightly on and all, I'm not sure why I should stay."

"Mmmm." Phanes tapped his cuff on the bench and a video feed of Vera Voloshama from Corporate Relations appeared on the monitor. She was reading off a reader in a room like the one they had given Demiana. Phanes said, "My personal trainer constantly tells me to eat just enough. Just enough, he always says. Not as much as you want, not so little that you fade away."

"You didn't learn this when you were five?" Demiana asked.

"It is one of the things you forget over the years. The food here is quite good." He made another video feed appear on the large monitor. This one showed a young man, prematurely bald, inspecting pipes. Both feeds shrunk so they could share the space.

"I can manage my appetites," Demiana said.

"What a shame." He threw another feed up on the screen. Another young man, this one with dark fluffy hair, working at the power plant. The monitor now divided into thirds. "The company likes to keep us all on the same diet. It doesn't care to explain everything all the time. The company probably can't, really, it has grown so bloated. I find, though, that too little information brings a risk. People talk, fill in blanks, make things up, and the results are most frequently worse than the realities."

"Anyway…" Demiana stretched out, hoping her companion would take over the sentence.

"Anyway," Phanes echoed, "I want to give you just enough."

"You're not my personal trainer."

Phanes added a fourth feed to the video mosaic. Brick, the op, walking atop the walls. "Why don't you ask me what you want to know?"

"I did."

"Right. Why should you remain here. Of course, I should ask you why not? It's lovely here. You've got a nice space, we cover your room and board. As I've mentioned, the food is excellent. What's the trouble?"

"A question is never an answer," Demiana said. "Besides. Just because I'm a priest doesn't mean I don't have a life. Friends, family, places to go, things to do. And to be extra honest, this place isn't all that lovely. It's eerie. Those walls, the guard towers, the dorms, the way no one comes and goes."

"You noticed that." Phanes tapped on his desk for a fifth time and Vananith's video feed appeared. He sat by himself in his room eating pizza.

Demiana said, "I didn't even mention the monster you're growing in the reactor core. What's that going to be? A 20-ton tarantula?"

"Not exactly." Phanes grinned. "You're oddly inquisitive."

"My original mission was to figure out what went on here."

"That is what you thought. The Bishop actually wanted you to screw up the tragedy-of-the-commons mediation."

The words seared. Demiana flushed. She knew it. She knew it all along. The Bishop wanted her to fail badly and take the whole operation down with her. She had no idea why. What would be the point? Not grasping a motive made it easy to ignore her instincts. She moved the little devil on her shoulder to a corner in the back of her head and let the angel stay and chat her up. You're terrific, girl. Stretch, grow, and learn. The Lord never gives you a cross you can't carry. The Bishop will, though. He'll give you a flaming cross and you can feel it right now on your neck and cheeks.

"Sorry," Phanes said.

"Really?" Demiana said. "What specifically is your regret? What do you feel sorry for? Nope. Store it. I don't care." She checked her cuff. "You've got 13 minutes. Throw your man-switch and tell me what kind of mess you've made here."

Phanes spun his chair and threw his arms up, formally presenting the collection of moving squares in his background.

"Here are your reasons," he said.

"For what?"

"Staying, Father DeFalco. These five souls are your reason for being here. If you leave now, they will die."

Demiana looked from feed to feed, each showing a person around the age of 30, going about their lives.

She said, with minimal mouth movement, "I take it you *are* one for making threats."

"Making and carrying out." Phanes lowered his arms. He put them on his knees. "The founder of your religion died to save people, right? I'm simply asking that you stick around for a few days. Have a drink. Read a book. That's nothing compared to expiring on a cross."

"So no one has to die."

Phanes pursed his lips. "Pretty much."

— «» —

McCallum knew that guy wasn't right. The computers disagreed. His own eyes didn't agree. Each point on Neelesh Fhor's face matched perfectly with the photo and his memory. Body size, voice, even the bastard's hair messed with McCallum's taut memory. He trusted his visual memory. It was one of the last things he trusted about himself. The snap and crackle of his joints, the bum left leg — that this guy made bum — the nagging notes from the back of his head telling him his whole job for his whole life amounted to shoveling sand onto a beach... he still had his ability to hold an image in his mind. That had not been dampened and smoothed and begun to wash away with the waves of time.

"What's this about?" Neelesh asked from the back of the cruiser.

"You tell me." McCallum drove. He'd yet to pick a way back to the station house downtown.

"I was the one being assaulted."

"Certainly looked that way."

"Why isn't Jack Qui in the back of this car?"

"I wasn't looking for Jack Qui."

"He just about blinded me!"

"Just about," McCallum said.

"This is nuts!"

McCallum drove passed the entrance ramp to the highway. He decided to stay on the ground streets. It would take longer.

"How did that guy get the best of you?" McCallum asked.

Neelesh directed his eyes at the rearview mirror. McCallum met them for a second.

"I don't know," Neelesh answered. "The man's nothing but muscle."

"You've fought better guys before."

There. McCallum only caught a sliver of it in the mirror. The sliver sufficed. The sneer had a familiar shadow, a deep landscape of anger, but mixed with indignant confusion.

"I've never been in a fight before in my life."

McCallum looked at the road. This Neelesh didn't have a double banded cuff, with a secret T-bar connected to a wire sharper than scalpels. He didn't carry himself carefully. He didn't pan his head, taking in possible threats.

"You got a brother?" McCallum asked.

Again, the indignant surprise. "No."

"You ever been treated for dissociative disorder?"

"What kind of question is that? If I did, I might not even know. If I did, I'd probably lie about it."

McCallum nodded.

"And why don't you know?" Neelesh continued. "I don't mean to be disrespectful. I really don't. It's just that you guys usually know everything. I will tell you that I'm spinning back here. I can't seem to connect with this moment. I am not used to dealing with Systems Security. I am an elementary school teacher and I have stayed out of trouble my entire life. You should know that, too. You can read back my whole life on that monitor. You should know I am an only child with no history of mental illness and that I have been tested for it, along with everything else. Repeatedly. I am clean and good and I don't know what that fuck I am doing zipped-tied in the back of an ASS car."

"It is a mystery," McCallum said, mostly to himself.

Chapter 24

"To Brick," some cute boy shouted, glass raised.

"To Brick," everyone else in the bar shouted back, which thundered through the place, which was not much bigger than Demiana's dorm room.

Demiana lowered her drink back down to head-level and threw back a sip. Brick nodded thank-yous to everyone, slobbered up a good cheek-full of beer and shook hands with the nearest of the very near, very tight band of well-wishers. She liked the crowd. It reminded her of the seminary. The closeness, the reverie and friendliness you couldn't avoid. The quarters forced it. It figured she couldn't find Van in the crowd. She did not have a clear line of sight in any direction and it did not matter. She knew he wasn't here. This was not his kind of event.

She oozed between two women and got next to Brick. "So you ship out tomorrow."

"Thanks for coming, Father," he returned.

"It's what I do," she said. "Where you headed?"

"Sydney Catchment."

"Holy batata, that's like half way around the world."

"It's going to take me forever to get there." Brick slammed down the rest of his beer. He held the mug high and someone yelled, "Beer the man!"

"Are you looking forward to it?" Demiana asked.

Brick lowered his head, getting closer to her face. He had a glint in his eye that hadn't been there before. She found him dull and sweet in their last two encounters. Now, despite the alcohol, he seemed sharper.

"Anywhere but here," he said.

"I know that feeling."

"I don't think you do."

"This place is off. I can say that, I've been a lot of places."

"I've never been anywhere else."

"Sing, Brick!" a woman yelled. Demiana glanced over at the source. Vera held up a tall, sweating glass.

Brick closed his eyes and shook a head full of shyness.

"Come on. Sing, Brick," another called out.

He shook some more but the crowd started chanting Brick, Brick, Brick… Demiana joined in. He opened his eyes and gave her a tiny smile. He started to clap a slow, forceful beat. Others joined and the beat grew, rolling out the noise of the crowd. When he'd decided the rhythm was right, he opened his mouth and sang:

"As we go marching, marching in the beauty of the day,

A million darkened kitchens, a thousand mill lofts gray

Are touched with all the radiance that a sudden sun discloses.

For the people hear us singing, bread and roses, bread and roses."

Demiana chided herself for thinking in cliché, but he really did have the voice of an angel.

"As we go marching, marching, we battle too for men.

For they are women's children and we mother them again.

Our lives shall not be sweetened from birth until life closes.

Hearts starve as well as bodies, give us bread, but give us roses."

She knew the song, the kind that existed now by oral tradition alone. Should Ambyr Policy Review decide to listen in on anyone's com-link right now, they'd be called in. Anyone but her, anyway. She could listen all she wanted. So she did, through to the end at which point she clapped and hooted with everyone.

"Beautiful, eh?"

Demiana twisted he head, feeling pressure on her shoulder. Phanes stood next to her, too close.

"Never would've guessed," she replied.

"Not this particular talent, no. Everyone's got something, though. Has that not been your experience? There's always a company man, and then another inside, capable of something that company could not care less about. Even when it is so painfully beautiful."

"So what's your flip side?" Demiana tried to keep her voice intimate despite the low, continuous thunder of the bar.

"Oh, I've got more than one." Phanes smirked. "None of which I want to discuss with my priest."

My priest, Demiana repeated in her head. Normally the phrase would mark him as a member of her congregation, but the way he said it made her feel like a pet. She lived in his big terrarium, like Brick. For how long, did he say? His whole life? The phrases shifted and started to make sense. The originals, the final five, the 30-year life sentence.

"How many?" escaped her mouth before she had a chance to catch it.

Phanes' smile flickered, threatening to go out.

"How many of these 30-year-olds did you start with?" she continued. "You're down to five. Well, four now, with Brick's departure. How many did you start with?"

"Father." Phanes brought his face closer to hers. "Why don't you go back to asking questions about human existence, morality, and why God allows evil to exist in the world?"

"That is exactly what I'm doing." Demiana jutted her face even closer to his. "I'm simply narrowing my scope to a highly defined set of humans, whose existence I care about, who are subject to what I fear is an abstract morality, and who I hope are not living examples of evil on this blessed earth."

Phanes stared into her eyes. She couldn't remember ever seeing that exact expression on a person, a smile not fully formed, stifled by anger, topped by eyes full of curiosity. He retook his full height and looked out over the crowd.

"Four," he said. "Let me find homes for my last four. Then you and I will talk."

— «» —

"How long are you going to leave him there?" Andrea thumbed in the direction of Neelesh Fhor.

"Ask him." McCallum thumbed in the direction of the door as Wayne Clement walked in to the squad room.

"Ask him what?" Wayne stopped and glanced over at Neelesh, sitting, arms behind him, head tipped far enough to rest on the chair back. "That the guy?"

"You called Econ?" Andrea asked.

"This shit's going to get pricey," McCallum replied.

"Captain." Wayne gave Andrea a nod.

Andrea nodded back, then glared at McCallum.

McCallum tapped the desk and bobbed his head in the direction of the big monitor on the wall. "Wayne's all right."

"I'm not saying otherwise." Andrea continued her glare, trying to beam some information through her eyes into McCallum's.

"I'm on a potty break," Wayne said.

"See?" McCallum said to Andrea. "Just three colleagues passing through the squad room."

"And me," Neelesh added.

"How could I forget?" McCallum pointed to the screen. "He counts for two."

The image on the monitor was split. The left side showed a still photo of Neelesh standing in classroom, arms out, mouth wide. The time stamp in the lower right corner read 20:12. The right side showed Neelesh at a pizza parlor, arms crossed, presumably waiting for an order. The second time stamp was the same as the first.

"I performed a deep-dive image search," McCallum said. "The computer's been spooling for a couple of hours."

"Oh," Wayne said, "That's why I got the call."

"This much chugging is going to cost," McCallum continued. "Though I don't know why the machine's chugging at all. Should've been two minutes. It keeps getting confused. Showing me crap like this."

"The time stamps match." Andrea took a step closer to the wall.

"Yeah," McCallum said. "There's a couple like that. The system doesn't want to ascribe the image to two separate events. Mr. Fhor here seems to frequently be in two places at once."

"Do you have a twin, Mr. Fhor?" Andrea asked.

"No," he answered. "I still don't."

"These two match up so perfectly the computer can't compute."

"Oh," Wayne repeated. "So *that's* why you called."

Andrea gave McCallum the 'I'm waiting' look.

"Images can be faked, manipulated, just plain wrong," McCallum said. "Not dollars."

"Nope." Wayne nodded. "You're right about that. The company tracks money to a much higher degree of accuracy than people. You can't fake funds."

"So if this guy's got a doppelganger," Andrea said, "it will show in his accounts?"

"Don't know what it will show," Wayne said. "Let me scratch around. I can tell you this: Bank accounts don't have look-a-likes."

"Do you have enough to go on?" McCallum asked.

"Nope," Wayne answered. "First, I'll need an account code. Sorry, but you were right. This won't be a slip of the key. I'll need to assign a resource and burn time. Is there a policy transgression I can cite?"

"Augh." Andrea sat on the edge of McCallum's desk.

McCallum said, "The Captain and I are still kicking that around."

"Is this really how you want to proceed?" Andrea asked McCallum. "Op-on-op quarrels beep red and lots of people see it. People lower grade than us."

"Internal Audit has a big budget," McCallum said.

"Yeah, and it's Internal Audit," she returned. "They turn your life inside out. You know what they say about IA."

"I know." McCallum lowered his head.

"Your call," Wayne said.

The three of them went silent, each gazing into a different space.

"What?" Neelesh asked. "What do they say about IA?"

McCallum tipped his head way back and stretched his arms. "It's the opposite of AI."

They all sat in silence for a moment.

"What can we do on the cheap?" Andrea asked Wayne.

"Focus," he replied. "Narrow your scope. Big data cost big money. Let's look at something small."

"Like the night Doc Cohen died," McCallum threw out.

"That's a good place to start," Wayne said.

"Mr. Fhor," Andrea said. "What were you doing Thursday, August 22, around midnight?"

"I… ah…" Neelesh stammered, "That was weeks ago. To be honest, wouldn't you all have a better idea?"

"Did you work?" McCallum asked. "Was it a school night?"

"Yes," Neelesh said. "My second shift ends just before midnight."

"The school's in Riverside," McCallum said. "The Doc lived near me. That is a tough timeline."

"Excepting that this guy's hobby is racing cars." Andrea tapped her cuff. McCallum assumed she had Neelesh's profile on her screen.

McCallum got up and walked over to Neelesh. He stood in front of him, looking down. "You've got to paint us a picture. What happens after school? You go out with buddies? Leave a bar tab behind you? How about a bus? We could dig up those charges."

"I don't do much after second shift," Neelesh said. "I'm usually exhausted. Sometimes I run."

"It was a hot night," McCallum said. "I remember it pretty damn well. Humid, with haze blocking most of the moon and starlight."

"Damp," Neelesh said without much push. "The car had condensation on it. And…"

He stopped. He looked McCallum right in the eyes and stopped everything he'd been doing inside his head. McCallum had seen the behavior before, especially on crappy-ass liars. The worse someone was at lying, the more pronounced the effect. This guy didn't want to say the words that just filed into his mouth.

"Say it," McCallum commanded. "Say it. Unless you just remembered you were killing someone else, you're better off telling us whatever you just remembered."

McCallum watched the teacher toss and turn inside. He'd made a bed and never expected to lie in it. McCallum usually didn't mind this part of the interrogation. It meant progress. In this case, though, he felt like he was putting a worm on a hook.

"I have an alibi." Neelesh looked at McCallum's boots.

"Most people say that with a sense of relief."

"It's a girl. A third grader."

McCallum had not been expecting that.

— «» —

Neelesh watched the others scurry about. The Economist tapped on his cuff. The Captain left the room, he thought maybe she went to her office. The Detective stared at him. Neelesh could not read a hint of anything on the man's face. He only knew the man remained alive by an occasional blink.

After a few minutes, the Captain returned and the three huddled up. They spoke so low he couldn't hear. After another few minutes of mumbles and grumbles, the Detective turned to him and said, "Your story's been proofed. The little girl remembers it like you said."

The Economist apologized that there was nothing else he could do at the moment and left. The Captain and the Detective returned to their big screens. They didn't seem to care that he had been alone, in his car, with a female child. They didn't care at all. They didn't seem to know what they wanted to do, which ran contrary to everything he imagined about Systems Security. They always seemed so... organized, at least in the movies. Snap decisions, always the right ones. One step ahead of the bad guys. Tracking people, arriving before them, going all Kung Fu and... well, that last part proved true. He'd seen that. He felt lucky to still be seeing anything out of both eyes. His brief attempt at being the tough guy did not go as hoped. No more tough guy. He would sit here quietly and let these jokers figure out that he had nothing to do with any kind of policy breach. He would sit. On his day off. Like an idiot.

Passive, he thought. He always let life take him like a leaf on a stream. It had worked out well for him so far. A nice car (if it got fixed) and nice apartment (thanks to his mother.) He had a job way beyond what he should have landed (thanks to...) He had to think about that. He had found all kinds of ways of thinking about anything else lately. Dr. Chesterfield Cohen had been quite a friend. So much a friend. His doctor since birth. Before birth, really. He saw Dr. Cohen two or three times a year, despite his perfect health. The doctor had given him all that sage advice, helped him prep for his exams, nudged him into teaching, and even gotten him a deal on his beloved sports car.

He helped him get his job. Neelesh said this to himself. He'd never completed the full thought before. Never allowed himself. He never wanted to think of the alternatives. Where would he have ended up? Scraping goo off city streets? He wanted to be self-made, self-actualized, a success on his merits, like his mother.

His mother had a great job, too. Very powerful. Very safe and lucrative and maybe too safe and lucrative. She never had to move physically to move up. They'd been in the Buffalo Catchment his whole life. They didn't get tossed around the globe like so many others. Like everybody else who made the single digit grades.

Doctors didn't have that kind of juice. Neelesh knew he had a limited understanding of company architecture. He had gone from school to school — learning to teaching — with nothing else in between. He never had to compete in the real vicious corporate arenas, trying to outdo the rest of his cohort, stabbing handholds into the backs of others to better his position. He'd only heard about the ordeals from friends who been dropped into different streams. He knew, though, that doctors didn't shoot high-pressure juice. Not outside of their fields. Respected, yes. String-pullers? Not normally. Not unless they were connected. How connected was the doctor?

He wanted more than anything to call Dr. Chesterfield Cohen right now. They had items to discuss. The medical tests, the special treatment, the influence. Neelesh felt, in that moment, that he had been propelled down the stream. A boat without any sense that it had a motor.

He wanted to call Dr. Cohen and, of course, could not — him being dead. He would have to settle for the next best option.

Good thing you ditched the tough guy routine, he said to himself. That makes this easier, eh?

"Detective?" Neelesh said. "I need to call my mom."

Chapter 25

The Captain and the Detective stopped what they were doing and looked up. Neelesh followed their lines of sight and saw his mother standing in the doorway to the squad room, unsure of the protocol. Waiting to be invited in, he assumed. She saw him, placed a hand over her mouth and marched over, no longer caring about formalities.

"Sukhbir Fhor?" the Detective asked.

Sukhbir nodded as she marched, not taking her eyes from her son.

"Hi, mom." Neelesh tried to sound casual, like he sat in ASS offices with his hands zip-tied behind his back every day.

"What happened?" she murmured.

"Ms. Fhor." The Captain moved to meet her. "Ms. Fhor, we have a couple of questions."

"So do I." Sukhbir knelt next to Neelesh. "Are you OK?"

"I'm fine," he answered. "Better than I should be, given the day I've had."

"What is happening here?"

"Funny you should ask," Neelesh said. "We were hoping you might know."

"Ms. Fhor," the Captain said. "We have some… discrepancies." She directed Sukhbir's attention to the large monitor on the wall.

Neelesh watched her. His mother stood and faced the wall in annoyance, irritated by the op's request. Her face held stern as she worked through the puzzle. Neelesh in two different places, with two slightly different haircuts, doing two very different things at the same time. A frown sprouted and hardened. She didn't show emotion outside, to others.

Emotions were hers, Neelesh knew. She did not feel they were for sharing with anyone. The frown baked on her face.

"The time stamps are wrong," she said in a sandy whisper.

"We believe them to be correct," the Captain said.

"They can't be." Sukhbir took a step towards one screen, then the other. "Can't be." She reached out a hand and touched the short-haired Neelesh waiting for his pizza. "Can-"

The Captain placed herself behind Sukhbir. Neelesh glanced over at the Detective, who sat and studied the scene. No one said a word. Neelesh wished he could see his mother's face. Read it. Get a clue as to what she knew because she always knew something. His whole life he had never seen her surprised. She gave off the sense that she knew exactly what you were going to say before you said it. She knew things you didn't. She knew about other places, far away. Other kinds of lives and living. She was wise and worldly, Neelesh always thought, until this afternoon, when he wondered if she wasn't simply secretive.

She collapsed against the screen. Her hand squeaked along the glass as she sank. The Captain grabbed her and helped her to a chair.

"Mom?" Neelesh called out.

Sukhbir tried to hide her face with her hands, then her arms, then her knees, balling up, wriggling on the little bamboo office chair, twisting side to side as the Captain hovered, hands out, keeping her from falling. His mother gurgled. Her lips emitted a bubbling sound. Her eyes disappeared under the tight, clay-red wrinkles.

"What is it?" the Captain asked.

Sukhbir turned in her seat again. She opened her mouth, but a hollow rush of air overcame any word she might have tried.

"I need to know," the Captain said with firmness.

Sukhbir squeezed her legs together and bent over, forehead to knees. She cradled herself and pushed out all the air in her lungs. She didn't move for a long time. Neelesh watched, unable to move himself. Then Sukhbir threw her head back, black hair flailing. She faced the ceiling, eyes still sealed. She took a breath.

"Where was that photo taken?" Her voice had a slick, mean edge Neelesh had not expected.

"Do you know this man?" the Captain asked.

"Where was it taken?"

Neelesh would've bet the op captain could have been just as cutting, but she chose a softer tone.

"Town of Albion," the Captain said. "On the edge of the Buffalo Catchment."

"Albion?" Sukhbir said. "Albion's no more than 60 miles from here."

"What can you tell us?" the Captain asked.

Sukhbir lowered her head and opened her eyes. She found Neelesh. "I'm so sorry."

"About what?" Neelesh returned.

"I actually believed this would never happen. I was assured of if."

"What?"

"That is your brother," Sukhbir said. "Your twin. The company took him at birth."

Neelesh felt as if his head were in a tunnel. A black tunnel with red spots around the edge. He stopped breathing.

"Dr. Cohen said he was gone forever. Never to think of him. I had you and that would be more than enough for most people. So I—"

"A twin?" Neelesh said.

"I'm so sorry." Sukhbir shook her head in movements just above a quiver.

"Ms. Fhor," the Detective started. "Did you kill Dr. Chesterfield Cohen?"

"No," Sukhbir said. "Though were he alive now, I most certainly would."

— «» —

Demiana watched Vaninath pass. She sat in a corner tower, back against the wall, tucked up to be unseen. The darkness helped. She waited for him to make his rounds on the wall, like he always did, more regular than a clock. An atomic clock. As diligent as he was, she noticed that he kept his attention on the grounds below on both sides, ever on the lookout, but never behind. She suspected his job — whatever it might be — got easier as the staff thinned out at the power plant. She also suspected he had no mechanism for handling the slowdown. He would make these rounds if he were the last guy on earth.

She rose and followed him, skipping to catch up.

"Hey," she said.

He spun, left foot forward, right back on its toe, arms tight to his body and raised, hands poised like he might give her the worst shampoo of her life. His face went gargoyle. She would have been terrified if it wasn't the effect she'd been after.

"Father DeFalco!" he barked. "You should not do that."

"What?"

"Startle me." He relaxed, arms dropping, each leg taking on equal weight.

"I wanted to see if I could."

Van's face returned to its usual stern nothingness.

"Sorry," Demiana said. "I shouldn't play games. I'm bored."

He turned and began walking, continuing his tour of the wall. Demiana hopped next to him, then matched his pace. The night air had a full chill, not enough for mittens and a hat, but she was happy to be moving. Crouching in the hard, unheated corner tower had become unpleasant.

"Aren't you going to ask what I'm doing up here?" she asked.

"You said you were bored," he returned.

"Yeah, but there must be better ways to deal with that, right?"

"That is your business."

"OK," she said. "I know you're not supposed to talk to me and all, but this doesn't have to count. We can be just two people strolling under the stars, chatting like humans, right?"

"Sure," he replied.

They continued down the rough concrete trough that ran along top of the walls surrounding the nuclear plant. She figured the walkway was extra coarse to prevent slipping under wetter circumstances.

"What do you do for fun?" Demiana asked. "That can't be a dangerous secret."

"I enjoy my work." Van continued to look left and down, then right and down, as he walked.

"Great answer." Demiana continued to look at him. "You must do something when you're not working. I know how the companies are about that stuff. I have a friend who's a recreational councilor for Hong Kong. She has a whole list of employees she has to meet with regularly to see how they're spending their time. Or, more importantly, their money. The companies like to keep it churning. Is Ambyr like that? Do they make sure you fish or go to soccer games or build little dollhouses modeled after famous homes from literature?"

Van stopped. He looked Demiana full in the face, eye-to-eye, serious as an oncologist. Clouds ambled in the distant background, between him and the stars. The shadows on his face blended into the night and made him seem not fully there. Unfinished.

"No," he said and resumed his patrol.

Demiana's eyes rolled all around their sockets. "You must do something," she said. "Do you ever leave the resort?"

"On occasion."

"What do you do?"

"The usual," he said. "Pick up... sundries."

Demiana smiled. She very possibly may have taught him that word. "Seriously? Shopping? Don't you even eat out once in a while?"

"I like pizza," Van said.

"*Finally*," Demiana exaggerated. "We're progressing. I love pizza. Is there a decent place in town? I know a couple in Buffalo that will kick your... um... bottom place."

"The pizza here is not that good."

"I haven't dared. I've taken a vow of poverty, so I'm far from being spoiled, but I have vowed nothing about substandard pizza. I won't do it."

Van stopped and looked down the smooth wall. Light from the moon and stars made the coat of dew glisten.

Demiana looked, but failed to see what caught his eye. He waited, so she waited. Something moved out of the shadow of the apron. A fox lilted off towards the tree line, two hundred yards away, bouncing as it moved, like the earth was a mattress. Van walked.

"So what about me?" Demiana stayed next to him. "Phanes didn't tell you not to ask *me* any questions."

"He did not."

"You must have some. Everybody does. What's it like being a priest, with no money and no sex? Do you pray all day? Do you hear God? How can you not work for a company? Can you buy anything? You must wonder about something?"

Vaninath moved his head side-to-side as he made his way across the wall top. He paused partway through one of his arcs and gave Demiana another of his contemplative stares.

"Would a good God create a man to do evil?"

Hurray, Demiana cheered in her mind, followed quickly by, *Crap. What the fu— fudge kind of question was that*? She'd meant to ambush the boy, catch him off guard while on guard, and now? Now the night darkened and the wind came with a sharper edge. She'd conveniently forgotten this was the guy who wanted to slice off Detective McCallum's head. Conveniently? Blessedly? Didn't matter. She trained for moments like this, right? Kind of? Around the edges? Counseling and encouraging any of God's children.

"God doesn't make mistakes," she said.

Van nodded. He returned to his walk.

Demiana paused. She'd let him go. She'd get back to her room and let this night fade. Except...

She ran up alongside Van. "Why are you last?"

"The last what?"

"The last of the 30-year-olds. Your cohort. Why does everyone get to go but you?"

"It is an honor," Van answered. "I earned the honor of staying to the end."

"The end of what?" Demiana asked.

Van turned in front of her, blocking her progress. His lips thinned. She so hoped she could get him to show emotion.

This particular emotion had not been her first choice. He looked pissed.

He said, "That is why I'm not supposed to talk to you."

— «» —

McCallum checked on Neelesh Fhor. He had snapped the zip ties and told the man he could use his communication link however he liked. He knew this guy hadn't killed the doctor or severed his left Achilles tendon. The guy had not fought him in Albion, outside that restaurant near the power plant. This guy was mixed up in something weird, but knew nothing about it. So he freed him up some.

Only some. McCallum stopped short of letting the teacher go home.

The Air and Sanchez, now at the Sergio, played in McCallum's ear. He set his coffee down on his desk and said "yes" to accept the call.

"What have you got for me?" Cherry pits pouring into a plastic jug — the voice of his favorite gallery owner, Aga Graber.

"What have you got for me?" McCallum answered.

"You've got to get me something by the end of the month. This Sanchez show is coming down. People look at mobiles. They don't buy mobiles unless they are for babies, over their cribs, which these most assuredly are not."

"I'm working here, Aga."

"Aren't we all, precious. Aren't we all, all the time?"

"The photos I sent you?"

"Yes, yes," the woman said. "If I can't do an Eddie McCallum retrospective, I'll take all of these at 15-percent."

"That wasn't..." McCallum stopped himself. "I just wanted to know what the Hell they are."

"Fertility statues," Aga replied. "This is a beautiful collection, or so it seems from the photos. I would obviously like to examine them in person."

"This is more than folk art?"

"It is folk art, but this curator had a theme. All of these pieces are meant to inspire reproduction, babies. Not reproductions as in fakes. I mean these are supposed to make the spirits give you kids after screwing."

"I've got to go, Aga."

"Sure you do. Use me up like a plastic cup. Do you treat all your women this way, Eddie?"

"Not because I want to."

McCallum ended the call. He spun and slouched in his chair, facing Neelesh. The teacher had fanned out a pocket screen to read off. McCallum had encouraged it. Four hours of boredom followed by the revelation you had a twin brother your mother neglected to tell you about should not be followed by more boredom. He hoped he had an escapist book on tap. McCallum didn't need him sparking up.

The man appeared calm, so he returned his attention to the big monitor. The data-drill had dug up 14 photos of the alternative Neelesh Fhor. The great and powerful Ambyr Systems Security computers could find the bastard's face, but they could not find any record of that face belonging to another human — let alone an SS operative. McCallum met the other Neelesh on duty, at the nuclear plant. He'd been in uniform, with another uniformed op. He seemed genuine. McCallum admitted he could be fooled, lots of people had done it. Still, the guy had a station and skills. It's a tough fake.

And why? McCallum thought, for a second, about the value of planting a fake. He knew the Catholic Church managed a negotiation with the three companies. They had interest in the place. Enough to send a spy? Sure, but they would've done a better job. Given the spy a background, probably fuller than his own.

No, this twin was not supposed to exist.

McCallum pulled the rest of the photos he'd taken from the fight. He found one of the other op. It wasn't great, but he had searched on worse. The computer started to chug. Again. He waited.

"Mr. Fhor," McCallum rotated his chair.

"Yes, sir." Neelesh lifted just his eyes.

"You don't have a father listed in your files."

"Well, at least that hasn't changed."

"Know anything about him?"

"My mother said I had no father."

"You left it at that?"

Neelesh blinked like his lids weighed two pounds each. "I did."

"You never wondered?" McCallum asked.

"All the time," Neelesh answered. "I created elaborate fantasies growing up. I was a space alien stranded on this planet. I was the son of the Hindu sun deity Surya hidden away as a secret weapon for an upcoming battle. Later, I thought he might be a low grade, like a one or a two, who couldn't have a bastard on the books. I also like the one in which I'm a descendant of the Maharajas of India and the company erased my history so that I'd never raise an army and take back my throne."

"That's a good one," McCallum said.

"I became a history teacher," Neelesh continued. "A friend of mine told me once that I appreciated history more than most because I didn't have one."

McCallum sat and listened for more. Neelesh's eyes went back to his screen, so McCallum returned to his. Nothing. The computer chugged. An operation that normally took all of two minutes just spooled along, giving him an image of a stopwatch, the secondhand jerking clockwise with each second. He'd last seen the graphic when he had searched on the image of Neelesh.

He sat way back and stared at the ceiling, forming pictures from the spray of random holes in the tiles. A knight on a horse. A dog eating a large donut. The sea.

The monitor on his desk flickered. He looked and saw the dossier on a person possessing the face of the second op from the Albion Nuclear Facility: Dawson Michaels, age 30, Seattle Catchment. The pharmacy tech lived more 2,000 miles away.

The monitor flickered again. A second dossier showed up, this one for Brick Smith, Sydney Catchment. This man had the uniform. Ambyr Systems Security, Grade 13. McCallum had met him. The hair, the smile — no way this kid lived in Sydney. Was there another Sydney? One of those little towns in the middle of an apple orchard 20 miles from here?

"You met my brother?" Neelesh asked.

McCallum didn't turn. "Never said that." He asked the computer for more details.

"I can tell that's you in the photos."

The computer confirmed SS operative Brick Smith had been assigned to the Sydney catchment. As of today.

"What?" McCallum said out loud.

The computer had taken the video feed McCallum recorded during his fight and created a comic book — still photos distilled from the blurry action. McCallum didn't appear in any of the photos.

"I can tell it's you. You can see a bit of your trench coat in a few of the pics."

McCallum read: Brick Smith was due to arrive in two days, assigned to a security detail at an automotive manufacturing facility. There were no older entries in his file.

"You have got to be kidding me," he said.

"No," Neelesh replied. "The coat is pretty damn clear."

McCallum tried a priority override. The dossier seemed to respond — it didn't give him a clearance warning or deny him access. It simply gave him a blank page. Brick Smith had no work history for the first 30 years of his life. No jobs, no training academy, no school, immunizations, physicals, or life of any kind.

"Never," McCallum said, mouth hanging open at the end.

"Are you talking to me?" Neelesh asked.

McCallum looked back over his shoulder. "Your brother's an asshole."

"Oh," Neelesh said.

McCallum interlaced his fingers and stretched his arms. He wanted to type more, but there was nothing to request. He had never seen a file like this one. He had heard rumors, SS myths, really. Crystal ops. He never gave them any thought. It was the type of myth rookies whispered about after the third beer. Ghost stories for security workers. The name had a double meaning: an op so transparent no one ever saw him; an op assigned to the kind of people who had crystal.

The ultralow. It took more than money to keep an op out of the database. It took real, true, power juice.

There were no regular ASS ops assigned to the Albion Nuclear Facility. It had spooks.

Futile as it was, McCallum killed the search, erased his history, and told the computer to reboot. The action didn't wipe his trail clean. No one could do that.

Except the people from whom he now wanted to hide.

Chapter 26

Demiana stood staring at the giant cocoon. The dull whirl in the pipes infringed on her hearing and she hated it. She couldn't hear everything in a full circle around her and she felt she needed all of her senses working at capacity. She had that tingle you get in an empty parking garage at night.

The whispers of the three 30-year-olds at the control console did nothing to quell the tingle. She recognized Vera, her former tour guide. She leaned over the U-shaped desk packed with monitors. The two men stationed there looked familiar, one with dark hair, one with none. All three huddled, glanced at Demiana, and whispered more. They were not passing gossip or talking about plans for later. They projected hard, tight tension.

The door behind the control table swooshed open. Phanes emerged, followed by Van, rolling a piece of luggage.

"Thank you." Phanes took just two steps in.

The three turned to give him their full attention.

Van rolled his black suitcase around the control center, stopping between it and the grand cocoon.

"Sorry to keep you waiting," Phanes said to Demiana, cold smile aimed right at her.

Something different, she said to herself. Out of place.

"I'm fine," Demiana replied. "This place is fascinating."

"You have no idea." He gazed up at the cocoon. "Or maybe you do. I don't truly know."

"I know you're breeding a giant spider." She walked in his direction.

Phanes laughed lightly. "Wouldn't that be amazing? Would you love to see the looks on everyone's faces when I opened the top of the silo and let it crawl out?"

"It would almost be worth it."

"Almost," Phanes said. "But not quite, I'm sure. This has not been easy for you and yet you have been a wonderful guest. I thank you for that. You managed to save a couple of lives and they would thank you if they knew."

Demiana's ears flushed. Her muscles went tight. Phanes spoke in the past tense but he hadn't said to meet her at the gate. Nope. Instead he brought her to dead center of the plant. She glanced at Van. He poked and swished his fingers on the control panels. Vera and the boys paid him no mind.

"How exactly did I save these lives?" Demiana asked.

"When you have something that is too big to hide you must keep people from looking."

"I get enough obtuse sentences from scripture," Demiana said. "How about you lay it right out there."

"I am," Phanes protested. "It is a corporate truth. Don't make them look. Unwanted attention is failure."

"This power plant got lots of attention. Moths to a flame."

"That's legerdemain," Phanes said. "The Kongers and the Groupies and even people in my own company want the secrets of this nuclear reactor. I have been much more concerned with the true treasure here. The people."

"The 30-year-olds?"

"Yes." Phanes motioned to Van. "Vaninath here, his brothers and sisters. 100 in all. They have been here since birth. Raised in the glow of this reactor. They have lived their whole lives on this compound. But now the experiment is over."

Run, Demiana shouted in her head. Beat the crowd. This band shell was coming down hard. All you can do is run.

"It proved difficult relocating the lot, what with none of them having any records of any kind. I couldn't just dump them out in the market. People would ask questions. It's funny, in a way. The company is all powerful, but it doesn't like to be disturbed. I had 89 individuals to slip out into company life and it took time."

"Not the full 100, huh?" Demiana hushed the part of her brain that yelled.

"There have been losses," Phanes replied. "There would have been more if not for you. If you hadn't extended your investigation. As it is, I'm down to five."

"Five?"

"It would have been zero if your detective had minded his leash."

"He's not that kind of breed," Demiana said.

"It's a shame. His hubris has forced a sad change in my schedule." Phanes bowed his head. "What a tragic accident."

"Accidents are usually, you know, accidental. There is an unforeseen component."

"Not this one," Phanes said. "I've known it was coming for a long time."

Van stood. "All set."

"Great," Phanes replied. He returned his attention to Demiana. "You pushed the timetable. I really had to scurry these last few days. All is forgiven, though. You also presented us with a new option."

"I'm not following you."

"No," Phanes said. "You are not."

Phanes raised his hand. He had no cuff. That's what was different. No bracelet. Who didn't wear their com link? Instead, he held a small silver cylinder. A flashlight? He pressed the end then tossed it.

"Time to go." Phanes spun and marched. Just two steps and he was on through the doorway.

The dark-haired man behind the panel jumped to his feet, "What the?!" The bald man smacked the table with both hands and swore. Vera opened her mouth, too stunned for anything to make its way out.

"You died to save others, Father," Phanes called out from the door. "Be content. Isn't that what you people aspire to?"

Van ran for the door, full out.

The door slammed behind Phanes. Van flattened against it.

Bolts hissed into place.

— «» —

All of the monitors McCallum used flashed yellow. Block letters began to scroll across his cuff, the desk screen and the inner wall of the office: Lock Down Enabled. Albion Medium Yield Nuclear Power Production Facility.

"What's that?" Neelesh asked.

"A trigger I set up." McCallum popped keys on his terminal, trying to raise more information.

"That's where my brother is."

"Among others." McCallum thwacked his index finger across his bracelet. "Call DeFalco. Voice. Priority."

The computer wrote 'Event Uncategorized' across his screen. It wasn't going to give him any more information about lock down. He heard "unable to connect" in his ear.

"What?" McCallum checked his cuff. He couldn't connect to Father DeFalco. He pressed the com link again and forced a priority call. The same response appeared. He stood up, crashing his chair into the desk behind him.

"What's lock down?" Neelesh asked.

"Don't know," McCallum answered. He could call the power plant, but the place was shady. He had no faith in any answers he might get out of the staff. He could call the local SS. He wasn't too sure they'd be highly cooperative either, him stealing their truck and all. He looked at his cuff again. He'd only seen that 'unable' message twice in his career. Once, the com link owner had had a disagreement with a drill press; the other had fallen under a sledgehammer because the owner's rapist needed time to attempt a get-away.

McCallum looked at Neelesh. "Your file says you run."

"Exercise."

"Let's see it."

— «» —

Demiana ran to the door. Bars the size of her arms crossed it. They had not been there before, nor did they look like they were going anywhere anytime soon. Van pounded on it. His palms made faint squishing slaps. No resonance. No vibration.

"Jesus Christ!" the bald man behind her said. He also pounded on whatever he could. He made more noise. That was it. Nothing but noise.

"It's fucking out," Vera said. "Dead. All of it."

"Phanes!" Van screamed.

Demiana decided the time had come to call in the—

Ice ran from the top of her head, down through her neck and into her legs. Her cuff was blank. She'd never seen it blank. She'd never seen any blank. That didn't happen. You couldn't turn them off. If you went to the shop for a battery they hooked them up so they were never, ever, couldn't be off.

Someone came running. Demiana thought it might me the guy with black hair. She didn't check. She gazed into the blank face of her bracelet. A gray abyss. A tiny, all-encompassing nothingness.

"The core is sealed!" A new voice shouted.

Van turned. Demiana looked up. The others hunched over the control console fidgeting, tapping, or crossing their arms.

"This is not good," the bald man said.

"Not good?" the man with black hair replied. "Are you fucking kidding me? Everything took a shit. A massive shit."

"There's no data?" Vera added.

Van slid down the door.

"Is there another way out?" Demiana asked.

"We're locked in, lady," the man with black hair said.

"It's Father," the bald man corrected him.

"Sorry, Father. Hate to piss off a priest right before I die." He hugged himself and twisted at the hips. Back and forth.

"We're not dying," Demiana protested.

"Soon enough," the black-haired man said.

"We're not." She slammed the counter. "There's been a mistake. They will open the seals shortly."

"All the controls are dead." The bald man dropped to the floor and started removing a maintenance panel underneath.

"The reactor's active," the black-haired man added. "But the water's stopped. It's going to melt down."

"Van," Demiana said with force. "Answers. Now."

Van gazed into the floor, eyes glossed over.

"They'll open it," Vera said. "They'll figure out the mistake."

"They won't." The black-haired man continued to sway. "They can't risk it."

"What did you do, Van?" Demiana said.

"What could he have done?" the man under the counter said. "My cuff's dead, too. I got nothing!"

"Van?" Demiana tried a calm voice.

Van lifted his head. He looked at each of them, one by one. "I'm very sorry."

"Tell 'em, Vaninath," the man with black hair said. "Tell 'em why we're here, our brother. Our watcher. Our PROTECTOR!"

Van closed his eyes. "EMP. In the suitcase."

Exclamations of "What!?" Slams, swearing, and noise — Demiana didn't sort it all out in her head. The three others blew out astonishment, anger, and fear all at once, all loudly, all losing any composure they had left.

The bald man scrambled across the floor like a spider and pounced on the reclining Van. Demiana had seen Van bat away much more elegant attacks with ease. This one he let in. The man straddled Van and clamped his hands around his throat.

"Toby!" Vera shouted.

"Kill him," the black-haired man said. "Kill him. Then do me."

Demiana took three steps and bent over the two men. Van gripped Toby's arms. He didn't pry them off. His mouth melted and drooled. Demiana reached down, folded Toby's ear into a taco and tugged him backwards. The man broke his grip. Van pushed him in the chest and wriggled from under him.

"Seriously," Demiana said. "Get a grip. Or not, actually. No grips. Not on anyone's neck."

"Too good for him anyway." Toby stood. He took a step back. "He should die slowly like the rest of us."

"No one's dying," Demiana said. "There are two kinds of people in this world and I aim to be one of them. Am I right? Are you with me? We're locked in a room, not a tomb."

"No." The man with black hair chuckled. "It's pretty much a tomb."

— 《》 —

They stopped running in the gym. Neelesh found that kind of funny. He would have mentioned it to the Detective if he thought the guy had any sense of humor. He stopped and surveyed the crowd. About 12 people worked out on machines, mats, and dull beach balls.

"Artie," the Detective yelled. "Stand up."

A man on a weight bench looked over at them.

"Go stand next to him," the Detective ordered. Neelesh figured he was now talking to him. Neelesh hurried over. The man in shorts and a sweaty tank got up from the bench, confused. They both stood facing the Detective.

"Good enough," he said. "Arty, which locker is yours?"

"Aaah…" The man's confusion grew.

"Cough it up. We're in a hurry."

The weightlifter took a couple of steps to the edge of the locker room. He pointed inside, to a locker in the middle of the row. "You need something, sir?"

"I'm afraid so," the Detective answered. "Neelesh, strip down. Artie, I'm borrowing your uniform."

"I, ah, don't have another here."

Neelesh took a couple of steps. "You want me to what?"

"I'll say it all again," the Detective announced. "But it won't change anything."

Neelesh looked at the man, shrugged and entered.

"Sorry," he heard the Detective say. "It's a pretty decent emergency."

Neelesh took off his jeans and shirt. He took out the Ambyr Systems Security Uniform. Black pants, with red piping down the legs, a shiny black shirt made of a silky ceramic polymer blend, and the jacket. More black and red, tight to the waist, with thick epaulets, the ensemble made the wearer look mean. Neelesh felt like a complete fraud. As usual.

"…behind us," the Detective said as Neelesh finished. He could tell the man was talking through his cuff. "I appreciate it."

Neelesh walked out of the locker-room. His sneakers didn't seem like company issue, but he wasn't about to change those.

"Let's go," the Detective ordered.

They jogged out of the gym, into the hall, and down another corridor. Nobody pointed fingers and complained. Nobody said, "What's he doing in that?" People just got out of the way.

They made another turn, ran up some stairs and came out in a large garage. There must have been close to a hundred gleaming black vehicles of various shapes and sizes, all in different states of repair. Technicians clinked away at cars up on lifts, backed small trucks into slots, and hooked wires up to the 'pancakes' — the flat, six-wheeled armored cars the company used to drive fear into the hearts of its employees.

"Moesh!" the Detective yelled.

An old woman picked her head up from under the engine cover a small patrol car. She had a light strapped to her head, puffing her gray hair into a muffin top.

"What you got?" the Detective asked.

"Nothing." She put her head back down.

The Detective walked towards her, scooting around a rolling workbench. "I've got to get out to Albion."

"I heard nothing about it."

"It's a hot flash. Can't talk."

She stood, the light giving her a bright third eye. "We're skimpy today, Eddie."

Neelesh took in all the makes and models. Two Unimogs, done up for foul weather. A mess of little Skoda Cubs. They were fun and efficient, but looked like containers you put leftovers in.

"I wouldn't be here if I wasn't in a hurry," the Detective said. "I'll do the forms from the road."

Neelesh walked passed them. The Vauxhall Minotaur would be fun. He doubted it was an op car. Looked like a low-grade liked having the op techs wax his ride. After that, he saw a large pickup truck — a Willys Powerwagon. You don't see those every day. Four motor drive. Not a sports car, but beastly on the road. Or off.

"If we're headed into the country," Neelesh said. "That's what you want."

Moesh cranked her head around, then returned to the Detective. "That's not mine."

"It's supposed to go back to Albion anyway. I'm going to return it." The Detective took off down the center of the garage. "Stealing a truck seems to be the best thing I've done lately."

The Detective opened the door to the cab of the truck and put a foot on the runner. Neelesh was about to move around to the passenger door and stopped. Maybe the uniform had begun to have its effect: it brought out that cockiness ops showed when they swaggered into a room, demanding answers, sure that you're going to answer. Maybe, he knew without thinking, that this op needed him at this moment, way more than Neelesh needed him in return. Or maybe the allure of a four-motor truck was so big and had so much power that fear and intimidation took a backseat. Neelesh didn't know and didn't care.

"I'll drive," Neelesh said.

The Detective stared him with that same pissed-off leathery look he'd been seeing all day.

"We don't know each other," Neelesh continued. "You might be a damn fine driver. I'm better."

Not one wrinkle changed on the Detective's face. Neelesh thought about spewing out all his track experience and race training and really making a plea for the driver's seat. Then he thought, no. This guy didn't work that way. Neelesh kept his mouth shut and met the op's eyes, telling himself he wouldn't blink. Don't even blink.

The Detective stepped down and ran around the front of the truck, trench coat flaring out behind him like a cape. Neelesh hurled himself into the cab and for the first time in... the first time ever? He fit. He fit just fine.

Chapter 27

The truck felt enormous on the city streets. Neelesh was sure it was a good two feet wider than his Saab and a good deal longer. Three times as heavy, four times the power. He plowed through the traffic, light bar flashing red and blue. He got to the on ramp for the elevated highway and pressed the accelerator to the floor. The truck launched, pinning Neelesh and the Detective to their seats.

No governor. On public roads! Ha! Neelesh smiled out the left side of his mouth so the Detective wouldn't see it.

"Shit, kid," the Detective said.

"I know."

He arced around the little boxy car in front of them and sailed down the left lane. Most cars pulled into the right lane immediately. Other's failed to see the pickup truck attack their rear-ends so quickly. Neelesh slid right, then left, oozing around them. Slowing down never occurred to him. The op wanted fast, he'd give him fast.

"Exigent circumstance," the Detective said, holding his left ear. "Report to follow." He paused, listening to other ops, Neelesh supposed. "Will return to normal speeds as soon as warranted."

The Detective dropped his arm and looked at his cuff. At least, that's what it looked like through the corner of Neelesh's right eye. He kept his attention on the road. They were now moving at 64 miles per hour. More than twice the speed of the ambient traffic.

"Call Station Chief Town of Albion, Buffalo Catchment," the Detective said. Neelesh listened through the pause. "Chief? It's Ed McCallum. Sorry to bother you."

Neelesh came up on a pack of seven cars plodding along, tight in a knot. No one on the right would slow to let the left ones over. Neelesh pulled way left, driver-side wheels on the shoulder, shooting up a fan of cinders and stones into a high arch. He passed the pack with no idea how much room he had. From his position, it looked like he'd crunched three cars in a row, though he felt no bumps or rubs.

"I'm sorry you feel that way," the Detective said. "I am bringing your truck back to you right now. Heard you might need it."

Neelesh cleared the knot of little single-motor hatchbacks and pressed the pedal to the floor. He knew this rig could reach 70. He knew it.

—— «» ——

Demiana pointed at the man with black hair. "What's your name?"

"Avad," he replied.

"And what do you do here?"

"I'm a service engineer."

She pointed at the bald man. "Tobby, right? What's your gig?"

"I'm an engineer, too," he answered, plowing his hands over his shiny, hairless head.

"Vera," Demiana said. "I know what you do."

"I don't even know why I'm here," Vera replied. "I never have to come here. I should've known when Phanes called. I don't belong here. I don't..."

"Sure you do," Avad said. "We are the last. We all belong here, except for her." He looked at Demiana.

"Yeah," Demiana said. "You'll get no argument from me there." She glanced at Van. "I know what you do, but not what you did."

"I discharged an electromagnetic pulse." Van sat on the floor. Demiana thought he looked relaxed. That was the wrong way to look.

"Anyone want to elaborate on that?" Demiana asked.

Avad paced, hugging himself. "He set off a nuclear bomb. The radiation toasted all the electricals in the room. The good news is the company makes them so they don't do much, if any, harm to humans. Can't depreciate an asset, you know. The bad news is, in here, the sensors took it as a core breach and went to emergency lockdown."

"So we're trapped in here?" Demiana asked.

"Absolutely," Avad continued. "Which wouldn't be terrible if we could communicate with the outside world and tell them the reactor is stable. At least for the moment. It won't be for long, because, like I said, he toasted all the electricals. We can't insert the control rods and stop the reaction, which also wouldn't be terrible if the water kept running."

Demiana listened. No droning noise in the background. No water rushing through pipes, continuously cooling the uranium.

"How long do we have?" she asked.

"I am certain I don't know," Avad answered.

"An hour," Toby offered. "Maybe 90 minutes. The silk hasn't been tested this way."

"But we know how it fails," Avad added.

"I don't." Demiana motioned for more words, more information. "You said 'silk'?" she asked.

"Spider silk," Toby said. "It's great for blocking radiation. Not so great dealing with the heat."

"The cocoon?"

"It's a spider web," Toby said. "That's what we've been testing for the last 30 years. A medium yield fission reactor made mostly of spider silk."

She looked at the cocoon, understanding the organic shape and hard, milky texture a little bit better. "That's a lot of spiders."

"Goats," Avad offered. "They have goats that produce the silk from genetically engineering mammary glands."

Demiana started walking. Staring at the thing would not help. "There's got to be another way out of here."

"Father," Toby said. "The containment facility is designed for just that. Containment. It keeps subatomic particles from escaping."

Demiana clinched her fists and walked, circling the reactor core, passing under the tubes and ducts spiraling in, closer and closer. The distance wouldn't matter now, not to radiation. She took measure of the great football-shaped spider web construct. She could see, now, the intricate weaving, threads so small that they couldn't be seen from even a couple of feet back. She walked, trying to outdistance her trail of fear by at least a step. *Stay ahead of the shadow*, she told herself. *Stay ahead of your shadow.*

They were cut off. Completely. It didn't happen, ever. In her whole life, she'd never been cut off. Hell, they put a band on babies seconds after they were born. The Monsignor, the Bishop, her parents. She could always, until this moment, run, hide, or call for help.

She had one avenue of communication left.

Hail Mary, full of grace
The Lord is with you.
Blessed art thou amongst women
And blessed is the fruit of thy womb, Jesus.
Holy Mary, Mother of God
Pray for our sins,
Now, and at the hour of our death
Amen.

Chapter 28

The open highway disappointed Neelesh. The traffic thinned and he wanted more cars to dodge. The Powerwagon topped out at 72. Probably the big (and useless) grill and slab body. Too much air resistance. The machine had not been designed for racing on a wide, paved strips of road. Still, the thrill of 72 miles per hour lingered. He kept his hands tight on the wheel and his foot to the floor. He would not slow down. He told this Detective he could halve the time to Albion and he would do everything in his power to impress him.

Impress him? Was that what he was doing? Trying to impress some lower grade again? Prove his worth? Again and again and again, as if anyone cared. Dr. Cohen, school administrators, his mother.

No. This mattered. The op had serious interests in Albion. Rule breaking, use-all-your-juice interests that involved his brother.

"Monsignor?" the Detective said. "There has been an incident at the Albion Nuclear Plant. I've been unable to contact Father DeFalco."

Nuclear power? Neelesh resisted the urge to glance over. Eyes on the road. Look as far down the road as you can see. They preach that in racing school. Focus far. Far is here real fast if you're doing it right.

"More than unusual," the Detective said. "It's unheard of. I don't know what's going on. Have you heard anything?"

The sun sat near the horizon behind them. The world took on a tinge of gray. Headlights sped through the blue glaze towards them, on the far side of the highway. Red lights shifted right before them, cowering in the path of their brilliant flashing monster.

"Yeah," the Detective sneered. "I'll be sure to do that." He pancaked his hand on his cuff. "Because the first thing I'm gonna feel like doing is reporting to you, you fat bastard."

Neelesh figured the call had ended. This time he chose to glance at the Detective. He wanted to see the seething, angry lines on the guys face. The dimming light made them worse than he'd expected.

"I... ah..." Neelesh did not want to talk to the man. He didn't think he could avoid it, either. "Could you set the map for this nuclear plant you mentioned? I'm trying to, you know, keep my hands on the wheel and all."

"Yes." The Detective poked the truck's computer center and told it to give them a direct route to the power plant.

Neelesh had a cord of questions. Enough to fill the back of the truck. All cut and stacked and ready. His load was so huge and heavy, with one leaning on another, questions wedged in, stuck up against each other, threatening to spill and crush if he pulled the wrong one that he didn't know where to start.

So he didn't. He drove, cutting between lanes, slowing for nothing.

"You were right," the Detective said.

Neelesh slid a look at the man.

"You're a fast driver," he continued.

"Thanks," Neelesh said, trying not to sound like one of his kids gazing at the 'A' on their exam.

"You're like him," the Detective said. "And you're not."

"What do you—"

"Excuse me." The Detective pressed his cuff. "Captain?"

Neelesh checked the estimated time of arrival on the truck's map. 42 minutes. He would start shaving that down. On a race course, he'd post to the apex of every turn, pick the most direct path. This long straight-away left him little to do but floor it and pass.

"Thanks," the Detective said. "Don't think I'm going to need a beefy budget for this. Should be a basic pick up and drop off. Another milk run."

Really? Neelesh thought. Like you all did this every day?

"I'll let you know." The Detective ended his call. "Neelesh, is it? Anyone call you Neel?"

"Neel always sounded like a command I didn't want to follow," Neelesh replied.

"I get that. What do your pals call you?"

"I don't have too many pals."

They whooshed through the twilight to the drum of tires and whistle of the wind.

"Neelesh," the Detective said. "When we get there, you've got to act like you own the place. Can you do that?"

"No," Neelesh replied. "Or, rather, that would've been my answer until 30 minutes ago."

— «» —

"So," Demiana said, "This place is locked solid."

"Tighter than a..." Avad didn't finish his phrase. He sat on the floor next to Van.

Demiana rolled her eyes. "But you and Toby are engineers. Can't you, you know, engineer us out of here?"

"I don't think so, Father." Toby sat at the control console, next to Vera.

"They were worried about keeping radioactive particles inside. Not people. Come on, let's think ourselves outside the box."

"We would need a concrete cutter," Toby said. "Or an acetylene torch."

"Or a bomb," Avad added.

Demiana said, "We've had enough of those for today, thank you very much." She circled around the rest, panning up and down and around she strolled. All those stories about the saints, they were always getting thrown in holes or prison or... who got stuck in an oven? Now there's a test of your faith. Tossed in an oven with a bunch of sinners.

"Come on," she said. "There must be tools and weak spots and that kind of thing."

"Sure." Toby stood. "We'll look around." He motioned for Avad and they walked toward the far side of the reactor. Demiana had seen other doors. She knew there was other stuff. Probably mops and buckets, but that was beside the point. These four needed inspiration. Direction. Anything to keep them from contemplating their fates.

Fate. Never a good use of your time.

Vera stared into blank screens. She talked to people for a living and right now she didn't have anyone to talk to.

"Vera," Demiana said. "You must be very smart to work in public affairs."

"If I were really smart, I wouldn't be here." Nothing moved but her mouth.

"We were tricked," Demiana said. "That doesn't count."

"I still should've known."

"How? How could any of us have known," Demiana said. "Except for Van, of course. But he was tricked, too."

"We knew what they were doing," Vera said. "Generally, anyway. Shedding the originals. I never, ever thought it would come to this."

Van sat up. "It's not your fault."

"You think I care about faults?" Vera said. "Same old Van. Right up until the end. He can land a punch anywhere on the human body, but he always misses the mark."

Van lifted his head, aiming his gaze at the ceiling.

"Vera," Demiana said. "Phanes called you treasures, maybe he—"

"One of those empty, stupid things Phanes says. He likes to pretend he's the wise, old head master at his school for the gifted whatnots. Yeah, we're his little treasures. That's why he spent the last the year slowly getting rid of us."

"He said he was saving you."

"From being incinerated!" Vera spat. "By him! You heard him, the experiment is over. He didn't want everyone in the world to know how bad he's been fucking with people. That's why he's been shipping us out one-by-one for a year. You can see us if we're concentrated here, not if we're dispersed out in the world. One part per 60 million."

Demiana felt the revelation grow inside her. A spirit, but not holy. She had served the spirit. The great delay. She had helped keep the inquisitors from the other companies at bay, giving Phanes time to cast out his tribe and burn his temple to the ground. She did it all by screwing up. She had been called in as a professional screw-up. The Bishop must have known everything. He wanted this flock to flee out into the safety of anonymity.

Avad and Toby walked back towards master control. They had no tools. Demiana could tell by the pitch of their heads that they had no hope, either.

"Why?" Demiana muttered. "What are you all hiding?"

"We don't know," Vera said, still staring blindly. "We all talked about it. We all came to realize over the years that this wasn't how the rest of the world lived, wrapped in tight little communes."

"Cocooned," Demiana said.

The men stopped.

"Not even a mop," Avad said.

"It doesn't matter, does it?" Vera said. "Even if we get out of here, it wouldn't extend our life expectancies by much, would it, Van?"

Demiana looked at the op, slumped on the floor. No reaction.

"They've got to kill us now," Vera said. "Once you try, you've got to carry it through. The company can't have us out there in the world interacting with other people after they attempted to kill us. We would be corrupting data. We need to be eliminated."

"I'm not sure that's true," Demiana said.

"Oh, now you don't want me to be smart, do you."

"Smart doesn't mean infallible."

"Tell her, Van," Vera said. "Tell her I'm wrong."

Demiana looked back and forth between the four. They all looked at nothing. They didn't have to look at each other. They didn't need to study each other's faces or read their glances and gestures. They knew each other. They all knew each other so well. All the 30-year-olds. They had been like a 100 siblings.

"Say it!" Vera shouted.

"If you had found way out," Van said. "I'd probably have to kill you."

Chapter 29

The sun abandoned them as they approached the nuclear plant. McCallum decided that was for the best. Sometimes the perfect light is little to none. They didn't need the map to call out the location of the main gate. Red and blue flashers marked that just fine. Systems Security had cordoned off the entrance with vehicles and human assets. Expensive.

McCallum looked at the map in the center of the dash one more time and nodded. "55 minutes, Neel. Probably a record."

"Thanks," the man replied. "Will there be a trophy and champagne?"

"I should've mentioned this before," McCallum said. "We'll be lucky to get out of this with our heads still attached."

They eased up to the gate. Two patrol cars with light bars warning most away. Uniformed ops stood on either side. The tall one on the left waved in the air, kind of lazy, like he couldn't believe anyone might attempt to come this way. He motioned for them to stop and Neelesh brought the pick-up to a halt. He lowered his window as the op sauntered to the truck.

"The facility is–" He caught himself. Startled. "Oh. Van. I thought you were inside..." The op might have been McCallum's age, from the town's ASS unit, he bet. He looked at the gate, confused. McCallum dipped his hand into the door release, just in case.

"This Powerwagon..." the op said, working through an equation that didn't add up.

"We need to get inside," Neelesh said.

The op looked at him, then at McCallum. "Who's the passenger?"

"Now," Neelesh said.

"Hey, I've got orders. No one in."

"Who gave the orders?"

The confusion grew across the op's face, deepening. "You."

Neelesh turned his face forward and made the window rise. McCallum fought the twitch of a smile under his nose. Asshole ran in the family. At least a little bit.

The op backed up, nodded to the other op and tapped his cuff. The entrance gate vibrated. Neelesh started driving as the great steel mesh barring entrance to the nuclear plant rose up between concrete towers to allow them to pass under.

"Whew," Neelesh said. "I did not think that would work."

McCallum pulled his hand from the door release and relaxed his muscles. "You're a history teacher?"

"Most days."

They drove through the gate and onto the power plant grounds.

—— «» ——

"Van," Demiana said. "You're not murdering anyone."

"I already did." He sat in the lotus position. He rested his hands on his knees and pressed his fingertips together.

"Stop talking like that." Demiana raised her voice. "All of you. Even the ones that aren't talking. Stop being like that. Our fates are not pre-determined. God's gift to all of us is free will. Freedom to do as we please and it would please me very much to get out of this place."

"I don't see how," Toby said. "No com, no controls, no tools—"

"Van has a tool." Demiana walked over to him. "You still have your cuff on."

"I never thought to take it off." He raised his arm and examined the black, carbon-fiber double-strap bracelet favored by ops. "Phanes told me the EMP had a timer."

"He lied to you about a lot of things," Demiana said.

"The cuff is shit now," Avad said.

Van pulled the end of the cuff. It released in a T shape, drawing a silvery string behind it, so thin Demiana could not quite see it. She only knew it existed by the shards of light it sliced, white and yellow and shades of violet.

"What the fuck, Van?" Avad said.

"Spider silk," Van said. "Same kind we used to make the reactor core."

"What the fuck do you do with that?"

"Whatever needs to be done." Van gave it a tug and it retracted back into the bracelet.

Avad pounded a control console. "God damn it. Sorry Father. But God, Van, can't you ditch the brooding shit for the last moments of your life?"

Demiana said, "I saw it cut through that cane. When you fought the Detective."

"It will cut through anything," Van said.

"We've got things. What can we cut?"

"Not a door," Van said.

"OK." Demiana began panning the room. "Not a door."

Toby stood and moved over to Van. "What have you cut with it?"

"Many things," Van answered. "It is an ultra-fine ribbon. It's not a thrusting weapon. It's only useful when you wrap it around a cane... a leg... a neck. I can't exactly wrap a door."

— «» —

McCallum pointed towards the center of the complex. Service roads winded around the various support buildings. Neelesh ignored them, choosing the most direct route over the grass and through the landscaping. A fleet of fire trucks and emergency vehicles flashed away near the tall dome in the middle of the facility. All kinds of trucks. Hong Kong and India Group had turned out. A three-company disaster. McCallum had never seen one. He picked the Ambyr mobile headquarters out of the heard. A jumbo egg pulling a loaf of bread, festooned with spotlights and antenna. He motioned Neelesh in its direction.

As the truck came to a stop McCallum said, "You got me this far, and that's plenty."

"This is where my brother works?"

"This ain't going to be the best time for a family reunion."

Neelesh opened his door. "It is the time I've been given."

McCallum opened his door and got out. "Stay close."

They moved toward the command vehicle. McCallum knew how to look and walk like he belonged. He ignored the people running around and shouting, laying cable and setting up gizmos and gadgets he could only assume would monitor the Hell brewing around them. He counted eight vehicles total and about 50 men and women in turnout gear or coveralls. Each company triplicating the efforts. Three of everything. No trust tonight, all needing verification. Deploying human assets in these numbers meant the company expected an extreme loss of capital or worse: compensation outside the company. He took a moment and gazed up at the domed cylinder covering the nuclear reactor. They'd lit it up nicely and that was never a good thing.

McCallum hopped up the three foldout steps leading to a door in the side of the mobile command center. He paused for second and looked back over his shoulder at Neelesh. He thought of 12 things to say and decided on "Keep your hands in your pockets."

"What?"

"Your cuff will give you away." McCallum opened the door and squinted at the garish light inside. White and lime. Monitors covering every vertical space. Men standing on every inch of horizontal space. A blond man in a suit had his back to him. The rest were either watching monitors or listening to the suit. One of the other guys noticed McCallum as he entered. Then another. Four looked past the golden-haired guy. McCallum recognized the white shirt and epaulets — a senior Ambyr emergency technician. The others must be Kong and Grouper Emergency Techs. Their shifting attention caused the suit to turn to see who could possibly upstage him.

The man didn't match his hair. His skin was too old. And crinkling into a new expression. McCallum couldn't say to what, exactly. Irritation with a pinch of surprise? The man rotated at the hip to continue whatever orders he'd been spouting. McCallum brought up his arm and tapped the face of his bracelet, ordering a scan of the room. The man turned again, thinning his eyes, accentuating his wrinkles, giving

McCallum a good, hard stare. Like he'd forgotten a detail and was trying his best to recall it.

"And you are?" he commanded.

McCallum watched the bios slide across his screen. Six various engineers and emergency response technicians. Six. McCallum looked up, and recounted. Seven. Mr. Golden-hair failed to come up in his sweep. He could work for one of the other companies and not be registered as emergency personnel, but that didn't fit.

"I'm going to ask you the same thing." McCallum took a step farther into the trailer, allowing Neelesh to enter behind him.

"I didn't call for more help," the man said.

"I won't be asking again."

The man completed his rotation and planted his legs and his hands on his hips. The rest of room went ridged. The four standing ETs puffed up and scowled. The suit opened his mouth to speak, stopped and bent his head left to peer around McCallum

"Van?" the golden-haired man asked. Then his face changed again. This time McCallum had a word for it: horrified. His eyes fired, hands went up, fingers splayed, he hunkered down like he was defending a goal. "Whoa," the man continued. "I don't know what you're doing here, but this is absolutely not the time."

McCallum pressed his com link in the upper right corner, the button programmed to broadcast. The men in room twitched at the tickle from their com links. They each glanced down to confirm what they had probably suspected. Their bracelets told them an Ambyr Systems Security operative, detective grade, stood before them. Six of them, at least. Not the old guy with a younger man's hair.

"Where's your cuff?" McCallum asked.

The man couldn't take his eyes off Neelesh. "There has been an accident."

"You are in violation of company policy."

"This is serious," the man protested. "Whatever you're doing—"

"I'm looking for Father Demiana DeFalco."

The man said out the side of his mouth. "Get the Chief over here. Now."

The Ambyr emergency tech brought his arm up and touched his bracelet.

"You adding insubordination to com link violation?" McCallum took another step forward and took on his full height. "Where's the priest?"

"Yeah, yeah," The man waved his hands. "That's what I'm trying to tell you. The nuclear reactor core is melting down inside the containment unit right alongside your priest."

"She's in there?"

The golden-haired man nodded. "She will be for the next twelve-hundred years."

McCallum shook his head. "Get her out."

"That's the thing. We can't. The dome is sealed up to keep the radiation in. It can never be opened again."

McCallum panned the monitors, not knowing what they might tell him. He panned the men's faces, and learned more. They all drooped in the shoulders, corners of their mouths and eyes. A couple of them nodded in slight degrees.

"She's alive?" McCallum tried to maintain his op voice. "Now?"

"Phanes," the man in the white shirt said. "The Chief's on his way."

"You can't open the door for a second?" McCallum's face creased in on itself.

"Not a millisecond," Phanes said. "The radiation would be lethal. But don't feel bad for her. It's her own fault."

"What?" McCallum spat.

"She sabotaged the core. That was her plan all along."

Chapter 30

McCallum wanted to sit down. The cramped drive, the cool night air, the suck of the day — the way the day kept taking all his thoughts and energy and flipping them. That's the tiring part, the keeping up. The twins, the nuclear meltdown, the saboteur priest. The picture he'd started in his head hung upside-down.

All the seats were taken. The mobile command center didn't have many to begin with. It didn't have much of anything, besides monitors and out-sized communication gear. McCallum flicked his chin towards the door. Neelesh caught the signal, stepped out of the trailer and down the steps. McCallum followed but stopped. At the bottom of the stairs stood the Albion Systems Security Station Chief — the man he swiped the truck from — and two uniformed operatives, barely visible in the hard shadows.

"Hey, buddy," the Chief said. "You got to be what they called about."

"You'd have to ask them," McCallum replied. "They're right inside."

"Van," the Chief addressed Neelesh. "You mind if I escort this operative to a 'safe' zone?" He snickered at the word safe. The other two ops painted McCallum with their eyes, analyzing the threat like legitimate pros.

Neelesh met McCallum's eyes. McCallum could tell the teacher didn't know what to do. He'd played his part damn well till this point, but the thought of bluffing a bunch of ASS ops was over-stressing him.

"Chief," McCallum said. "I don't know what kind of arrangement you have with Phanes, but it's coming to an end."

"Is it now?" The Chief patted his belly, face exaggerating surprise.

"After that reactor melts down," McCallum continued, "the facility's going to be canned up. Sealed like strawberry preserves. You follow me? Phanes is not going to be around. The company's going to relocate him."

The Chief sneered. "That's got nothing to do with you taking my truck."

"You and I know this is becoming an empty field. Why don't you try making a score, here?"

"That's funny," the Chief said. "I want to even one."

"You've got a distinct opportunity. A major catch. Sabotage." McCallum tried to put some drama in the word.

"That would be great, if the insubordinate weren't about to get deep-fried along with all the evidence."

McCallum put up his left arm. "Why doesn't Phanes have a cuff on?"

"Don't care."

"Ask yourself," McCallum said. "Why? It didn't get damaged in the accident, otherwise he'd be inside. Stuck like the priest."

"You want me to pick him up for a com link infraction? I think I'm looking at a much bigger get. You're a thief and I'm pretty sure a general asshole."

"He did it!" Neelesh blurted. "Phanes took his cuff off because he planned to sabotage the reactor. He knew the radiation would cook his cuff, so he took it off beforehand."

The Chief slowly rolled his eyes from McCallum to Neelesh. "Of course he did, Van. You thinking I don't know all that? You thinking I got here 'cuz of my looks? Where the Hell you think he got the EMP in the first place?"

"EMP?" McCallum mumbled. "EMP?"

"We pin it on the priest and everyone goes home happy," the Chief finished.

"You gave Phanes an EMP?" McCallum said-asked-realized. Systems Security kept them around, he knew. He'd even trained on one a couple of years ago. They were not used often, and only in special circumstances. The company liked to control data, not erase it. It liked destroying electronic assets even less.

The picture came into focus. Phanes set off an EMP in the containment silo, tricking the facility into thinking it had a radiation leak. The facility went into lockdown automatically.

"Tricked," McCallum repeated out loud. "There's no leak. At least not yet. We've got to get her out of there?"

"Boys," the Chief said. "I'm all done talking."

He reached behind his back and drew out a LTL-40 stun baton.

"Shit," McCallum said, "Not this again."

—— ⟨⟩ ——

Demiana brushed her fingers along the steel door to the containment silo. So smooth, all the edges rounded, as with every corner of the place. No corners. No nooks or creases. Nothing to collect radioactive dust.

No place for Van to entwine in a scalpel-sharp filament and pull.

The others scoped out the walls as well. Toby put his nose to the door jam, peering into the airtight seams. Avad took to the floor on the far wall, near the pipes. Even Vera exhibited a faint pulse of hope. She hadn't moved, but her head turned and searched — she thought, at least faintly, that they might be able to cut their way out of this tomb. Only Van failed to roam. He fixed on the reactor — the two story-high cocoon, its heart getting ready to have an attack.

Avad and Toby called back and forth to each other, each reaffirming the other's negative response. Nothing. Nowhere. The engineers had not intentionally made the containment dome impervious to harm from a spider silk garrote. Demiana knew making it fend off subatomic particles just kind of led to that sort of thing. Smooth, hard, and dense. Like her. Irony. Demiana had always thought irony, as opposed to cleanliness, was next to Godliness. God wasn't exactly clean; he put more dirt in the world than just about anything else. Irony? He must have made that for himself.

She heard someone running. She didn't look up from the bars crossing the back of the door. Maybe they could thread the silk down there? She couldn't see any space.

"First thing I thought of," Toby said. "If the gap were big enough and we could somehow — I don't know how — detach one end of the spider silk and weave it down we might have had a chance. I can't get one of my hairs into the gap, though. There is nothing to snare with Van's evil little toy."

"Not nothing," Avad said from the center of the chamber.

Demiana and Toby spun. Vera perked up. Even Van gave Avad his attention.

"We've got three problems," Avad said. "First, we can't get out. Second, there's no water flow to cool the core. Third, we can't stop the reaction in the core. We've got no computers to tell the control rods to lower and turn this bad boy off. At least, that's what we thought. That last assessment is flawed."

"Can you hurry this along," Vera said.

"What can I cut?" Van asked.

"I'm hoping web," Avad answered. "I'm hoping web cuts web."

"How does that help?" Demiana scanned the cocoon trying to see what Avad saw.

"This is a good news-bad news thing," Avad continued.

"I'll do it," Toby started walking towards Avad.

"Whoa, buddy," Avad put out a palm. "That's not how we do things."

"Do what?" Demiana insisted.

"It's got to be somebody," Toby said.

"This conduit." Avad pointed a pipe running into the cocoon near the bottom. "It's for control and sensor output. It's not large, but I think a person could squeeze in."

"In?" Vera said. "To the core? For what? A quicker death?"

"To lower the rods." Toby dropped to the floor. He measured the junction with his eyes. "Manually."

Demiana ran. "We can do that?"

"Yep," Toby said. "Nature's finally helping us out."

"Gravity," Avad added.

Demiana slid into home, stopping next to Tobby.

"This reactor is not that large." Toby spread his hands, eyeing up the possible entrance.

"Used to be on a war ship," Avad said.

"So it is manageable," Toby said. "I can get through there."

"Not as easily as I can." Demiana stood. "What do you guys do when we open this? Radiation's going to pour out?"

"We go in the maintenance closet," Avad said. "It's protected. We wait 30 minutes, come out and pray the bastards outside eventually realize we halted the meltdown."

"We?" Van's voice made them all turn. No one had seen him approach. "How noble."

"Hey," Avad spat. "I'm working here. What are you doing?"

Van crouched next to conduit and drew the silk out of his bracelet.

"Van?" Demiana blurted.

He stopped pulling when he approximated the diameter of the opening. He held the silk at the measured length and stood. "Line up."

Toby and Avad glanced at each other, nodded, then squared themselves off.

"You too, Vera," Van said. "We're going to see who can enter the hole and who can't."

Vera walked over, hugging herself tightly. The streaks down each cheek glimmered. She kept her lips pressed together.

Demiana met her with an embrace. "It's going to be OK. I'm not doling out priestly fluff, either. You and your friends are going to walk out of here tonight."

"Boy, girl," Van commanded.

Avad stepped between Demiana and Vera. They all faced the op.

"This is unnecessary." Demiana held out her hand. "Give me your cuff. I'm the smallest and I'm going in."

"Toby, Avad…" Van said. "If you could each take the priest's arms please."

"What?" Demiana scowled. The men took her arms.

"Hold on to her." Van let go of the line. It zipped back into his bracelet. "My duty has always been to keep them safe."

Demiana tried to jerk forward. The men held her. Vera huffed twice, sharp and rapid.

"I'm not happy with all the things I've done in pursuit of that… mission." Van paused. "If I could keep these last three safe? Do you think it would balance out?"

"You don't need to do this," Demiana pleaded. "Don't you see? That's why I'm here! It's my fate. God wanted me, here, now, to save you."

Van stepped up to Demiana. He brought his right hand up and cradled her cheek. "You were brought here to bear witness that, in the end, I tried to balance out my life. I don't know about Catholics and priests. You are like this conduit, right? You have a line up to God?"

"Van," Demiana burbled. "Please."

"You will tell him I tried to get it right."

He kissed Demiana on the mouth.

— «» —

The young ops marched towards Neelesh and the Detective, paying Neelesh no mind. They thought he was on their side. He knew it was a strategic advantage… of which he could not take advantage. These were the real ASS ops. Deadly fighters. He couldn't even take a middle-aged mechanic. Was that today? The Detective had the high ground, still up on the steps. The fat one had a stick. It didn't look friendly. The two other ops? They looked even less friendly. Holy crap they were going to beat the soul out of the Detective and all the poor guy wanted to do was rescue a priest. Even if you're not Catholic, that's got to be good karma.

"Van." The fat one pulled his club, telescoping it to a good three feet. "Get on him or get out the way."

The three ops closed in on the trailer steps. Neelesh needed to step through their semi-circle. He had to move. He couldn't fight these guys. He couldn't even pretend. The young ones brought their arms in, made their hands like claws. The fat one took the left flank. He planned to poke at the Detective with the stick. Poke and prod. That's what that stick was. A cattle prod. The ends put out a jolt of electricity strong enough to knock a man out.

The Detective would last five seconds. The man who had saved his eye, if not his life. The man who had trudged through all those photos when the easier thing would have been sending Neelesh off to a chain-gang for the rest of his life. Hard labor for something his brother did. This was the guy who told him about his brother, Van.

Ha, Neelesh said in his head. I've still got one solid life skill: pretending I'm something I'm not.

Neelesh held his hand out to the fat op. "Give me the prod."

"No can do," he replied. "This one's all mine."

Neelesh stepped up to him, chest-to-chest, the baton pointed up and to the left between them. "Not what I asked."

The roly-poly op's eye twitched. He sensed something — the voice, the hair, the stance — the cuff. Neelesh's hands were out. The op was old and out of shape, but he was still an op. He saw Neelesh's pretty gold bracelet.

The op checked him hard against the chest. Neelesh stumbled backwards, hitting the fold-out railing. Neelesh brought his arms up. The cattle prod slid through them. He felt a log hit his chest. His head lurched back. The stars spun into a circle.

Chapter 31

McCallum leapt onto the railing, spun, and grabbed the edge of the command trailer. He bounced on his bad leg, letting the spring of the brace give him some lift. He yanked himself higher and threw his legs up over the edge.

"Get 'em!" the Chief yelled beneath him.

McCallum rolled and rolled, arms over this head. The slick top made it easy. The darkness and the spinning made it impossible to see the edge. He felt it with his shoulder and kept going. He tried to use his arms to slow his fall, but only a little. No time. He needed each quarter second. The uniforms would be fast.

He collapsed on the ground, letting his leg brace soak up most of the shock. The pain made it to his mouth. He crushed his teeth, keeping it in, and rolled under the trailer. With all the blood rushing and the tumbling, he couldn't hear the others. He saw Neelesh crumpled by the steps. The Chief standing over him, undecided on a direction.

McCallum rolled out from under the trailer and launched. To his credit, the Chief caught on. He took a fighting stance and raised the baton. "Boys!" he shouted. McCallum's kick came under the cattle prod, landing the tip of his boot in the older op's groin. McCallum planted his legs and dodged left, avoiding the baton crashing downward, still in the Chief's hands as he doubled over. McCallum elbowed the man in the jaw and levered the weapon out of his grasp.

Four or five discharges, McCallum thought. If the weapon had been properly juiced. One on Neelesh. He jabbed the baton into the Chief's neck. One on the Chief.

McCallum could feel the other two coming. They shouted something to each other, about 'under' or 'around'.

He took the railing and whipped himself up the stairs and through the door of the mobile command center. He heard the uniforms behind him. Great. They were all fired up. Leaving good sense behind them.

The first one came through the door like a bear, roaring with his teeth out, as if he were going to rip and tear. McCallum crouched under his claws and brought the stun baton up into the man's chest. The jacket might have protected him, if he'd had it zipped all the way. McCallum reposted so his weapon wouldn't get caught up in the falling body.

The last op used the doorway to stop. He looked a little stunned without even getting the stick. He needed a second. This didn't seem to be going... McCallum thrust the baton at him. He dipped back, holding the doorjamb like he was a slingshot. McCallum twisted his grip and zapped the man's right hand. The op's muscles constricted so hard he hung in the doorway, stuck, face contorted. McCallum stepped on the op's partner, jumped, and kicked op number two full in the chest. He flew out and down.

McCallum turned to the men at the other end of the trailer. Each gawked, mouths like melting candles.

"Open the silo," McCallum said.

Phanes took a step forward, arms wide, palms up. McCallum thought he might bow. "We can't do that."

"You set off an EMP," McCallum said. "There's no radiation leak."

"We don't—"

McCallum jabbed the cattle prod into Phanes' forehead. The man jerked, made a coughing sound, and fell like timber.

"Who can open the door?" McCallum swished the baton through the air.

Six men inched away, guppy-faced. The two in the chairs didn't move. The four standing cowered a little, though they probably didn't know it.

"Seriously." The guy in a white shirt waved his hands. "There's nothing we can do."

"It was an EMP," McCallum said.

"Even so, it would've locked everything up. There's no water flow for cooling. There's no way to lower the control rods. Even if it was an EMP, a meltdown is inevitable."

"But... there's a woman in there. Alive."

"Actually, there are five people," one of the other men said. "We don't know that they're still alive."

"A plan?" McCallum closed his mouth a tried to drum up some moisture. "What's the plan?"

"We monitor the temperature of the containment facility and hope it holds."

"That's your... Watch people bake like muffins?"

The man in the white shirt — a senior emergency response tech, McCallum assumed, based on the tags and epaulets — lowed his arms and shrugged. His look went low and left. Shame. McCallum knew the posture. The guy probably spent his life training for fires and rescues and not this. He never trained for inaction.

McCallum lowered the stun baton. He let it slip from his hand and tinkle on the floor.

McCallum walked outside. His left leg throbbed. Too much running and leaping and crap. His right trapezius muscle hurt when he looked to the right. He wrenched something good with that stupid lift up and over the trailer. He could feel the adrenaline being swept from his body, leaving the ache and thirst and chill. The night air made it worse, drying old sweat on his neck and wrists. He pulled his trench coat tight. He'd stroll down to the river and keep going. Forever.

Emergency techs crawled around the Chief and Neelesh like ants on a candy. They were thrilled to have a task. No one wanted to watch a thermometer stuck to a nuclear plant, all keyed up and helpless. Skills and training bottled up and shaken. Dormant frustration to bubbling anger then to flat — that's what he felt now, flat. He was glad they weren't flat yet. Neelesh especially needed the aluminum foil blanket they tucked around him.

The rest of the chaos had settled. The teams from the other companies pulled back. McCallum didn't see anyone near the silo. They didn't need to be, he figured. Watching a screen would be way wiser than strolling out here hoping the lead-lined concrete did its job — that everyone involved in building it did their jobs. That nobody hurried, cut a corner, mixed a little less stone in the base because a friend of a friend would trade a cord of firewood for a load of decent backfill.

A big cylinder with a round top, the silo had no artistic menace. It didn't look its part. Round signaled soft and safe to people. This building should look like the bottom of a Burmese mantrap — a mess of spikes jutting up from the earth. Although maybe this shape would be more appropriate as it took on the role of mausoleum.

McCallum stopped at the door. He pictured Father DeFalco's face, saw her sitting inside, on the floor, hands together, praying to God for... he couldn't picture that part. He couldn't understand right now. He refused it. He could picture her face, though. Placid and sad, trying really, really hard for peace. Demiana and the others sat in a circle, waiting for the flash. Maybe she got them all to pray—

He heard a muffled boom. His heart stopped. This was it. The rupture of the core. He wasn't safe here.

There it was again.

McCallum held frozen, legs cocked, arms bent, ready to sprint. He heard the tiniest pillow of a blow for a third time. Then a fourth. The core would not explode repeatedly, if it exploded at all — he had no idea what a meltdown was like — but it wouldn't do so over and over in a steady rhythm.

He ran.

Chapter 32

Demiana reclined in a frosted plastic tent, dressed in a sweat suit three sizes too big. The Hong Kong paramedics had given it to her, as her clothes had been entombed in lead. She'd been a little shy at first, stripping in front of two men in white suits with huge bee-keeper helmets veiling their faces, but getting blasted with cold, sugary goo cleared away that feeling. It is tough to be shy when you're freezing and angry and relieved and stinging in spots that don't often see a lot of water jets. Now that they had given her a cot and turned up the heat, she kind of liked lounging about in the sea of cotton. What the Hell. She was fu— freakin' alive. Praise the Lord.

And the others, they made it, too. Praise be to God.

Poor Van. May the Lord accept him into his loving arms.

The Kongers also gave her a loaner cuff. Ceramic. The color and texture of an elephant tusk. It weighed more than she wanted. She lifted her arm up and down, contemplating the mass. Yep. Way too heavy. It was nice to complain about that. She'd spend the rest of her night complaining about this wan, weighty, wickedly without-style bracelet because that was a much better than—

Screw it.

Praise be to God.

Demiana pressed her finger to her communication link and called the Bishop. She felt a prickle in her tummy. One did not call the Bishop. He had channels and protocols and all of that went to cinder in a flash. Burned away in the nuclear fire.

"Father DeFalco," the Bishop answered.

"Sorry to bother you," she replied.

"You have not been far from my thoughts as of late."

"So I was bothering you anyway? Even without calling you?"

A pause. She wanted to put her wrist to the pause, try to take its temperature. Hot, cold, what?

"You sound well," the Bishop said.

"You could have told me," she shot out. She had to be fast. Get it out before she remembered you can't talk to the Bishop this way.

"I could have," the Bishop said with a cordial calm. "Then you would have had a choice. You could have gone the way of Monsignor Bujold and come down, understandably but most unfortunately, on the side of transparency and neutrality. I decided to trust in your nature, rather than your reason."

"My nature. You knew I'd make a mess."

"Forgive me."

"That's what we do, right?"

— «» —

Phanes sat on a bed inside an ambulance. They'd raised the back so he seemed more asleep than dead. McCallum watched the medical technician eject fluid into the man's arm. The tech checked a couple of dials and gauges as Phanes moved his lips, sucking like a newborn. His tongue made a lap around his mouth then his eyelids split. Just a hair. McCallum moved to the edge of the bed. He wanted to be the first thing the man saw.

"I got this," McCallum said to the med tech.

"I'd rather—"

McCallum gave him the look. The tech exited through the back doors of the truck.

"You," Phanes said. His eyeballs darted around under droopy lids.

"Me," McCallum confirmed. "You know your name yet."

"Mine," he replied. "And your boss' boss' boss."

"Huh. You'll have to tell me who that is. I've got a couple of other questions first."

"Good luck with that."

"We got the Priest out," McCallum said. "Along with three others. Seems your boy Vaninath didn't make it."

Phanes opened his eyes. He brought up his right hand to block some of the light.

"An inspector from the India Group and the local Hong Kong station chief debriefed the gang. They were pretty happy to talk."

"Van?" Phanes' mouth hardly moved.

"Not sure my boss' boss' boss is going to be taking your call."

"How? The radiation. What did you do?"

"Why?" McCallum asked. "Why'd you try to kill them all and blow up your damn nuclear plant?"

"That's your question? You want me to dribble out the details of my life's work to slake your curiosity? I've spent more than 30 years keeping secrets. Very large, very dark, and very dirty secrets. It is what I do. It is not a habit, it is a lifestyle."

"Yeah." McCallum tapped his com link. He turned to look at the back of the ambulance.

One side of the split doors opened and Neelesh climbed in, still wearing his Systems Security uniform.

"Van?" Phanes said in a rush of weak air.

McCallum stood so they could both loom over Phanes.

"That was my brother," Neelesh said.

"Oh."

"You killed my brother."

"I gave your brother — and you — your lives in the first place," Phanes said.

"That means you can take them back?"

"Now this." Phanes rolled his head. "What are you going to do, exact vengeance? Strangle me where I lay?"

"I didn't even get to meet him." Neelesh's voice tightened.

"He was just like you. Loyal, passionate, and willing to kill for a cause. See? Now you met him."

"You lump of shit!" Neelesh dove into Phane's neck. His hands locked around his neck and crushed in the flesh they found. McCallum counted in his head. He'd been strangled once. It left him with a fair understanding of the timing involved. You had to keep squeezing long after the passing out for death to set in. Phanes gurgled and purpled, slapping the teacher's forearms in a total waste of energy. The slapping turned to flapping and the man's eyes shut.

"Plenty," McCallum said. He reached up under Neelesh's arms and separated them, breaking his grip on Phanes' windpipe.

Phanes gasped, coughed and pounded the bed. He reeled side to side like he was trying to wriggle out of a tight hole.

"No need," McCallum said to Neelesh.

"He's shit."

"He's worse now. He's brought the spotlights. To the company, he's a liability."

— «» —

Neelesh stood next to the Detective, who stood facing a woman on a cot, curled up in someone else's gym clothes. They were separated by plastic so thick it bent the light passing through it, like a waterfall. A super slow waterfall. On this side, technicians darted about, reading their cuffs, setting up gizmos and lights, endlessly chatting with each other. Four tents had been set up in a cross, with a makeshift monitoring station at the center. The Detective seemed interested only in this one.

"She's going to be fine," a man in a white shirt with epaulets said as he strolled out of the shadows and into the field of electric lights Neelesh decided were brighter than any day he'd ever had.

"Thanks," the Detective replied.

"We found the EMP. Seems the Chief gave it to Phanes."

"The Priest is clear, then?"

"Her people are coming to get her," the tech said.

"Guess I'm done." The Detective didn't move.

"You know," the tech said. "If you hadn't heard them pounding inside the core, I don't know that we would've ever popped that seal."

"If they'd made that thing right," the Detective said, "I'd never have heard them."

The emergency technician smirked. "If they made it right, none of us would be here in the first place."

As the emergency tech continued on, the Detective tapped his cuff. Despite three yards and the stupidly thick plastic, he could see the woman on the cot roll her eyes and tap her own cuff

"You're going to be…"

Neelesh didn't want to overhear. He stepped back, looked around, tried not to pay attention, then her heard—

"…twins?" McCallum said. "All of them?"

He had a twin; others had twins. Quivering wrongness rang his belly.

"Phanes, too?" The Detective looked surprised. Neelesh enjoyed it for a second, then realized neither one of them needed any more surprises for the night. They didn't need anything from this night except its end. He tuned out of the conversation, trying to give the op as much privacy as the maze of tarps and wires and floodlights would allow.

"Neel." The Detective drew a finger across the face of his cuff. Neelesh hated when people called him Neel, but this guy got a pass. "You feel like driving?" he asked.

"My specialty."

He put his hand on Neelesh's shoulder and leaned in. "First we've got to find a car. The one we came in is pretty damn dead."

"That Chief had to get here in something, right?" Neelesh said.

The Detective smiled. "Hope it's something fast."

They walked out of the light in the direction of the main gate.

"Sorry about your brother," the Detective said.

"I didn't know him," Neelesh replied.

"The survivors said he saved them. He was a hero."

"So I know that," Neelesh said. "Funny, huh? He escaped all the other junk. I'd be pretty happy if my family only knew me for the best thing I ever did."

Epilogue

Neelesh knelt at the rear of his Saab. Sam Qui squatted next to the back driver's side tire, hanging a good eight inches off the ground. Sam checked each of the five lug nuts with a torque-wrench and Neelesh watched. He tried not to let surrounding activity distract him. People yelling for tools, pushing cars on to the track, stomping their feet in the sunny cold. He wanted to look around, he wanted to suck in all the data — who else would run today, how did their cars look, would the weather hold, how much debris littered the track — all the stuff that made racing more important than math or science or even history. The factors that made it the perfect mixture of everything you could know or do, shaken with a dash of chaos. Sweet.

"All set," Sam said.

"Grand," Neelesh replied. "Take her down. Then check the lugs again."

Neelesh stood and stretched. Sam released the air in the pneumatic jack and the car lowered to the ground. Neelesh glanced at his cuff. 12 minutes to start.

"You want to steer it up to the line?" he asked Sam.

The kid's face opened like a flower.

"Jack?" Neelesh turned to Jack Qui, who sat on a stack of two tires, focused on a reader.

"One second," Jack said. "I'm running another model."

"Oh." Neelesh slid over to him. "What's different?"

"I recalibrated your rear generators," Jack said. "Here's the thing most people don't realize. You are only as fast as your brakes. There are guys who spend thousands and thousands trying to get more out of their motors. They should be lookin' around at everything, know what I'm sayin'? Tighter brakes are going to let you go into them turns faster."

"Faster by going slower." Neelesh grinned.

Jack grinned back. "Going slower faster, actually. But you get the idea."

"Yeah. From you," Neelesh said. "I never would've thought of it."

Jack stood and closed up his reader. He and Neelesh watched Sam pushing on the torque-wrench with his all of his body.

Jack said, "All the racers go 'round the track their own way."

"And there are lots of ways to win."

Neelesh put on his helmet.

— «» —

Demiana didn't care for running outside in the cold. Ok, it wasn't like you could see your breath or snot poured out your nose, but still. If the trees had no leaves, she had no business being outside. Except when she had business best conducted outside. Far away from curious ears and diligent note takers. She loved her fellow clergy, but Holy Thursday she was convinced the Gospels started out as the Gossips, and the tradition continued strong and long in the devout. The only thing worse than running in the cold was running off the path.

She pounded across the grass, leaping over a depression, dodging between a bench and a trio of trash cans, one for each company, a value of the commons that made her happy. She caught the running path again and found her target. Now she had to make sure she had enough breath to talk or the whole excursion would be a freakin' waste of coziness.

Monsignor Bujold jogged along, black tracksuit pressed to the front of him, flapping a bit in his wake. Demiana ran up alongside him and slowed to his pace. She looked over in time to see his eyebrows arch like scared cats and his mouth pop an 'O.'

"Father DeFalco?" He tried to hide his surprise but the physical exertion wouldn't allow it.

"Monsignor." Demiana smiled. "Looking good."

"Thank you. I'm surprised."

"At all kinds of things, probably," she said, trying not to huff.

"I'm glad your ordeal seems to have," he took an extra breath, "done you no harm."

"Yes," she agreed. "I'm no worse, anyway."

"Well, it's a lovely day for a run," the Monsignor got out before returning to his regular breathing.

"Too frosty for me," Demiana said. "I'm here for you."

The Monsignor looked at her from the corners of his eyes. Demiana let him look. She didn't want him to squirm, necessarily, but she could use a little more oxygen. This running and chatting got real stale, real fast.

"I couldn't figure out why you wanted me to find in favor for opening the nuclear plant," she said, paused, swallowed, let he lungs loosen. "I mean, what's it to you, right?"

The Monsignor said nothing. Demiana couldn't get a good look at his face. She hadn't considered that when she thought up this meeting. It wouldn't be a face-to-face after all. Crap.

"Then I figured," she continued, "you were just like me. Somebody told you to care. Somebody lower up than the Bishop."

The Monsignor continued to run, unwavering and steady. Demiana couldn't tell whether or not he even heard her.

She took another deep breath and continued. "Cardinal? No, too distant. I'd put my chips on the Arch Bishop, were I a gamblin' gal, which I am not. Aside from bingo." She exhaled and inhaled and shook out her hands. "I'm thinking it spells out like he tells you to settle this power plant thing 'cuz the Bishop is dragging his miter? Am I right?"

"Is there a point to this?" The Monsignor's voice came out punching. She thought she saw a little spittle spray forth. Cool.

"A couple of points," Demiana said. "First, I'm not a chump. I don't want you thinking anything else."

"Fine," the Monsignor threw out.

"Third," Demiana went on, "I don't care. Score all the points you want."

"You skipped second," the Monsignor said.

"Right, yeah, I want off the desk. No more arbitrage," Demiana said. "I'm a mediator now."

"Ah," the Monsignor said. "Finally. Some ambition."

"Nope." Demiana shot. "I don't have ambition. I have a calling."

The Monsignor slowed up a bit, he turned a few degrees at the waist. Demiana assumed he wanted her to see his amused expression.

"Your fist and only mediation," he said, "was a catastrophe."

"I'm terrible, I know. Why do think I'm using veiled threats? If I were good, you'd reassign me all on your own."

"And..." He stopped that thought. "But..." It looked as though he might say something else, but shut that down too.

They ran in silence for a while, winding past the fallen stones and rusted gates of what Demiana had heard had once been a zoo.

"I may not be good," Demiana said. "But I'm fair. I figure every mediation I do will at least benefit from that."

"And if I say no?"

"I don't know. The threats were veiled. Even from me."

"Then let's keep it that way," the Monsignor said.

Demiana stopped talking and ran for real.

— ⟨⟩ —

McCallum wore his gray shark-skin suit with a black silk shirt. He didn't know if the outfit worked. He had nothing more appropriate for matching the Priest's description of the place. She had been right about him liking it. The Albright had wide hallways, stark white walls and careful lighting, all to make the art collection look its best. The collect certainly beat any outfit he owned.

He had to release his credentials to get in, which he never liked doing. He hated when ops bragged about getting floor passes or front rows or into places like this. These circumstances were special enough, he decided. He continued that line of reasoning right up to the bar, where he ordered a beer and put it on the tab of Horace Marigold. The Priest said he wouldn't mind.

McCallum strolled through the club. Back in the day, it must have been a fantastic gallery. Rothko, Rothenberg, Magritte, his personal favorite, Jackson Pollock. *Convergence* hung right there before him. A wall of intricate, weaving drip-lines of paint. He could touch it if he wanted. He didn't. He couldn't. He moved on.

He was impressed that the club had managed to retain so many icons of art history. The exquisite had a tendency to disappear into the homes of the very low grades, the ones and twos, never to be seen again. Even by them, he figured. This place must have had a special arrangement. The ultra lows must want nice things at their sex clubs. Kind of the point.

McCallum stopped at an older painting. It hung next to a few other elderly oils, in a hallway that linked larger rooms. The plaque next to the piece read *Cupid as a Link Boy* by Sir Joshua Reynolds. 1771. An oil painting, it looked like coal soot had been worked right into the medium. It depicted a small boy, not yet ten, with little bat wings. He held a torch shaped like a penis. He didn't seem happy about it.

He'd wait here for the man who'd bought him a drink. McCallum figured he could stare at this work of genius for a couple of hours if that's what it took.

It didn't take that long. What looked like Phanes Larkspur in a better suit walked down the hallway, rocks glass dangling from his fingers like the gondola of a hot air balloon.

"I like to meet the people I'm helping to inebriate," he said as he approached.

"I was counting on it." McCallum looked at Horace Marigold. He might have turned away quick, so as not to be rude, but the man looked McCallum up and down like he was trying to decide what to bid and where to hang him. McCallum took the opportunity to stare. Horace looked exactly like his brother. Even up close.

"The staff says you are an ASS op," Horace said. "I can certainly see where they come by that idea."

"The staff is astute. What else do they say?"

"That you have poor taste in beer." Horace turned to the face the painting. "You seem to have excellent taste in art, however. Are you a Reynolds fan?"

"I am now," McCallum said. "This is not the usual 18th century portrait."

"How true. That's no lord or lady. Link boys were used to guide the wealthy through streets of London Catchment during the dark and dangerous hours."

"Putting Cupid on that job would suggest more."

"I know, right?" Horace's face lit up. "The duality. It speaks to me. None of us are just one thing, are we? Moonlighters and side-jobbers, all of us. That look on his face. He is not comfortable with at least one of his jobs. I can certainly relate to that."

"It's haunting," McCallum said. "I have an attraction to haunts. Ghosts. Things that are unsettled."

"What unsettles you, officer."

"Detective."

"Sorry, Detective."

"I reprimanded your brother."

"I was sort of getting that idea."

"It left me with a few open questions."

"You came to the wrong place," Horace said. "The delights offered here will make you question all kinds of things."

"Your brother had a doctor murdered," McCallum said. "Cohen."

"I thought that question remained… unsettled."

"Why kill the doctor?" McCallum decided to apply and pry. "If Phanes was shipping out all the twins, why bother with Cohen? Why risk it?"

"Had you thought of asking him?" Horace took a sip of his cloudy drink.

"He's unavailable at the moment." McCallum took a sip of his beer, a warm slurp. He neared the bottom. "I think that doctor was a link and I don't think he liked it."

"A link between what?"

McCallum glanced at Horace. "There's a question for you. Got to have two dots for a connection, right? Your brother works for Ecron, a division of Ambyr energy. They were paying him for a long-term study on the use of exotic materials in nuclear energy production. You work for

Cellprog, Division of Ambyr Medical. They've been doing generational twin studies since before the Buy-Ups. If a person could sell one set of results to two different studies, well, that could be very enriching, couldn't it?"

"Getting paid twice for the same work is a very serious policy breach," Horace said.

"There is nothing the Company hates more than double-dipping."

"I wouldn't know anything about doubles." Horace grinned at the painting.

"The doc knew study results were going to two different branches."

"You'd have to ask him."

"Once you got rid of the kids and closed down the plant, he was the only other connection. These studies are blind, and the divisions share about as well as toddlers. The whole disgusting nature of the project made the divisions want to keep it all a secret. You just about pulled this off."

"If I had any idea what we're talking about, I might be amused." Horace turned to face McCallum. "I'm not. It appears you need another beer. Why don't you grab one on your way out?"

McCallum held his beer bottle up and eyed the bottom. "You are most generous. Thanks." He lowered the bottle and found Horace's eyes. "You think you can relax because you kept your records in the reactor control room. When that EMP went off, it did more than fry the equipment. It erased the evidence. Funny thing about this case, though. I find duplicates everywhere I look."

McCallum turned and strolled back down the hall. "I'm not done looking."

If you enjoyed this read

Please leave a review on Amazon, Facebook, Good Reads or Instagram.

It takes less than five minutes and it really does make a difference.

If you're not sure how to leave a review on Amazon:

1. *Go to amazon.com.*

2. *Type in The Link Boy by Michael J. Martineck and when you see it, click on it.*

3. *Scroll down to Customer Reviews. Nearby you'll see a box labeled Write a Review. Click it.*

4. *Now, if you've never written a review before on Amazon, they might ask you to create a name for yourself.*

5. *Reviews can be as simple as, "Loved the book! Can't wait for the Next!" (Please don't give the story away.)*

And that's it!

Brian Hades, publisher

About the Author

Michael J. Martineck started writing stories when he was seven. Over the years he's written short stories, comic book scripts, articles and novels.

Michael's previous novel - The Milkman (EDGE Science Fiction and Fantasy), a murder mystery set in a world with no governments – won a gold medal from the Independent Publisher Book Awards and was a finalist in the Eric Hoffer awards, given for salient writing from small presses. His previous novel, Cinco de Mayo, was a finalist for an Alberta Reader's Choice Award. He has written for DC Comics, several magazines (fiction and non-fiction) the Urban Green Man anthology and two urban fantasy novels for young readers. Michael has a degree in English and Economics, but has worked in advertising for several years. He lives with his wife and two children on Grand Island, NY. Visit him at:
http://michaelmartineck.blogspot.ca/

Here's a peek at some of the other novels by Michael J. Martineck.

The Milkman
A Freeworld Novel

by Michael J. Martineck

In the near future, corporation rules every possible freedom. Without government, there can be no crime. And every act is measured against competing interests, hidden loyalties and the ever-upward pressure of the corporate ladder.

Any quest for transparency is as punishable as an act of murder. But one man has managed to slip the system, a future-day Robin Hood who tests dairy milk outside of corporate control and posts the results to the world.

When the Milkman is framed for a young girl's murder and anonymous funding comes through for a documentary filmmaker in search of true art beneath corporate propaganda, eyes begin to turn and soon the hunt is on.

Can the man who created the symbol of the Milkman, the only one who knows what really happened that bloody night, escape the corporate rat maze closing around him? Or is it already too late?

Praise for The Milkman:

The Milkman won the Independent Publisher Book Award (IPPY) as the best science fiction novel at the national level. The novel was also a finalist in the Eric Hoffer awards, given each year for salient writing from small presses.

"Reminiscent of the novels of Michael Coney, Frederik Pohl and Cyril Kornbluth as well as Terry Gilliam's Brazil, although with less bitter humor and more outrage than those luminaries, the work is a reductio ad absurdum examination of the increasingly corporatized world in which we all live, an impressive demonstration of the author's skills."
-- Publisher's Weekly

"I have a fascination for the art of writing; this author grabbed me at the first paragraph, relating crimes to works of art. His creative use of dialogue, description, and plotline moved the story along smoothly. Thought provoking ideas added depth to this powerful dystopian tale of murder in a corporate world, but did not get in the way of this futuristic noir style detective story. With believable, sympathetic characters and page turning action, I highly recommend this fascinating thriller."
— Paul Fruehauf

For more on The Milkman visit:
http://tinyurl.com/edge2075

Cinco de Mayo

by Michael J. Martineck

Secrets: some feel freed having them out.
Others will kill to keep them.

On May 5, in a flash of pain, every man, woman and child on the planet receives a second set of memories. A new name, a new language, a whole new life slips into their minds, along side their own.

- In Chicago, a transit worker knows enough about the Aryan Brotherhood to mark him for death.
- In Abu Dhabi, a playboy experiences modern day slavery.
- In New York an advertising executive shares the memories of a blind railroad worker in China.

In this transparent world of instant intimacy, no one is left untouched... Everyone has secrets!

Praise for Cinco de Mayo:

"Read this book...but don't start it on your lunch hour because you won't want to put it down and go back to work. A fast-paced story, interesting, multi-cultural characters, a thriliing, scary chase, and even some hilarious moments, make this a wonderful read. Martineck's characters step out of the book fully engaged. Treat yourself!"
— Phoebe Wray

"The premise of every person earth sharing memories with one other person, sounded interesting but I wasn't expecting much more than a contrived "what if" story and it was cheap. I was pleasantly surprised. The author fully developed and used the memory swap as a device to explore social and philosophical subjects including racism, sexism, child labor, slavery, totalitarian oppression, ageism, income inequality, religion etc. without preaching or bogging down his fascinating story lines. The only fault I found was that it ended too soon. Then again, the story was so big, that I think any ending would have seemed too soon."
— Paul Fruehauf

"I really enjoyed this book. Fast-paced, an intriguing concept, and I really got drawn into the characters' stories. It kept me eagerly turning pages right till the end! Great science fiction and a very enjoyable read."
J. A. McLachlan

For more on Cinco de Mayo visit:
http://tinyurl.com/edge2038

Need something new to read?

If you liked The Link Boy, you should also
consider these other EDGE-Lite titles:

The Rosetta Man

by Claire McCague

Wanted:
Translator for first contact.
Immediate opening.
Danger pay allowance.

Estlin Hume lives in Twin Butte, Alberta surrounded by a horde of affectionate squirrels. His involuntary squirrel-attracting talent leaves him evicted, expelled, fired and near penniless until two aliens arrive and adopt him as their translator. Yanked around the world at the center of the first contact crisis, Estlin finds his new employers incomprehensible. As he faces the ultimate language barrier, unsympathetic military forces converging in the South Pacific keep threatening to kill the messenger. The question on everyone's mind is: Why are the aliens here? But Estlin's starting to think we'll happily blow ourselves up in the process of finding that out.

Praise for The Rosetta Man:

"The cover and synopsis had me expecting a light-hearted comedy. I didn't realize I was getting a geopolitical first contact thriller that somehow still managed to be a light-hearted comedy. I really enjoyed this book! The characters are rich and diverse. Estlin and Harry are great, Beth and Bomani made me cry. The story is fast paced and engaging and again, completely unexpected. Great book for fans of first contact scifi, but also fans of thrillers and mysteries. And so well-executed that I give it a solid 5 stars."
— Scott Burtness, author of Wisconsin Vamp (Monsters in the Midwest)

"This book ranks up there with many of the classic sci-fi "first contact" stories and Claire McCague's scientific background comes through in waves."
— Cameron Arsenault, Amazon Reviewer

"A completely enjoyable read. Good action, lots of humor, and a global setting. Strongly recommended."
— Diane Lacey, Amazon Reviewer

For more on The Rosetta Man visit:
tinyurl.com/edge6004

Beltrunner

by Sean O'Brien

As an independent beltrunner mining asteroids in the frontier of space, Collier South is a dying breed. Scrounging and cutting corners to work cheap, Collier isn't a stranger to lean times and make-do repairs; in fact his onboard computer hasn't had outside maintenance in years and its beginning to show its personal quirks.

When Collier finds an asteroid that shows promise, he thinks he's bought himself some time. But his claim is stolen out from under him by his vindictive ex-lover and her shiny new corporate ship. Powerless against the omnipotent mining corporations, Collier has always been too stubborn to give-up without a fight. Broke and desperate, Collier has one last chance to land a strike. If he doesn't come back with ore, he'll end up destitute and trading his own biologicals for his next meal.

What he discovers in the farthest reaches of the belt has the power to change his life and the fate of the entire system forever. That is, if Collier and his onboard computer can keep his discovery out of corporate hands.

Praise for Beltrunner

"This is a fast moving book that leaves you breathless with hair-raising action and unexpected twists. The world creation is well-developed and highly creative. The interactions between Collier and Sancho are particularly

entertaining - with Collier coming up with implusive dangerous plans and Sancho trying to talk him out of them. Highly recommended for action space lovers."
— Patricia Humphreys

"Scavenging known space makes for a hard life, and surviving outside of the Corporations in the Belt makes it all the harder. It is not surprising that Collier and his unusual companion Sancho hit bottom, like many before them, until they make the discovery of their lives…or deaths, as it may turn out to be.

"Beltrunner is a solidly enjoyable science fiction adventure, fast paced, and filled with the kind of characters that make you smile, break your heart, or just make you clench your jaw. I read it in one sitting and thoroughly enjoyed it. O'Brien builds a universe to get lost in that is as hard, gritty, and unforgiving as deep space itself. It is a well-written romp around space like many others, yet plenty of surprising elements give the story a depth and purpose all its own without the heavy strain of space melodrama. Read it because it is both light fun and thoughtful reading."
— A. Volmer

For more on Beltrunner visit:
tinyurl.com/edge6010

For more EDGE titles and information about upcoming speculative fiction please visit us at:

www.edgewebsite.com

Don't forget to sign-up for our Special Offers

www.ingramcontent.com/pod-product-compliance
Lightning Source LLC
Chambersburg PA
CBHW050247110726
47898CB00007B/2311